I0603762

a healing spirit

Riverview Series Book 2

Melissa A. Hanson

Copyright © 2015 Melissa A. Hanson
All rights reserved.
www.mahwriting.com
First Printing 2015

ISBN-13: 978-0-9965485-2-6 /
ISBN-13: 978-0-9965485-7-1
EPUB: 978-0-9965485-3-3

Cover Layout & Design: Melissa A. Hanson
Image: Alex Sun/shutterstock.com
Editing: Erica Orloff

Though inspired by an actual medical event, this is a work of fiction. Names, characters, businesses, places, events, and incidents are either the products of the author's imagination or used in a fictitious manner. Any resemblance to actual persons, living or dead, or actual events is purely coincidental.

All rights reserved. Without limiting the rights under copyright reserved above, no part of this publication may be reproduced, stored in or introduced into a retrieval system, or transmitted, in any form, or by any means (electronic, mechanical, photocopying, recording, or otherwise) without the prior written permission of both the copyright owner and the above publisher of this book.

Please do not participate in or encourage piracy of copyrighted materials in violation of the author's rights. Purchase only authorized editions.

Table of Contents:

Dedication:

For Keely Proctor:
an amazing, strong young lady,
who survived,
and lives each day to the fullest.
You have indeed been an inspiration to so many.

"You gain strength, courage, and confidence by every experience in which you really stop to look fear in the face. You must do the thing which you think you cannot do."   Eleanor Roosevelt

PROLOGUE

Voices drift in and out of a fuzzy grayness. The immense pressure and pain in my chest and abdomen is unbearable. I try to speak, but a sense of panic overwhelms me as I realize there is a hard object in my mouth. I try to resist; I'm freaking out as I realize it's not only in my mouth, but down into my throat. No matter what I try, I can't dislodge it. My breathing is difficult and shallow as I try to resist. It feels weird, and I try to push against the air that flows into my lungs, fighting against the pressure. The urge to wake up from this nightmare is intense, but I can't seem to free myself from the nothingness that I'm floating in.

A calming voice, thick with a southern accent floats in my subconscious. The memory of vivid green eyes and a handsome stranger is just beyond my grasp as I try to reel the memory in. A small light appears in the distance, skinny rays pouring through the fuzziness. It's warm and comforting, almost hypnotic. I try to move toward it, but just as quickly as it appeared it's gone. The light is replaced with a vague sense of no color, no light, but neither is it dark. Concentrating hard on the steady beeps nearby, I find a sense of peace and drift into a deep sleep.

CHAPTER ONE

~ *Mia* ~

It was the day before Thanksgiving, and a freak storm had blown in the previous weekend, dumping a significant amount of new snow in the local mountains. I was bursting with excitement to get up the mountain and enjoy the first snowboard run of the season. To make things even better, my best friends, Bailey and Natasha were home from college for Thanksgiving break. I hadn't seen either of them since they left back in August, and I really missed them. Things hadn't been the same since they left. We had been inseparable during our junior and senior years in high school. Having them so far away was like a piece of me was missing. Though we Skyped and texted, it just wasn't the same as having them nearby.

Natasha had gotten a full architectural scholarship at a school in Oregon, and Bailey had left for Las Vegas to attend college near her boyfriend Collin. Sometimes I wished I'd been able to get away from Riverview, which was located in the inland valley of Southern California. The excitement of a new town, new places, and new people was really appealing, but if I was honest, Riverview wasn't a bad place to live. We were about an hour from the mountains and ski resorts, an hour from the desert, and a little over an hour from the beaches. Not many places around could boast such a variety of sceneries.

I was enrolled at the local community college—unlike my friends, I had no idea what I wanted to do "when I grew up." Thankfully, my parents were supportive and didn't pressure me, which had been a huge relief. I was taking my general eds, and hoping I'd find something that I really wanted to do. Eventually, something would click—at least I sure hoped so—and that's what I kept telling myself.

Between classes and studying, I worked part-time as a receptionist at a local hair salon. It wasn't super exciting, but the people I worked with were nice and it gave me extra spending money. My favorite job though was babysitting little Riley. He was four, and the son of one of the hairstylists who worked at the salon. Bailey had been his main babysitter until she left for Las Vegas. Over the past couple of months since she'd been gone, Riley and I had bonded and he was a lot of fun to watch. He was energetic and so cute. His favorite thing was spending time at the park. He was so outgoing, practically every time we were out he made some new friends.

As I finished getting dressed, the smell of bacon wafted through the house, and my stomach growled in response. I grabbed the last of my snowboarding gear on my way towards the kitchen. The living area of the house was open to the kitchen. My dad relaxed in his recliner as he flipped through the channels. While my mom stood at the stove as she fried the tantalizing bacon. She was still dressed in her pink satin pj's, with her shoulder-length brown hair pulled back into a ponytail. Everyone told us that we looked more like sisters.

"Morning Mia, would you like some bacon and eggs before you head out?"

"Sure, but I've got to hurry. I'm supposed to pick up Tasha in fifteen minutes."

"It's almost finished. Grab a plate. I wish you guys would go up over the weekend. We've got a lot of family coming tomorrow, and I've got no one to help prep the food now."

"I'll be home early and can help you then. I haven't seen my friends in months, and we don't always get snow this early in the season."

"I know, but it would be nice to have the help today. I'll need you to help when you get home tonight and tomorrow before everyone gets here, okay?"

"I promise." Turning from the kitchen I walked over to the adjacent living area where my dad was still engrossed in his TV show. "Morning, Dad." I leaned over as I gave him a quick peck on the cheek.

"Morning," he mumbled.

I chuckled as I walked back into the kitchen to grab the plate my mom had set out for me. As I ate, it was hard not to glance at the time that blinked over the stove every few minutes. My mom finished dishing up bacon, eggs, and toast and served it to my dad, as he remained focused on his news, then she set out another plate on the table next to me.

"Zach! Breakfast!" my mom yelled upstairs to my ten-year old brother.

"Be right down." Zach answered as the sound of his feet thumped down the stairs.

I finished the last of my eggs, took my plate, and slid the dishes into the dishwasher.

"Okay, I'm out of here. See you guys later." I crossed the kitchen and gave my mom a hug on my way out.

"Be careful! The roads are probably going to be icy when you head back down."

"I know. I've got the chains too. You've taught me well, Mama." I smiled.

"I still worry, honey. Have fun. And call me when you get there and when you leave, okay?"

"Yes, Mom. Bye, Dad."

"Bye, Mia."

As I walked out of the kitchen I practically ran over Zach as he came bounding down the stairs. "Hey, watch it, buddy."

"Sorry. Hey, where are you going?"

"Snowboarding with Tasha and Bailey."

"What? Why can't I come?"

"Sorry, dude, not this time. Maybe next weekend if the snow holds?" I ruffled his dark hair in affection as he stalked by, his shoulders hunched over with disappointment.

"Ah, man. Not fair! Mom! Why can't I go with Mia?" He stomped into the kitchen.

"Zach, not today. Let Mia have fun with her friends. Now come here and eat before your food is cold."

"All right I'm out of here! See you guys later!"

I grabbed my board and backpack and walked excitedly to my parents' Tahoe. Tossing everything in the back, I jumped in the truck and drove to Natasha's house first. The truck had barely pulled into the driveway when Natasha, her older brother Quinn, and Bailey's boyfriend Collin were out the door loaded down with their stuff. Leaving the truck on, I jumped out to help.

"Tasha!" I reached my friend and took her duffle bag, as I wrapped her in my arms in a big hug, all in one graceful move.

"Mia! I've missed you! I'm so excited to be home! It's good to have everybody together again."

"I've missed you guys too. It's just not the same around here without everyone."

"Guess we know where we rate, huh Collin? We don't even get a hello," Quinn teased.

"Hi, Quinn. Hi, Collin. I just saw Quinn the other day, but I've missed you too. Collin, when did you and Bailey get in … last night?"

"Late, we hit a ton of traffic on the drive. Usually everyone is headed to Vegas for the holidays not leaving. Not sure what the hold-up was. Maybe there was an accident. Who knows? It added a good hour and a half to our drive."

"I'm glad you guys could finally get back here. I'll have to drive out there to visit soon."

"Bailey would love that. She misses you," Collin replied

"Well, let's get this stuff loaded so we can go get her," Quinn said as he restacked the snowboards.

My friends jumped into the truck. Natasha slid into the front passenger seat while Quinn and Collin got in the back. The quick drive to Bailey's aunt and uncle's house was filled with excited chatter and laughter. It felt good to have everyone back together again, but at the same time I realized even more how much I'd missed having them close. When we reached Bailey's house she was standing on the front porch waiting for us, her snowboard propped up against the porch railing.

As I pulled into the driveway Bailey grabbed her stuff and was at the truck by the time Natasha and I got out. The three of us hugged while Collin chuckled as he loaded Bailey's stuff in the back. Bailey jumped in the back with Collin and Quinn and our group was complete. We started the steady climb up the mountain into the white, snowy bliss.

"Is the main road still washed out from the storm last year?" Collin asked.

I glanced in my rearview mirror as we passed the turn-off for our regular route. "It's still closed, they might not even have it opened until next year. The landslide took out a huge chunk of the road. At least we still have the other two ways up the mountain."

Bailey groaned from the backseat, "yeah, but it takes almost twice as long, and I hate the mountain roads."

I looked back at my friend as she sat cuddled next to Collin. A couple years previous her entire family had been killed in a car accident on a winter night. She'd moved to Riverview to live with her aunt and uncle, Natasha and I had befriended her right away, and the three of us were inseparable. Then Collin came into her life and helped turn it upside down in a good way. They had a few bumps along the way, but ultimately they seemed to have been meant for each other and they were happy. Maybe someday I'd be lucky to find someone as caring and attentive as Collin was to Bailey.

Natasha turned from her place in the passenger seat to look back at Bailey. "At least you have the best company. So tell us … how's Vegas anyways? I don't know how you can stand it out there with all the heat, and the desert. I'm loving the green forests up in Oregon."

The banter between my friends went back and forth as each one listed all the great things about their current schools and cities. Quinn chimed in listing why staying in Riverview was the best decision and that everyone else but him and I were crazy.

Halfway up the mountain it got real quiet in the backseat. I glanced in the rearview mirror to see what was going on. Bailey's face was white as a sheet, and Collin had his arm around her trying to soothe her.

"What's wrong?" I asked, keeping my attention on the winding road ahead.

"Mia, pull over, quick! I think Bailey's going to throw up."

"Oh, no. Okay, hold on, Bailey; there is a turn-out just ahead."

"Hurry." Bailey's voice quivered.

Reaching the turn-out I quickly pulled over. Before I'd even put the truck in park Bailey was out of the car and at the side of the road bent over. Collin quickly followed after her and stood with one hand holding her hair back away from her face while the other rubbed her back.

"Oh geez, that's not good. I hope she's okay," Natasha commented. "Maybe I should sit in the back so she can see the road ahead better. I didn't realize she got carsick."

"I didn't know either, but then again I think most times we've come up here she's either been driving or in the front seat." I sat watching Bailey with sympathy.

"Hey Quinn, can you reach my bag? There's a bottle of water in it. Bailey's going to need it when she gets done."

"This one, Mia?"

"Yeah, the bottle should be in the front pouch."

"Got it."

After about ten minutes Bailey slowly walked back over to the Tahoe with Collin's arm on her shoulder. Natasha got out of the front seat and climbed in the back next to Quinn.

"Jump in front. It will be easier for you to keep your eyes on the road," Natasha told Bailey as she opened the back door.

With a slight smile Bailey eased herself into the seat. "Thanks, Tasha. I think maybe it was my breakfast and not paying attention to the curves. I'm usually okay if I watch the road."

Natasha leaned forward handing Bailey the water bottle.

"Here, this should help. Always an adventure, huh, guys?"

"Yep." I laughed as I maneuvered the Tahoe back on the road and we were on our way again.

The cool crisp air stung my face as I sat on the chairlift, sandwiched in the middle between Bailey and Natasha. The wind had picked up considerably since we had gotten to the resort. It was late morning, and we were getting ready for one last run before lunch. My stomach growled, and I was looking forward to hot chocolate and hamburgers in the lodge. My feet were numb, and frozen in my heavy boots. That was one thing I hated about skiing and snowboarding was my feet always got so cold. I had forgotten my heat packs today that I usually shoved in my boots to help keep them warm. But really it didn't matter, I loved snowboarding and skiing, I'd suffer through a little bit of cold.

My family had been skiing since I was little. I loved the icy mountain air and rush of racing down the snow covered slopes. I especially enjoyed the adventure with my close friends. I smiled as Collin's and Quinn's laughter drifted on the wind from the chair behind. I knew how lucky I was to have such a very special group of friends, and I'd missed them immensely.

A slight uneasiness rippled through me. Sitting in the middle had always made me a little nervous since there was nothing to hold on to. Being so far above the slopes in the open chair was kind of freaky if I let myself think about it. I shoved the nervousness aside. I'd been on lifts since I was four, and I'd never had any trouble before.

I watched the bright-colored specks of people below as they traversed the bright white trails. I shifted slightly in my seat. At that moment the chair came to a stop. The momentum shifted my balance forward— much too far forward. I tried to readjusted myself. With the added weight of the board attached to my foot, my balance was off. In the pit of my stomach I knew something was wrong.

Before I could even scream I knew I was falling. It was unreal, the snow-packed ground rapidly approaching. All I could hear was the wind as it rushed in my ears, and the pounding of my heartbeat. Then I felt nothing as I impacted on the middle of a snow drift below. First my knees, then the rest of my body as it fell forward and everything went eerily quiet.

CHAPTER TWO

~ Dylan ~

The ski patrol hut was warm as I sat drinking a cup of coffee. Across the table lounged my ski patrol partner, and best friend, Corey Easton. We had started ski patrol together two years previously, and I loved my job. For the most part it was lighthearted and fun. Our typical duties included watching for skiers and snowboarders who were in closed areas of the resort, or taking care of sprained wrists and ankles. It wasn't often that we had a severe injury, but we did have our share of broken bones and concussions. Corey and I both loved the outdoors, and we even worked up at the resort during the summer months.

It was a nice change to have snow so early this season. I really hoped it would stay. Earlier in the morning we had caught a family in a closed portion and had to warn them to get back on the trail or they'd be removed from the resort. So far we hadn't come across them again so hopefully they had listened. I hated to be the bad guy, but I was only doing my job and looking out for their safety.

I glanced up at the clock mounted on the wall; it was almost time for our lunch break. The door to the hut was open as we watched the packed slopes, our radios silent for once when I heard a loud thud. I looked at Corey startled.

"What the heck was that?" Corey asked, as faint screams could be heard from above.

"I'm not sure, but it didn't sound good."

Our coffee cups forgotten, and our gloves in hand we raced outside. I was shocked when I realized there was a girl curled in a ball, face first in the snow just a short distance away. I grabbed my skies, with Corey right behind me and ran the few feet down the slope to the girl. As I reached her I unclipped my radio.

"Base, this is Hut 2. We are responding to a snowboarder down. This is a possible fall from the lift near tower 20. Start the trauma gear and additional personnel to this location."

"Roger that."

Shoving my skis upright in the snow I kneeled down next to the girl. Her burgundy jacket contrasted against the brilliant white snow. Her face and helmet were almost completely covered by the snow, I gently brushed back her blonde strands of hair.

"Miss, can you hear me? My name is Dylan, ski patrol. I'm going to help you. I need to know where you hurt."

A slight moan escaped from the girl's lips. I quickly ran my hands over the areas that were exposed. Corey circled us as he kept back the onlookers that had gathered.

"Miss, what's your name?" I asked as I reached for her wrist to check her pulse.

"Mia." She quietly answered as she tried to shift in the snow. A cry of pain escaped.

"Hi Mia, please don't move, we need to stabilize you first. Do you know what happened?" Corey asked, as he knelt beside me.

"I fell, I think. I hurt."

"Where does it hurt?"

"My stomach, my stomach, burning."

"What about your head, your neck, arms, or legs?" I asked as I continued to run my hands carefully over her.

"No, my stomach, my stomach. Please."

"Mia, how old are you?" Corey asked.

"Umm, nineteen."

"Do you know what day it is?" I asked next.

"Wednesday."

"Yes, good. Are you here with someone?"

"Friends, up there." She tried to point to the lift high above.

I looked up, squinting into the sun, at the chair lift that had stopped overhead. I could hear screaming from above which must be the friends that Mia was talking about.

"We'll find them. Don't move though okay." Corey said as he began to carefully unfasten her snowboard.

Examining her board I was amazed that it didn't even appear cracked. "Base, this is P-122. We have a nineteen-year-old female complaining of severe abdominal pain secondary to a fall from approximately thirty feet. She is lethargic, but oriented, breathing is 24 and shallow, pulse about 120. We recommend you request an airship." As I finished with my report, Justin, another of our ski patrollers finally arrived on skis with the trauma bag and toboggan.

"Her name is Mia. She's complaining of abdominal pain." I informed Justin as he unsnapped from his skis and hurried over with the trauma bag.

"Can you feel your toes?" Corey asked.

I noticed that her gloves moved slightly as they lay on the snow. "I see you can move your fingers. That's good. What about your toes?" I asked her.

"I think so."

"Good." Justin replied as he prepped the backboard.

"I'm going to take your helmet off before we put you on the backboard, okay?" I told her.

"Okay."

I removed her helmet and inspected it for cracks and fractures. I was surprised that it seemed to be completely intact, which was a good sign, a very good sign. She wasn't out of the woods yet, as unseen injuries could be far more serious than obvious ones. Thankfully, she had been wearing a helmet, her injuries could have been even worse if she hadn't been wearing one. There were still those that refused to wear helmets even though it was safer to wear them.

I glanced again at the staggering distance of the chairlift above. It hadn't started moving yet, I'm sure her friends were probably worried, and it didn't help that they were stuck waiting for the lift to start moving. Around us more people had stopped to watch; so far they seemed to be staying back so that we could do our job.

Justin, Corey, and I methodically prepared her for transport. I carefully applied the cervical collar as Corey held her head and neck steady. Justin placed the backboard against her back on its side. While we held her in place, the three of us rolled the board, so that Mia was lying on her back. We had so many training sessions we worked as one unit, knowing what each of us was going to do without having to even vocalize the next step.

I checked movement and sensation to Mia's limbs now that she was lying flat on the board. We continued to secure Mia, moving from her legs to her head. As Corey tightened the strap around her torso Mia choked back a sob. I caught Corey's eye, and we both knew without saying a word that we were racing against a time clock. We had no idea if that clock was going to run out on us.

"Mia, can you still feel your legs, arms?" I asked as I rechecked her pulse and breathing rate, alarmed that both were quicker.

"Yes."

"Good. We're going to move you to the toboggan so we can get you down the mountain, okay?" I knew keeping her informed of every step would help keep her focused and hopefully calmer. The three of us picked Mia up and positioned her on the toboggan, securing the board for her trip down the mountain.

"Okay."

Her response was so faint I barely even heard it. I looked down at her deep brown eyes as they watched me intently. I saw tears forming as they slowly began to slip down the side of her cheek and ran toward her ear. I yanked off one of my gloves and gently wiped it away. She was pretty; her blonde hair was shoulder length and there appeared to be slight indentations in her cheeks. I wondered if she had dimples when she smiled.

Corey handed me the oxygen mask as I positioned the elastic to go over her head. "I'm going to place this over your mouth. It will help you breathe, okay?"

"Okay." Her voice was shaky.

I looked over all the attachments and everything looked good. Justin had snapped his skis back on and was positioning himself in front of the toboggan. I unclipped my radio to call in our status. "Base, this is P-122, patient is on backboard, and we have oxygen in place. We are load and go to base. P-122 out."

Reattaching my radio, I put my gloves back on and snapped into my skis. Corey and I took their places on each side of the toboggan, where Mia lay immobilized. We navigated the hill quickly, just like the drills we regularly practiced.

⌒⌒⌒

~ Bailey ~

Screams from both Natasha and I echoed through the frigid air.

"Mia!"

"Tasha, is she moving? Oh my God, how did that happen?" I grasped Natasha's arm tightly.

"I don't know! We've got to get to her." Natasha cried out.

I quickly glanced back at Collin and Quinn, their faces white with fear as they watched the ski patrol below move toward Mia.

"Why's the lift stopped? What are we going to do? She's got to be okay!" I was in a complete state of panic as I tried to grasp what had happened.

Natasha and I clung to each other in painful silence. Well over thirty feet below us Mia lay in a ball, a small burgundy imprint in the snow. We watched as two ski patrol members in bright red jackets moved around her quickly and efficiently. The fun and excitement had vanished in a second. Instead we now sat in the icy cold wind. Chilled to the bone, not only physically, but emotionally as well. We were worried and scared for Mia, and felt completely helpless as all we could do was sit and watch.

"Look, I think she moved!" I squeezed Natasha's arm that I still had wrapped against me, holding for dear life.

"That's got to be a good sign right?"

"Why won't this thing move?" I was frustrated as I smacked the cold metal next to me.

Every excruciating minute we sat there was another minute it would take for us to get to our friend. Finally, the lift began to move again. We turned to look behind us as we continued our ascent up the hill. We watched as Mia was loaded onto a sled and started her journey down the snow-covered slope. Mia was no longer visible when we reached the top of the mountain. Natasha and I exited the lift and immediately located the first resort employee we came across, his radio crackled with chatter.

"Excuse me, sir, can you help us? Please, our friend just fell off the chairlift. We need to get to her." Natasha asked, as Collin and Quinn quickly joined them.

"Hold on; let me see where they've got her." He grabbed his radio and spoke quickly into it.

I felt Collin's arms as he wrapped them around me. I leaned into their warmth and comfort, tears streaming down my face.

"Oh, Collin! She fell so far. Do you think she's okay?"

"Babe, she's strong—and a fighter. She's going to be fine. What happened anyways? One minute she was on the lift with you and the next she was in the snow. We didn't even see it, just heard you both scream."

"I don't know, we were talking one minute. The chair swayed slightly as it came to a stop, but it wasn't anything too jarring. Then she was just gone," I replied.

"Okay, she's awake. They are almost to the bottom of the slope. They are taking her to a local hospital via helicopter," the resort employee informed us.

"Helicopter? It's that bad?" Natasha's voice was barely a whisper.

"Miss, we're taking all precaution. We don't know for sure how severe her injuries are."

"Can you get us to her?" Quinn asked.

"Yes, wait a minute. We'll get you all down the slope."

CHAPTER THREE

~ *Mia* ~

I tried to pay attention to what the three ski patrollers were saying, but it was difficult to concentrate on anything other than the screaming pain from deep within my stomach. Darkness was trying to close in, and I was frantically trying to push it away. I focused on the quiet southern drawl of the handsome guy above me. Dylan, I was pretty sure that's what he said his name was. His voice was calm and soothing. He asked the same questions over and over. His brown hair was cut short and spiky with blond highlights. His green eyes were clear and intense.

They had rolled me over and had me secure against the backboard. It was uncomfortable as it pressed against my spine. I was unable to move my head, or most of my body once they had secured the straps. Visibility was severely limited to only what was directly above me. I looked up into the bright sunlight, as the shadows moved efficiently above. I knew I was probably in shock. I closed my eyes and wished that I was having a horrible dream, but the searing pain in my stomach was too intense. Tears welled up in my eyes, and I felt them begin to slip down the side of my face as they streamed toward my neck.

I felt warm fingertips gently brush my tears away, I opened my eyes and stared into vivid green depths. I could tell he was concerned, and while I felt comforted by this it also frightened me. If he was concerned, I was probably in worse condition than I thought. Fear raced through me, and I struggled to stay positive, to not let the fear consume me. I would be fine, it was just a little fall. I continued to tell myself that over and over.

I could see the chairlift in the distance. It looked like it was stopped. I wondered if my friends were stuck up there watching me, or if they were on their way down the slope. I knew that they would be worried. I knew no matter what they would find me as soon as they could.

It was getting harder to breathe, and my green-eyed rescuer placed an oxygen mask over my nose and mouth. Shortly after the sled began to move and we were moving down the slope. I stared into the bright blue sky above me; the snow-covered pine trees flew by in a blur. The cold air that whipped across me no longer brought me happiness. My tears were swept away with the wind to land somewhere out in the iciness that surrounded me. The severe burning in my stomach grew stronger. All I wanted to do was to pull my knees up to my chest, and curl into a ball. But my legs were securely strapped down flat onto the hard, unmoving board beneath me. The stiff plastic collar that they had wrapped under my chin immobilized my neck. The back of my head throbbed with the pressure of being secured against the unyielding wood. The toboggan slowed and then finally stopped. My vision was blurred with the tears that overflowed into streams down my cheeks.

"Mia, can you still hear me?"

It was that soothing, voice again. His southern drawl was unforgettable. "Yes." My voice was muffled by the oxygen mask.

"Good, I need you to stay focused, okay. Do you remember what day it is?"

"Yes, Wednesday."

"How old are you?"

"Nineteen."

"What is your name?"

"Mia."

"Good. How are you feeling?"

"Stomach, it hurts really bad."

"Anywhere else?"

"Not really. Where are my friends? They're going to be worried. And my parents, I have to call them." Each word I uttered was harder to get out than the previous. I felt out of breath, like I'd run for miles. I tried to focus on anything but the ripping feeling in my stomach.

"We'll find them when we get down to the lodge. We need to focus on you first though, okay?"

"Okay."

"How many fingers am I holding up?"

"Three."

"Good."

One of my rescuers continued the questions over and over again until we reached the lodge where several medical staff were waiting for us. The flutter of activity around me was overwhelming. I felt like a specimen, or freak of nature, as they touched every part of my arms, legs, and stomach, and they continued their questions. With my visual sphere restricted, I couldn't see everything that was going on, and I hated not knowing what was happening. Resting and staying still were not things that I did well. Being completely strapped down and unable to move was starting to cause me to panic inside. Different faces swarmed above me and became nothing but a blur. I just wanted to wake up and be in my bed, with this whole thing a nightmare. I tried to stay focused on the calming southern drawl that kept speaking to me. I found comfort as I watched his intense green eyes as they moved above me. Pain instantly shot through me from deep within. It was like nothing I'd ever felt before in my life. I clenched my eyes shut, refusing to break down and sob. Coldness was overtaking my body, as it slowly seeped through every vein.

~ Bailey~

After we reached the bottom of the slope, Collin, Quinn, Natasha, and I followed quickly behind the ski patrol. They led us through the lodge and into a small medical room where Mia lay. Several employees moved around her asking questions. Two ski patrol members were talking to the medic staff. Natasha and I left the guys and walked quickly over to Mia, where she lay so still. It looked like they had her strapped against a board and had secured it onto a gurney.

"Hey Mia, are you okay?" Natasha asked quietly, as she grabbed Mia's hand.

"My stomach hurts, really bad." Her voice was muffled through the oxygen mask.

"You're going to be fine. We're here for you. What do you need us to do?" I asked as I stood opposite of Natasha.

"Call my parents."

"We will. Are your keys in your backpack?" Natasha asked.

"Yes." Mia quietly groaned.

"We'll meet you at the hospital." Collin stated.

I felt him behind me as his hand rested against my waist. I leaned slightly into him hoping to steal some strength and warmth, as I had suddenly gotten unbearably cold. One of the ski patrol members stood at the head of the stretcher and quietly watched us. A second one approached Mia.

"The airship is in route. We're ready to take her now." The second ski patrol member stated.

"Wow, see she gets all the fun! A helicopter ride, cool." Quinn piped in.

"Come on Quinn, stop!" Natasha slapped her brother's arm.

"What? I'm just trying to make her laugh a little."

Mia tried to smile. But it wasn't a success. I watched my friend shut her eyes, and I knew she was hurting, and it broke my heart. Watching her lying there was quickly bringing back memories I didn't want to deal with again. She had to be okay; there was no other option. I wouldn't let my thoughts drift into the darkness. Mia's breathing seemed very shallow, like she was gasping for air even with the oxygen mask that she had over her nose and mouth.

"Mia, are you sure you're okay? Sir, can one of us go with her?" I asked.

"Sorry miss, there's not enough room. We need to get her loaded up now and to the hospital. The helicopter is meeting us midway down the mountain. They can't land up here today, it's just too windy."

I pulled my phone out and glanced at the time. It had only been twenty minutes since Mia had fallen, but it already felt like a lifetime had passed. "Okay, Mia, we'll get there as quickly as we can; we'll call your parents on our way."

We stood there helpless, as Mia was wheeled into the waiting ambulance. A paramedic and one of the ski patrollers climbed in the back with her. The ambulance left the resort and began its journey to meet the helicopter. After it was no longer in sight we could still hear the high-pitched siren as it echoed in the breeze. We scrambled to get our belongings packed up in the Tahoe and began the long journey down the windy, icy road.

CHAPTER FOUR

~ *Mia* ~

The ambulance siren was constant, the deep ache within me so strong, I wanted to beg for relief. I stared at the ambulance ceiling as I listened to voices around me. Bits of information registered, my description, possible injuries, time elapsed, but other terminology was too hard to focus on. It was too scary to dwell on. I felt the strength and warmth as the rescuer, with the southern drawl, held my hand. The connection gave my comfort, and I squeezed it tight, holding onto it like a lifeline.

The paramedic that rode in the back with us had taken my blood pressure, and he was inserting an IV into my arm as he spoke rapidly and efficiently to the hospital dispatch.

"Mia, I'm going to give you a little something to help dull the pain."

I nodded slightly–well the best I could do–considering my head was strapped down. I didn't think I could form any more words right now. Every bump in the road jarred me, and I wasn't sure how much more I could take. The IV needle stung as they inserted it into my arm. I gripped the warm hand I was holding even tighter.

"We're almost to the helicopter landing site. It won't be much longer okay?"

I studied his handsome face as he sat next to me, and I couldn't utter a response. His soothing voice had become familiar and helped calm me. I didn't feel so alone knowing that he was still with me. I shut my eyes tight as the tears continued to slide down the side of my face, finding their way inside my ear. The burning pain was getting worse, and it felt like it was radiating throughout my body. I continued to focus on the warmth of the hand that I held and tried to block everything else out. I felt the ambulance slow, and finally stopped.

"We've arrived at the transfer location," the paramedic stated.

"Where are we?" the words were difficult, but I was curious where they had brought me.

The ski patroller placed his other hand on top of our linked hands. "We're at the washed out road that they're rebuilding. It was the fastest way to get you in a location for the helicopter to pick up you. It's still very dangerous here though. The wind is strong, even at this lower location and there are electrical wires that they have to miss."

The back door opened; I felt the frigid wind as it blasted into the ambulance. Both my rescuer and the paramedic prepared to move the gurney I was attached to. Once I was out of the ambulance the wind whipped snow flurries and the freezing cold momentarily distracted me from the excruciating pain. The two of them ran next to the gurney as they transported me quickly to the helicopter. Each jolt intensified the ache that was centered inside of me. I looked up into concerned, deep green eyes gazed down at me.

"Mia, the helicopter will take you now. You're almost there. It'll be a short ride. You're going to be fine, okay?"

I squeezed his hand one last time before he let go. I felt like my lifeline had been severed as he stepped away from the helicopter and I could no longer see him as I was slid into the small cabin. I really hated flying and I'd never been in a helicopter before. I was frightened and I sure hoped it would be quick.

The helicopter noise was deafening. I was poked and prodded during the flight. The radio crackled with communication from the trauma center to the helicopter. Even with the flight crew next to me, I felt alone and scared. I wished that my green-eyed rescuer was still by my side. I was so cold, I bit down on my molars in an attempt to keep my teeth from chattering out of control. I continued to fight the darkness that tried to tug and pull me into its murky depths. I instinctively knew that I could not succumb to it. If I did, I might never be able to shake loose from it.

Instead, I focused on the vibrant green eyes, as I tried to remember every detail of my rescuer's face. The slight stubble of facial hair gave him a rugged appearance. His hair was dark with blond streaked thru it, short, and a little spiky. His voice was so calming, the southern drawl unforgettable. I searched my memory for his name. I knew he mentioned it, but I couldn't pull it to the surface. I felt fuzzy; it was difficult for me to focus. The pain within overwhelmed me.

Finally the helicopter landed at the trauma center. Nurses and doctors scrambled to the helicopter and quickly ran next to the gurney until we were inside. Wind from the helicopter was warmer now that we were down the mountain. Medical staff immediately surrounded me. I bit back a scream as they moved me to a different gurney. All I could do was watch the flurry of activity as it moved above me. The white-gridded ceiling and bright lights above me were just a blur as I was wheeled into a room and the questions started all over again.

"Mia, you're nineteen correct?"

"Yes."

"Where do you hurt?"

"Stomach, awful, burning pain."

"Can you move your toes?"

I struggled to focus on moving my toes. The pain blinded me. All I wanted to do was to pull my knees up to my chest. But I was still strapped to the hard backboard; I was completely immobile.

"We need to get a CT immediately," a voice from across the room stated.

I didn't even know what they were doing to me. I knew they took my blood pressure, and pulse, and checked my heartbeat, but it all became such a blur. I gave up trying to follow it all. I just wanted the pain to end. I was rushed down several wide hallways. A sharp turn to the right, and I was in a frigid room with a large machine in the center. A woman's voice explained the procedure, but it was confusing. My brain was so fuzzy that nothing registered. By the time they rushed me back down the hall I couldn't fight the overwhelming pain any longer, and I succumbed to the waiting darkness.

A HEALING SPIRIT

Folding the last of the laundry I sat watching a TV movie. I had pies that were about ready to come out of the oven, and I had a good start on the prep work for the bulk of our thanksgiving meal. I wished Mia had stayed home to help, but I knew how much she'd been missing her friends.

Mia had always been such a social butterfly. Her friends were very important to her. Natasha and Mia had been close since they were little and when Bailey arrived she became one of them. When they both left for college I could tell how rough it had been for Mia to be left without them.

Quinn was the only one left out of the group that was still in the area. I was glad that she had at least one friend still nearby. The two of them had been hanging out a lot lately and I wondered if they were more than just friends, but every time I asked Mia she just laughed and said that he was like a brother to her. But I wondered sometimes when they were together if there might not be more than friendship between them.

I was enjoying the few spare minutes I had to myself since they were so rare. Even if I was doing the never-ending laundry. I knew that Trevor was in the garage working on his project car. Zach had moped around for a while after Mia had left but finally got over it and joined Trevor in the garage.

I set aside the last of the jeans I was folding and stretched out on the couch for a few minutes to relax. I knew I'd be busy tomorrow when a number of family members arrived for Thanksgiving that we were having this year at our house. The ringing of my cell phone pulled my attention from the TV. I looked at the caller ID expecting it to be Mia, but was a little surprised that it was her friend Bailey instead.

"Hi, Bailey."

"Hi, Gretchen, umm I don't know how to say this." Bailey was struggling to get the words out, her voice broken.

"Bailey, what's wrong, honey?"

"It's Mia. She's on her way to the hospital."

"What?! What happened?" my heart pounded, as I raced through horrific possibilities.

"She fell from the chairlift."

"She WHAT?!"

"She fell. I don't know how it happened. One minute she was there; the next she was gone."

"Bailey, where are they taking her?" Trying to rein in my fear, I bolted off the couch and ran toward the garage.

"Riverview Medical Center is what they told us. They sent her on a helicopter. She'll probably be there soon. We're on our way back down the mountain, but it's going to take us awhile to get there since we've got to take the longer road down."

"We're on our way. We'll meet you at the hospital."

I ended the call as I yanked the garage door open. "TREVOR!" I screamed as I stepped into the garage.

"What? You look like you're about to pass out. What's wrong?" he looked at me as he wiped his hands on a dirty cloth.

"We have to go now! To the hospital. Mia fell from the chairlift. She's in a helicopter on her way to the emergency room."

"Oh my God. Grab my wallet. Zach, grab a jacket —we need to go now!"

I ran back into the kitchen and grabbed my purse, Trevor's wallet, and the car keys. The oven caught my eye as I flew out of the kitchen. I turned back and shut it off knowing my pies weren't done, but the last thing we needed was a fire in the house.

We sped to the hospital in almost complete silence. I sat in the passenger seat as Trevor drove. My mind was a million miles away. I couldn't understand how she had fallen. Mia was a black diamond skier, she'd been on those lifts since she was little. Trevor found a parking spot near the emergency entrance and we ran inside. Just inside the entrance was a reception desk.

"My daughter. They're bringing her in on a helicopter. Where is she? Is she okay?" Trevor asked a red-headed receptionist.

"Sir, just wait a minute. Let me get some information first. What is your daughter's name?"

"Mia Kinney," Trevor answered.

We stood there at the counter while she worked on her computer. If felt like forever while we waited for any news. I found Trevor's hand and grasped it tightly.

"We have a transport that just arrived. It looks like she's the patient they brought in. Please come with me."

We followed behind the nurse to a private waiting room that was located down the corridor. Sunlight streamed in from the window. A couch and several chairs furnished the room, with a TV mounted on one of the walls.

"Please wait here. I'll bring you any updates as I get them. I have some forms you'll need to fill out."

Trevor pulled me into his arms. I tucked my head under his chin. I was shaking, and I couldn't seem to stop.

"It's going to be okay. She's in good hands." Trevor whispered into my ear.

"Trevor, she fell from a chairlift!" I sobbed.

"We have to think positive." He walked me over to the couch and sat me down, while Zach slumped into the adjacent chair.

The red-headed nurse was back with a clipboard and a stack of papers.

"Please fill these out for us as quickly as you can. They are assessing your daughter's injuries. We'll know more shortly. I'll be back with an update."

I reached for the clipboard, anything to keep my mind and body busy. The forms were long, words like "liability" and "release" blurred over and over. It seemed like forever, but as I looked up at the clock I realized it had only been less than twenty minutes.

"Mr. and Mrs. Kinney?"

"Yes."

I looked up as a doctor appeared in the doorway. He was in green scrubs. I searched his face for any information. But his expression didn't give anything away either good or bad.

"I'm Dr. Blake. Your daughter needs exploratory abdominal surgery immediately. Her X-ray's are good. Nothing's broken, but the CT shows she has internal bleeding, and we won't know the severity of her condition until we take her to surgery and can see what is happening."

"Oh my God. Is she going to be okay? Can I see her?"

"Mrs. Kinney, she's being prepped for surgery now. I need those papers signed so we can proceed."

I stared at the lengthy paperwork in front of me as the doctor continued to explain the risks and benefits of the surgery, but I was having trouble focusing. The words on the forms began to swim in front of me as tears streamed down my face.

"You need to sign them now. Every minute we waste is life-threatening. Your daughter is very critical right now. We're doing everything we can, but we need to get her into surgery."

My hands shook uncontrollably as I finished reading through the paperwork. I signed the sheets and handed the clipboard to Dr. Blake.

"Thank you. I will send someone with updates, but it could be awhile. I have a daughter just a bit younger than Mia. The staff and facilities here are the best in the area. I assure you, we will do everything we can. She's in good hands."

Dr. Blake turned and quickly left the room. Trevor pulled me tightly against his side, taking my shaking hands in his.

"She's going to be okay, honey. She's strong–and stubborn."

"We can't lose her, Trevor."

"We won't; she's going to make it."

"You heard the doctor. She's in critical condition."

"And people survive critical conditions all the time."

I couldn't shake my fear. Images of Mia through the years flashed through my memory. Tears continued to roll down my face. I leaned against Trevor, needing his strength. I looked over at Zachary. His face was pale. I reached out for him. He quickly sat on the other side of me and laid his head against my side. I pulled him tight and the three of us sat there in each other's arms.

CHAPTER FIVE

~ Bailey ~

I sat slumped against the side window in the passenger seat of the Tahoe. Collin drove as quickly as he dared on the twisting roads. An accident was the last thing that we needed, but we were all anxious to get down the mountain. I was frustrated that we weren't able to use the shorter road. It hadn't bothered me so much when we had driven up the mountain this morning since we were all having a good time in the car together. But now we needed to get back down the mountain as fast as possible and it was going to take us a lot longer than it should have. We also had afternoon traffic, which kept slowing us down. The silence was deafening, a complete opposite of our trip up the mountain.

The snow-covered trees and hills no longer held the beauty and excitement they had just a few precious hours prior. Unwanted memories began to flood my thoughts. Back to a few years previous, when my entire family had been ripped from me in a car accident. Those fears and the crushing pain were creeping back into my heart.

"Babe, she's going to be okay." Collin reached his right hand over to grab my left hand. He held it tight over the console that separated the two front seats.

"Yeah, Mia's a stubborn one. She's probably giving the nurses and doctors a hard time by now." Quinn added from the back seat.

"She was awake when they took her in the ambulance. That's got to be a good sign right?" Natasha asked.

"I hope so," I whispered. Thoughts of my younger brother as he lay in the hospital bed after the car accident ran through my head. The doctors had all thought he was going to make it and he didn't. I knew first hand that nothing was a guaranteed in the world.

The drive down the mountain took just short of two hours. Almost twice as long as it should have. With the shorter road closed, traffic was heavier on the two remaining roads that accessed the mountain communities.

Collin finally pulled into the emergency room parking lot and the four of us entered the crowded waiting room. Collin still had my clammy hand held tightly in his own. He looked down at me as we walked through the automatic doors. Quinn and Natasha were right behind us.

"I hate hospitals, Collin. I can't believe I'm back in one." I whispered.

"I know, baby."

We reached the registration desk. A red-headed woman in scrubs looked up from her computer.

"Can I help you?"

"Our friend was brought in by helicopter a couple of hours ago. Her name is Mia Kinney."

"I can't give out any information since you aren't family, but step over by those double doors and I can take you back to the waiting room where her family is. I'll be right there."

"Thank you."

We walked through the large, stark, and cold emergency room. It was packed. Several people sat in wheelchairs, while others slumped in chairs. Several sat along the edge of the room coughing, one mother had a little boy curled up in her lap, his cheeks bright red. The room was relatively quiet considering the number of people who occupied the space. We walked quickly to the double doors located on the opposite side of the room and waited for the nurse. There were several TVs mounted throughout that were playing a made-for-TV movie.

"Why is the ER always so cold?" Natasha asked. "I've got goose bumps."

"I've heard it's supposed to keep the spread of germs down," Quinn answered.

"Oh, I guess that makes sense."

We didn't wait long before the double doors opened, and the woman from the reception desk appeared. "This way, please."

The hallways were full of activity. Gurneys were being pushed from one area to another. Nurses and hospital staff rushed from room to room. Hospital volunteers brought blankets to those that waited in the ER and lab technicians was pushing a cart with several bags of lab specimens sitting on top. After a short walk with several turns, they reached a door marked "Family Waiting Area."

"They're in here. There's a vending area just down the hall to the right, and the cafeteria is upstairs on the second floor. The wait could be a while."

"Thanks," Collin said as he pushed the door open.

Collin's hand squeezed mine as we entered the room, Quinn and Natasha followed. I had a horrible sense of deja-vu. We had walked into the exact same waiting room that I'd spent way too many hours in when Collin had gotten into a car accident. Shortly after we'd started dating he'd lost control of his car. The roads were wet and another car had slid to his side of the road. When he swerved to miss the other car the backend collided with the other car and his car ended up wrapped around a pole. Luckily he only really suffered a broken leg.

Mia's parents and Zachary looked up immediately when the door opened. The four of us sat down in the chairs opposite the couch where Mia's parents sat.

"Is she okay?" I asked.

"She's in surgery. She's critical. They are doing exploratory abdominal surgery to determine the extent of her injuries," Mia's dad answered.

"Oh no," my grip on Collin's hand tightened.

"What happened?" Mia's mom asked, her eyes were red and swollen from crying.

"Mia, Bailey, and I were on the lift together. Mia was in the middle; we were doing one last run before lunch. Collin and Quinn were in the chair behind us. We were just talking and laughing, looking down at everyone on the slopes.

"Mia leaned slightly forward. It looked like she was trying to adjust the position of her snowboard. The chair came to a stop, and it swung a bit backward and then she was gone. She didn't make any noise; she was just there one minute and gone the next.

"It looked like we were close to thirty feet above the ground. From where we could see, she landed in like a ball. She was right next to a patrol hut. They got to her immediately and had her loaded on a toboggan and headed down the hill before we started moving again."

"Thirty feet? Oh my God. I can't believe she didn't break anything." Mia's mom whispered.

"She didn't break anything?" I asked.

"No, the doctor came in before she went into surgery. He said her X-rays were fine, but that they were concerned about internal injuries."

"We saw her before they loaded her into the ambulance. She was awake. She said her stomach hurt," Natasha added.

"The doctor said he'd give us updates, but we haven't heard anything yet. She's been in surgery for almost two hours now. They wouldn't let us see her. They were prepping her for surgery."

The door to the waiting room opened, and a man in scrubs entered. He looked tired, but calm. Everyone immediately stood as they waited for news.

"Mr. and Mrs. Kinney, I wish I had better news. Mia is bleeding internally. We haven't been able to stop it completely. She continues to lose blood. We've stabilized her with blood products and fluids for now, but she's not out of the woods. We need to get the bleeding under control before we can go back into surgery.

"She has a lacerated kidney, and she's bleeding from her liver. We've given her a medication called Factor VIIa that is still experimental for use in trauma patients. We are hoping it will help her blood clot so we can go take her back to the OR. This medication has been used on the front lines in combat to help stop bleeding. There is some thought that it may help in cases of blunt trauma such as your daughter suffered from her fall. We still need to remove the damaged kidney and repair her liver, but we can't do that until she's more stable.

"We've packed her abdominal wound, and they are taking her to ICU. A nurse will come get you after they get her settled into ICU. You can visit her very briefly then."

I watched the anguish flood Mia's parents; they were in a parent's worst nightmare. Mia's mom sagged against her husband as he held her around her waist. Tears streaked down both of their faces.

"Can I see my sister too, doctor?" Zachary asked quietly as he stood next to his mom.

The doctor looked down at Zachary; his eyes were full of sympathy. I'd seen that look too many times myself and if I never saw it again it would be too soon.

"I'm sorry, son. You'll have to wait until she's moved to a different unit. Only your mom and dad will be able to go in. But I promise, I'll let you see her as soon as possible okay?" Zachary nodded as the doctor turned his attention back to Mia's parents. "Mr. and Mrs. Kinney, do you have any questions?"

"Is she going to make it?" Mia's mom asked, her voice shaky.

"She's strong, she's made it this far. Staying positive for her is important. She's getting the very best possible care."

"Thank you, Dr. Blake, for everything. Please keep our daughter safe." Mia's dad reached out to shake the doctor's hand.

"I promise we'll do everything we possibly can. If you need anything there is a nurses' station right across the hall. Any of them will be able to help you. A nurse will be in shortly to take you to the ICU."

~ *Gretchen* ~

I sat in that waiting room for the nurse to take me back to see my daughter. I knew Mia was fighting for her life. I tried to not dwell on what could happen and kept telling myself everything was going to be okay. It was the only thing I could do. The door opened and the same red-headed nurse that had brought us to the waiting room entered.

"Mr. and Mrs. Kinney. I can take you back to see Mia."

"Zach, stay here with Mia's friends, okay? We'll be back soon," I said as I stood to follow Trevor. I gave Zachary a big hug, and kissed the top of his head.

"Please tell Mia I love her, and she needs to get better quickly." Zachary whispered.

"I will." I told him.

"Zach, here come sit next to me." Bailey patted the empty chair next to her as Zachary pulled from my embrace and walked over to Bailey.

Trevor put his arm around me, and we followed the nurse quietly out the door and down several hallways until they arrived at the ICU.

"Mia's this way."

We followed the nurse as they walked past the nurses' station and through double doors. The smell of antiseptic was strong. The noise of so many beeping machines nearby was distracting. The nurse walked over to bed one and pulled the curtains aside. I sucked in a breath, and the tears flowed. I quickly walked to Mia's side and gently took her right hand in mine. Trevor stood just behind me, his hand rested on my waist. I could feel his tension. I knew he was as worried about our daughter as I was.

"I'll leave you alone with her, I'll be back shortly." The nurse pulled the curtain around the bed to give us some privacy and walked away.

"Oh Mia, baby. Look at you." I whispered.

I gazed down at my only daughter. Mia's face was pale, but there were no scratches or bruises anywhere to be seen. She had a breathing tube and a machine on her left that quietly pushed air into her lungs. Another machine beeped as it monitored her heartbeat. She looked peaceful. It was hard to believe she had fallen so far. I could see bulges under her hospital gown. They were probably bandages, but I couldn't make myself look at them. The sight of the IV tubes attached to Mia's arm and the tube in her mouth was hard enough.

"Sweetheart, you're going to be okay. You're going to fight through this. You are strong. Don't give up. Zach says to tell you he loves you, and you have to get better quickly." Carefully I pushed aside Mia's hair from her face and leaned over to give her a light kiss on her forehead. "I love you, my baby girl."

Trevor pulled a chair next to the bed for me and I sat there, my hand holding Mia's tightly. Trevor's strong hand was clasped over mine, the three of us linked together. The sight of Mia lying so still on the bed tore through my soul. This couldn't be happening. No parent should have to see their child like this. I looked up at Trevor, and my heart broke even more as tears flowed unchecked from his eyes.

I continued to whisper softly words of encouragement to her. I knew there was a possibility that she could hear me.

"I love you, pumpkin. You need to fight; you can't leave us," Trevor pleaded.

Mia's chest moved up and down. The machine continued to help her breathe, while her body rested. Her eyelids began to twitch, and I felt her arm jerk slightly. Then there was a horrible alarm sounding on her machines. Nurses and doctors were rushing in, pushing us aside.

"What's going on? What's happening?" I cried out.

The red-headed nurse was pulling us aside, "I'm sorry; you both need to go back to the waiting room."

"Tell me what's happening to her?" Trevor yelled.

"I'll come let you know as soon as I know something more. I know it's hard to leave her, but please—you need to let them do their jobs."

We left the curtained room and stood against the wall for support. We were able to hear the nurses and doctors barking orders. Their voices were clipped, but professional. Fear surged through me.

"Oh my God. She's got to make it, Trevor; she's too young."

"I know, honey, I know." His words were barely a raspy whisper as his arms circled me and pulled me tightly to his chest.

CHAPTER SIX

~ *Dylan* ~

The paramedic and I ducked as we ran back to the ambulance. The blades from the helicopter continued to whip the snow up into a fury nearby. The overhead electrical wires that ran through the area were dangerously close. The two of us climbed into the back of the ambulance. The memory of Mia's pain-filled brown eyes continued to haunt me as we waited for the helicopter to take off. I glanced at my watch and noted that it had been forty minutes since Mia's impact.

"That's weird. Why did the sheriff volunteer helicopter come out to do the transport?" I asked the paramedic.

"I'm not sure. That's not normal. Probably was a blessing though. The wind is pretty harsh up here today. The sheriff pilots are able to get into locations that normal medical transports sometimes can't get to. That poor girl has a long road ahead of her."

"I know." I watched as the helicopter lifted off and became just a dot on the horizon.

"Well, we better get you back up to the resort."

"Yeah, I think I've had enough excitement for the day."

A HEALING SPIRIT

The ambulance ride back to the resort was quieter than the ride down. I sat in the back thinking about Mia. Her brown eyes had been so full of fear. Yet she had tried to keep calm. She was a strong one that was for sure. Serious emergencies, like Mia's, were ones that we trained for constantly. But when it happened, no matter how much training they did, it never made it any easier.

Most of the time my job was fun. The most common injuries typically were sprained wrists, dislocated shoulders, and concussions—usually caused by catching an edge or falling. We did see our share of more serious traumas usually caused during collisions. Falls from chairlifts did happen as well, but typically they were usually at the loading areas where heights weren't so great. Seeing Mia's curled-up body in the snow today would be burned into my memory for a very long time.

We reached the resort, and I opened the back door of the ambulance and jumped out. I thanked the crew for the lift and walked back to the ski patrol office. Corey was sitting at a table with a cup of coffee in his hand talking to Justin. They both looked up as I entered the room.

"Hey, how's she doing?" Corey.

I slid into the chair opposite Corey; my adrenaline burst was beginning to wear off. "She was still awake when they loaded her. I haven't heard anything else. I take it nothing's been reported up here?"

"No, we haven't gotten any updates. She took a nasty fall. That was a long way down."

"I know. It must have been close to thirty feet. What were the chances though that she landed right next to our hut?"

"I'd call it luck. Every minute counts. If she'd been anywhere else on the slope, our arrival time would have been longer."

"Let's hope her luck holds."

I tried to push her out of my mind and concentrate on the rest of my shift. My thoughts, however, kept finding their way back to her. I wondered how she was doing, was she even still alive? By the time my shift was done I found myself in my jeep driving down the mountain. I kept telling myself that I just needed to make sure she was okay. I didn't even take time to stop by my cabin to change.

⁓⸺⸺⸺⁓

~ Quinn~

The waiting room was eerily quiet. Cups of coffee and untouched food from the nearby vending machines sat scattered around on the adjacent side tables. Mia's parents had reclaimed the sofa with Zachary. Bailey's aunt and uncle had arrived for support. Bailey leaned against Collin's shoulder, their hands tightly twined together. Natasha was seated next to Bailey while I paced the room. There was no way I could sit calmly in a chair. I had to keep moving. We had been informed that Mia had been stabilized enough that they were taking her back into surgery. All we could do at this point was wait, and I hated waiting.

The TV on the wall in the waiting room was broadcasting the latest news, the volume on low. I looked up in time to see a shot of the ski resort and the exact area that we had been snowboarding.

"Look, isn't that where we were today?" I asked.

Everyone in the room turned to watch the news. A snowboarder was taking a video of the slope when I realized that the chairlift we had been on was at the edge of the screen. As skiers and snowboarders flew down the slope in the corner of the video they had captured Mia falling from the chair. Bailey and Natasha both screamed as they watched Mia fall from the lift.

"Oh my God. Someone caught it on tape!" Mia's mom sobbed.

It was bad enough knowing she'd fallen from such a height but actually seeing her fall was even worse. The news broadcasters had zoomed in on that small portion and replayed it. They were reporting that a female snowboarder had fallen and had been air transported to a local trauma center. At this time her condition was critical.

I couldn't believe the feelings that were raging within me. Mia was like another little sister. Mia and Natasha had practically grown up together, sleepovers, and play dates. As they grew up Mia and I had been friends, but that was it, nothing more. Seeing her lying in the snow, so far beneath me though had shaken me to my core. I watched her slim body as it was strapped to the wooden backboard and I had felt like something had been ripped from inside.

When we saw her before they loaded her in the ambulance I couldn't believe how pale her face had been. It had scared me, Mia had always been the vibrant, bubbly one. She lived life to the fullest. I had tried to joke with her when they were getting ready to load her in the ambulance. But the reality of it was that watching as she was pushed into the ambulance had to have been one of the worst moments in my life.

The past couple of years we had spent more time together after Bailey and my best friend Collin started dating. Over the past few months after Natasha and Bailey had left for college I still met her for coffee occasionally. Since I had also stayed in town, while most of my friends had gone away to college. It was nice to have someone I could call up and hang out with.

I was working on my associate's degree in computer programming from the same local community college where Mia was going. During the day I worked full-time at a computer software company. With our group of friends scattered to different towns I had told myself that I was just looking out for Mia. But now I wondered if there wasn't something more to our friendship. I glanced one more time, impatiently towards the door that remained closed. It had been at least another couple of hours since they had heard anything new. What was taking so long?

~ *Dylan* ~

I had made good time down the snow-covered mountain. The entire trip was filled with images of Mia. There was something about her that pulled at me. I tried to shake it off, and tell myself that I was just concerned. I was going to stop in and see how she was doing. Nothing more; I'd do it for anyone right? However, if I was really honest with myself I wasn't sure. I knew I'd typically call the hospital to see how things were with any patient, but to actually visit in person? Probably not.

Mia had been so calm, yet I could tell she was in a full state of panic. Her eyes were warm and comforting even though I could see she was scared. Her voice, as it softly answered my questions, stirred something within me that I thought I'd buried a long time ago. She was strong, but I wasn't sure if that would be enough to pull her through.

The receptionist at the entry lobby directed me back to a secluded waiting room. As I maneuvered through the busy halls, I reached the designated waiting room. I pushed open the heavy door. I immediately felt all eyes focus on me as soon as the door swung open. A group in ski clothing sat in the chairs on one side. I recognized them from the resort when they were loading Mia into the ambulance. There were a couple of older couples in the room as well. I assumed one of them must be Mia's parents.

"Umm, hi … I'm Dylan. I'm one of the ski patrol that assisted Mia. I just stopped in to see how she was doing."

A woman got up from her chair and walked over to me. Her eyes were swollen from crying. "I'm Mia's mom, Gretchen." She surprised me with a hug.

I felt incredibly awkward; I carefully placed my arm around her patting her back. I wondered if maybe I was too late and Mia hadn't made it after all. Mia's mom moved back out of my embrace and looked up. She looked a lot like Mia; the resemblance was actually quite stunning. She had the same warm, brown eyes that had haunted me the past several hours.

"Thank you for taking care of her. We don't have any new updates. She's back in surgery. They can't stop the bleeding. One of her kidneys is damaged, as well as part of her liver. Amazingly though, she doesn't have any broken bones."

An older man moved beside Mia's mom. He reached his hand out to me. I took it as he introduced himself. "I'm Trevor, Mia's dad. Please come have a seat; we're just waiting for any updates."

I crossed the room towards the group that had been at the resort with Mia. One of the guys motioned to an empty chair next to him.

"I'm Collin. We were with Mia at the resort. This is my girlfriend Bailey, my best friend Quinn, and his sister Natasha."

"You were there when we loaded her into the ambulance," I stated.

"Yes, Bailey and Natasha had been on the same chair as Mia. She had been sitting in the middle. Quinn and I were in the chair behind them."

"How'd she fall off?" I asked.

"We're not sure. She is an expert skier and snowboarder. She's been on the slopes since she was little. The girls said she had been leaning just slightly forward adjusting her board when the lift stopped. It swung slightly, then she was gone."

"She's lucky she fell so close to the patrol hut and not further up the slope. My partner Corey and I heard her land. She was conscious the entire time. That was a good sign, and we couldn't see any cracking on her helmet. But it looked like she had landed on top of her snowboard."

"Do people fall off the lifts often, Dylan?" Bailey asked.

"Sadly, we do have quite a few reports throughout the state each season of people who have fallen."

The door to the waiting room opened. The room fell silent as a doctor walked in briskly. His mask around his neck, surgical hat still in place. Mia's parents jumped up from the sofa; they faced the doctor.

"Mia's out of surgery. She's not out of the woods. She started bleeding out. She's lost a lot of blood, and her body is traumatized. We were able to finally stop the bleeding. But she'll still need another surgery to remove the damaged kidney and repair the liver. She wasn't stable enough to do that now.

"She's still with us, and she's fighting. That's all we can ask of her right now. The next twenty-four to forty-eight hours are going to be critical. We need to give her body enough time to rest, but it's a delicate line. We can't wait too long either to go in and repair the damaged organs."

"When can we see her?" Mia's mom asked.

"Family only right now," he stated as he scanned the full room. "I know everyone is concerned, but we have to keep the visitors down, so she can rest. I'd suggest you go home and get some sleep. There's nothing you can do to help her if you're exhausted as well."

"I can't leave her; what if something happens while we're gone?" Mia's mom's voice trembled.

"Take shifts then. But make sure you try to get rest and eat too. She's got a tough road ahead of her. We'll keep you updated. For now, she's resting, and that's the best thing for her. Do you have more questions?"

"Not right at this minute, but I'm sure we will have some after the shock wears off. Thank you, Dr. Blake." Mia's dad shook the doctor's hand as his other arm was wrapped around Mia's mom.

"You're welcome. We'll keep you posted."

The doctor turned and left the room. Mia's parents were still in each other's arms. I guess I was driving back up the mountain. At least I knew she was still alive and while she was still in critical condition she was fighting. I knew she'd be a fighter, it was something I'd known from the moment I met her. How I knew that–I had no idea.

Bailey stood up and walked over to the other older couple that was in the waiting room.

"Her parents?" I asked Collin.

"No, her aunt and uncle. Her parents were killed in a car accident a few years ago." Collin answered.

"Oh, wow. I'm so sorry."

"Yeah, it was pretty rough for her, her younger brother and sister were killed too. She was the only survivor."

"That's horrible."

"Her aunt and uncle have been great during it all. Her aunt is the twin sister of her mom."

"Really? That must be kinda hard sometimes."

"I'm sure it has been. But I think in some ways it might have helped her too. Let her feel like her mom was still there with her."

"You guys talking about me?" Bailey asked as she walked back to us and slid under Collin's arm.

"A little." Collin said as he kissed the top of her head.

"My aunt and uncle are headed home. They've offered to drop us all off."

"Okay, well I guess we better head out. I'll go see what Mia's parents want to do with their Tahoe." Collin stated.

"Thanks for driving down to check on Mia." Quinn stated as he stood from his chair.

"We hadn't heard anything up at the resort yet." I answered as I stood up to leave. "It was nice to meet you. I'm going to head home now."

I felt slightly out of place and moved quickly out of the waiting room. But not before Mia's mom caught me one more time in a hug and thanked me again for helping her daughter. I hurried down the busy hallways anxious to be back in my jeep.

CHAPTER SEVEN

~ Mia ~

The steady beeping wouldn't go away. I was groggy, in a fitful sleep full of dark nightmares. I struggled to move under an intense weight that I felt on my chest. It was like something heavy was crushing me. The immense weight caused my breathing to be difficult. My only focus was to turn off the frustrating alarm clock and make the beeping go away. Why couldn't I open my eyes? It was like they were stuck shut. Where was that damn clock? It continued to beep.

This was all a horrible nightmare; I just needed to wake myself up. My breathing quickened. The pressure in my chest fought against each breath I took. Something was holding me down … I was sure of it. There was a burning deep in my stomach, cramps, and sharp pains shot through me like I'd never felt before. Where was I, and why couldn't I wake up?

A HEALING SPIRIT

I sat curled up in the chair next to Mia's bed. I'd been there most of the night with her. My neck ached from the odd angle that I'd fallen asleep in. It was still early. I glanced through the glass door into the open area where the nurse's station was located. It appeared that the nurses must be getting ready for a shift change. I turned back to Mia and watched her steady breathing. Mia was so still, her face and skin were ghostly pale. I fought back yet another batch of tears as I took Mia's hand. It was frighteningly cold. I began rubbing my hands over Mia's cold one as I tried to give it warmth. I felt her hand twitch. I wasn't sure if I had imagined it. I waited, holding my hands still over Mia's, but there was no movement. I wanted her to wake up so badly that I must be imagining things. Then I noticed Mia's eyes. Her eyelids were fluttering like she was trying to open them.

"Mia, can you hear me? If you can hear me squeeze my hand."

Nothing, but the fluttering was getting stronger, and her hand twitched again. This time I was sure. Then I noticed Mia's heart rate quickened, the beeping increased.

"Mia, can you hear me? It's Mom. I'm here with you. You're going to be okay, sweetheart."

I turned as I heard the door open behind me. The red-headed nurse who had been with Mia since she was brought in entered the room.

"Mrs. Kinney, I'm going home," the redhead said.

"Okay, thank you. I think she's waking up. Is that possible?"

The nurse walked closer to the bed. She reviewed the read-out on the nearby machine. "It's doubtful that's she's waking up. We still have her sedated. Why do you think she's waking?"

"I thought her hand twitched, and her eyelids were fluttering."

"That's normal. She's in a deep sleep. It looks like her heart rate increased, but it's back down. Everything looks good right now. Dr. Blake will be doing rounds soon and will check in with you. He's one of the best here in the hospital. Your daughter is in good hands."

"Thanks. I'll stay with her until my husband gets here."

"When he gets here, please try to go home and get a little rest. You will need it."

"We'll see."

I gave the nurse a slight smile as she left the room. I focused back on Mia as I continued to rub her chilly hand.

~ Dylan~

I had always been an early riser. It didn't matter what time I'd gotten to bed the night before. By the time Mia had gotten out of surgery it had been late. The small cabin that I rented was back up the mountain near the resort. The roads had been treacherous and icy, making the drive take twice as long as usual. It had been early morning before I'd been able to finally get to bed.

Thanksgiving was always a busy day at the resort, but this year I'd actually gotten the day off. I had promised my mom, that I'd stop by for lunch. She was having her new boyfriend Elliot over and a couple of their friends. I groaned as I turned in my bed. I wasn't looking forward to spending the day with my mom's friends.

While I grabbed my morning coffee and got ready for the day all I could think about was Mia. I wondered how she was doing today. I couldn't shake her out of my head. I figured I must be crazy. I'd had the strangest dreams with her in them, and I usually never remembered my dreams in the morning. However, these were still vivid in my mind.

Just before noon I finally ventured over to my mom's house. I cringed as I entered. It was going to be a long afternoon. I should have taken Corey up on his invitation to join his family today, but I knew I'd never hear the end of it from my mom. Before she started dating Elliot a few months back it had just been the two of us for the past several years. It was good to see my mom happy for the first time in her life. My early childhood years were not full of fun memories. In fact, most of them I tried to shut away into the deepest corner and keep them locked down. I swore I'd never be like my father, and I lived every day trying to prove to myself that I was different.

"Dylan! Come here, give me a hug."

"Hey, Mom. How's it going?"

"I swear you get bigger every time I see you!"

I chuckled as I pulled my mom into a hug. Her head barely came to my chin. "It smells good in here. Did you make fresh apple pie too?"

"I sure did. I know it's your favorite. Come in. Everyone is already here, and I've got almost everything set out."

Surprisingly, I enjoyed the company. My mom's friends were funny and full of energy. I helped my mom clear the table and loaded the dishes for her. I stood at the sink and watched the birds flitter from one snow-covered branch to another as they flung soft white flakes to the ground. The sun was out today. The bright rays reflected off of the snow. It was beautiful here, peaceful. My thoughts turned again to Mia. Was she sleeping peacefully? Or was she still fighting for her life?

My mom walked into the kitchen carrying the last of the plates. She was laughing as she set the plates down next to me. I rinsed the dishes and placed the last of them in the dishwasher. She placed her hand on my shoulder.

"Are you okay, honey? You seem distant."

"I'm fine, Mom, just thinking."

"About?"

I looked down into my mom's green eyes, so much like mine. "Just a girl. She fell from the chairlift yesterday. Corey and I were the ones who took care of her. She's critical down at Riverview Community Hospital."

"Oh Dylan, I'm sorry. I'm sure you and Corey did everything you could. You're very good at what you do. How old was she?"

"A few years younger than I am. There's just something about her I can't shake. I even went down to the hospital to check on her yesterday after I got off work. I never do that Mom, ever. Work is work. I never get involved."

"You know what I always say … things happen for reasons. We just don't always know why. Follow your instincts, honey. Listen to your heart."

"I feel like I need to be there at the hospital, but I don't know why. I don't know her or her family."

"Then go. I'll even save you some pie. You can get it later."

"Thanks, Mom. I love you."

"I know. I love you too. Now go! And keep me posted. I want to hear all about this girl."

"It's not like that Mom. She probably has a boyfriend."

"Well, you're never going to find out standing here in my kitchen."

"I'm going. I'll call you later." I leaned over and gave her a hug.

"Bye, honey. Drive safe; the roads are still icy."

"I will."

Behind the wheel of my jeep I couldn't believe I was once again driving down the mountain. I must really be losing it. The uneasiness I'd felt all morning began to lessen the closer I got to the hospital. It was still early afternoon when I arrived at the hospital and was directed back to the same waiting room. I pushed the door open and couldn't believe how packed it was. Mia must have a very large family. I noticed that Mia's friends, Collin and his girlfriend Bailey were in the room. I crossed the room to where they sat.

Collin stood up and reached his hand out. "It's Dylan, right?"

"Yes. How's she doing?" I asked as I shook Collin's hand.

"She's resting. They say she's stable. If things keep going like they have been, they'll be able to go back in soon to remove her kidney and repair her liver. Her dad comes and gives us updates. Her mom won't leave her side."

"That's good news then. Is everyone here part of her family?"

"Mostly; many of them were already in town for Thanksgiving. There are a few of our classmates here from high school, but mostly it's family. I don't know everyone. Here, sit with us. So what brings you down here on Thanksgiving?"

"To be honest, I don't really know. I guess I just felt like I needed to see how she was doing."

"Mia's a special girl. She's always been full of life. Nothing has ever been able to keep her down. She's loyal, and she might seem quiet and reserved, but when she's riled up she's a force to reckon with. Trust me, I've experienced her wrath firsthand." Collin laughed as Bailey slugged him playfully on his shoulder.

"Please. Collin, you had that coming. Mia was only standing up for me," Bailey chimed in.

"Sounds like there's a story behind that," I replied.

"Let's just say guys can be oblivious sometimes." Bailey commented with a smile.

"Yeah, I guess so," I said as I watched Collin and Bailey. I could tell they were close, and completely in love with each other.

The door swung open and Mia's dad walked in. He looked exhausted, the strain he was under was obvious. Everyone quit talking at once and waited for the update.

"Mia's stable. They've decided it's time to do the third surgery. They'll be taking her in shortly. If they can remove the kidney and repair the liver without further complications, they are hopeful that they won't need to go back in after that."

Before anyone could even ask questions he was out the door.

~~~

It was almost midnight. Hours had passed since they'd taken Mia into surgery. Mia's parents sat stiffly on the couch with Mia's little brother who had fallen asleep. His head rested against his mom's arm. The group had received a few text messages from the OR saying that the procedures were going as planned. But it was taking longer than they had originally expected.

I glanced at my watch for what must have been the hundredth time. I really needed to get home. I had work the next morning, bright and early, but I couldn't pull myself away. Not until I knew that Mia had made it through surgery.

I'd spent most of the afternoon getting to know Collin and Bailey. They were easygoing and very friendly. It seemed like Mia had some really great friends and family. Bailey had opened up more about her past. I learned that Mia and Natasha had befriended her after she had moved in with her aunt and uncle after her family's deaths. Apparently the three of them had been inseparable after that.

Natasha and Quinn arrived after dinner. They were a tight-knit group of friends. I never really had that growing up. My family had moved around a lot while I was growing up, and I'd had a hard time making friends. I always seemed to feel like an outsider. Once my mom and I had moved to Southern California to Snow Ridge, a small mountain town, I had finally settled in and made some friends. Corey and I had done our Outdoor Emergency Care training together. Spending hours
~~~

together studying and participating in various scenarios as we learned how to survive in not only outdoor winter environments, but the wilderness in general. We had classes in ski and snowboard injuries, different types of illness that could happen at high-altitudes and cold weather. We were taught and educated about the special equipment that is used during emergencies and how to transport patients.

Many of the ski patrol members were certified EMTs or paramedics and both Corey and I were working toward that level of medical certification. We were required to maintain our medical training either through refresher courses or expanding our medical and outdoor skills. We had also joined the local search and rescue team along with a few others from our ski patrol.

The ski patrol had become family to me. We had to trust each other with our lives. We worked as a team, a complete unit. Corey and I had become closer because of all the time we spent during our initial training. We were not just close friends at work but also outside of work.

Dr. Blake entered the waiting room a little after midnight. He had dark circles under his eyes. He was rubbing his neck as the door shut behind him.

"Mia is stable, out of surgery and in recovery. The surgery went as planned. It just took longer than we had hoped. She may be awake as early as tomorrow morning. Visitation is still restricted to family only. She needs to rest."

Mia's parents stood and quickly crossed the room to where Dr. Blake stood.

"Thank you, Dr. Blake." Mia's dad shook his hand.

Mia's mom reached out and hugged him. "Thank you for saving my daughter."

"You're welcome. I'll check in with you tomorrow." Dr. Blake exited the waiting room. The door shut quietly behind him.

There was a collective sigh of relief throughout. I sat quietly as I watched the relief flood Mia's parents' faces. As many of Mia's family members started leaving, I quickly said goodbye to Mia's friends and slipped out. I moved through the halls in search of Corey's older sister Chelsea. She usually worked the night shift. I was almost positive she worked as a nurse in the ICU. I wanted to see Mia for just a minute before I left. I knew only family was allowed in, but maybe I'd get lucky.

My luck held. Chelsea was working that night. I found her at the ICU nurses' station.

"Hey, Dylan. What brings you here, and this late?"

"Hey, Chelsea. I have a huge favor."

"Uh-oh, I hate to even ask."

"Can you let me in to see Mia Kinney? Just for a couple of minutes? I promise I'll be in and out."

"Dylan, I can't do that. You're not family."

"Please, Chelsea. Corey and I were the ones that treated her on the slope. I just want to see her before I head home. She wasn't in such great shape when they loaded her into the helicopter."

"Okay, two minutes. That's it, Dylan. Make it quick. She's this way." Chelsea got up from her chair and turned towards the rooms behind her.

"Thanks, Chelsea. You're the best."

"Yeah, well you're too cute to say no to. Besides, I know you keep my brother out of trouble all the time." She grinned.

"I guess there is that." I smiled. Chelsea had accepted me into her family like another little brother. We reached Mia's room, and Chelsea pulled the curtain back allowing me to walk to the bed.

Chelsea pulled the curtain shut and whispered "Two minutes, Dylan. I mean it."

Mia's blonde hair lay in tangles on the pillow. Her face was pale, the breathing tube in her mouth was taped in place. Dark shadows were under her eyes. I remembered them being a deep brown, with a few light gold flecks. Her arms lay at her side. A probe was on one index finger, I knew monitored her oxygen saturation, an IV was attached to her other hand. There was a machine that monitored her heartbeat. The beeping had been turned off. I knew they often did that because the sound often caused sleep deprivation for a patient.

I picked up her icy hand and carefully held it in my own. I didn't understand my need to touch her, to have a physical connection with her.

"Hey Mia … it's Dylan, from the slopes and the ambulance ride. I just wanted to stop in and see how you were doing. Keep fighting. You're doing great. You have lots of friends and family here supporting you. … Well, I better go before I get in trouble. Bye, Mia."

I released her hand and stood up to leave. I didn't understand the pull she had on me. Before I left, I leaned down and my lips lightly brushed her forehead. I reached the curtain that surrounded her bed and gazed back at her one last time.

CHAPTER EIGHT

~ *Mia* ~

My throat was scratchy and dry. My eyes felt puffy and swollen. My body was sore. It felt like I'd been crushed. It was hard to think and focus. *Where was I? Why did everything hurt so bad?* As words swirled around me I tried to focus on them. *What was being said? And who was doing the talking?* My right hand felt warm, and fingers rubbed lightly against my skin. *Why couldn't I just wake up?* I felt something in my mouth as I tried to spit it out. I was starting to panic. *What was in my mouth?*

I tried to focus on just my eyes. I willed them to open. I blinked several times before I could finally see a dim light. Everything was blurry, but I noticed a dark shadow to my right. I tried to turn my head toward the shadow. My eyes were starting to focus, and a woman began to take shape. She appeared older. Brown hair skimmed her shoulders. She was crying, tears were streaming down her face. There was something taped to my face, and it felt like a wide straw was shoved in my mouth deep into my throat. I reached up to try to pull it out. Immediately my arm was held down by a balding guy wearing scrubs. He stood next to the side of my bed. My eyes flashed to him alarmed.

"Mia, we need you to stay calm. I'm one of the ICU doctors. You have a breathing tube in your mouth. We're going to remove it for you, but we need you to stay still and help us okay?"

Mia? Yes, that was my name. I thought to myself, but things weren't making sense. *A breathing tube? What the heck? Now I was really starting to freak out.* I felt the tape being removed from my face as the doctor stood over me.

"I need you to try to relax, don't fight it okay. Here we go."

I felt the tube as it slipped from my throat.

"Good girl, we're almost done."

I watched his deep blue eyes and tried to stay calm. The reassuring instructions I was given tugged at a memory, but I couldn't recall it for the life of me.

"There we are, can you cough for me? It will help clear your airways."

I coughed, and my throat was sore and raw. But being able to breathe without something shoved in my mouth was a relief.

The lady who had been crying in the corner was standing next to the doctor. Her hand held mine.

"Oh Mia, we've been so worried," the lady said.

"How are you feeling?" the balding guy asked.

Who was this lady? A shiver of fear ran through me. *How was I feeling?* I didn't know. I didn't even know where I was. *Think Mia, think!* I focused on my body.

"I'm sore, my body aches. It hurts to talk," I answered.

My voice was horse and raspy. I didn't even recognize it.

"That's to be expected. Your body has been through three surgeries. You are going to be sore for a while. Your throat should start feeling better soon. That is from the breathing tube. You need to rest. I'll be back to check on you at the end of rounds."

The doctor left, and I focused on the lady standing next to me. She seemed familiar, but I had no idea who she was. I tried to pull my hand away.

"Who are you?" I asked in a whisper.

"What do you mean who am I? Mia, I'm your Mom. Don't you recognize me?" the lady questioned, her voice shook.

"No."

"Do you remember anything? Do you know your name?"

"My name's Mia, Mia Kinney."

"Mia, how old are you?"

"I'm nineteen."

"Do you remember the accident?"

"Accident? What type of accident?"

"You fell from a chairlift."

Memories flooded me. The sudden impact when I landed in the snow, the green eyes of someone helping me. Gentle words of encouragement that were whispered to me, the slight southern accent that had soothed me. A hard, unyielding board that had been pressed tightly against the back of my head. An ambulance ride, and fierce pain that burned deep in my stomach, like it had been on fire. I remembered the noisy helicopter blades as they whipped snow in the air and a quick flight. Being rushed into the emergency room, and then nothing, but pure blackness.

Panic began to take control as I tried to move my arms, was I paralyzed? I didn't know. Could I feel my feet? I moved my fingers. Then focused on the feeling in my feet. I willed my toes to move. I could see the blanket twitch, and I could feel my feet. *That had to be a good sign right?* I sighed slightly as just that bit of movement caused me to feel exhausted.

Then the sharp pain in my stomach became almost unbearable. I reached my hand to settle on my stomach and almost cried out. The IV burned on the top of my hand and the knife-like, piercing pain that radiated from my stomach took my breath away.

I looked over at the lady. How could I not remember my own mom? What else did I not remember?

"I remember some things. How long have I been here?"

"It's the Saturday after Thanksgiving. You went snowboarding with your friends on Wednesday. You've had three surgeries: two almost back to back, when you first arrived on Wednesday, and a third one on Thanksgiving. You've been sleeping since then. Your dad and I have been taking turns sitting with you. Your friends have spent a lot of time in the waiting room. You've been through a tremendous ordeal."

"I'm so tired."

"Just rest, sweetheart. I'm going go get your dad okay?"

"Okay." I closed my eyes once more and drifted into a fitful sleep.

A HEALING SPIRIT

~ Gretchen ~

I walked through the hallways towards the waiting room where Trevor waited. I was relieved that Mia was awake, but how could she not even recognize me? Her own mother? I knew she'd been through a lot and it was probably normal that not all her memories were there. But they said she hadn't suffered any head trauma, so why didn't Mia know me? The doctors hadn't said anything about her possibly missing some memories. What else did she not remember?

Opening the door to the waiting room I spotted Trevor seated next to Zachary. One look at my husband's face and the tears started all over again. Trevor bolted from his chair and pulled me tightly to his warm chest. I hugged him tightly, so thankful that I still had the love of my life by my side.

"What's wrong, sweetheart? Is she okay?"

"She woke up."

"What? But that's good news, honey!"

"Trevor, she doesn't remember me. She didn't even know who I was."

"What do you mean she didn't know you? Are you sure she was awake?"

"Yes, she knew her name, and age. She said she remembered some things. She asked how long she'd been here, but she didn't know who I was."

"I'm sure that's normal; could just be a side effect from something. Honey, she's been through a lot the past couple of days. At least she woke up, and she's alive."

"I know. I am so grateful. I couldn't even imagine her not making it."

Trevor guided me to the nearby couch as we sat next to Zachary.

"What happened?" Zachary asked.

I looked at my son and knew how worried he'd been about Mia. Now that she was awake I'd try to see if we could let him visit her. I knew he wanted to see with his own eyes that his sister was going to be okay.

"She woke up, and the doctor took the breathing tube out. Then the doctor left. That was when she asked who I was and where she was. I told her and then she said she remembered a few things. She was tired, and I told her to get some sleep.

"I left the room and talked to her nurse. They were going to notify Dr. Blake immediately. They said that sometimes patients react differently to the different drugs and anesthesia. That we shouldn't worry right now, and that sleep is a good thing for her."

"Well then, let's focus on the positive." Trevor stated.

"You're right. She's strong. She's going to pull through okay."

"I got a call from one of the guys I work with. He and his wife had gone down to the blood bank to donate blood in honor of Mia."

"That was sweet of them."

"He said the entire waiting room was full of kids from Mia's high school and people from town who were also giving blood in honor of Mia. The staff told him that they've never seen such a huge community outpouring like that."

"Really? How amazing to have such support from everyone. I'm in shock; I don't even know what to say."

"Collin, Bailey, Natasha, and Quinn started it. They reached out to their classmates. It has spread like wildfire. They are even planning a blood drive at the school next week when everyone comes back to class."

"Mia's got some very special friends. They've been here almost as much as we have the past few days. And that cute ski patroller, Dylan, has even stopped in several times."

"Cute, huh? Should I be worried Mrs. Kinney?" he teased.

"No, I have eyes only for you." I smiled as I leaned against his shoulder.

"Oh no, you're not trying to play matchmaker are you?"

"Who me?" I asked innocently, while Trevor just chuckled.

CHAPTER NINE

~ *Mia* ~

The wind was cold and crisp, my cheeks burned. My arms were in front of me. I was falling, falling into the whiteness so far below. My stomach was queasy like I was on a roller coaster. The ground was coming toward my face, and I couldn't stop it. I screamed before I felt the impact.

The scream woke me up from the nightmare, and I bolted up in bed, pain shot through my stomach. I glanced at the curtains surrounding my bed. I had to get up and get out of here. I flipped my legs over the edge of the bed. My toes touched the cold floor, and I tried to stand. I ignored the IV stand next to me that was still connected to my hand. The curtain flew to the side, and a young nurse rushed into the room.

"Mia, are you okay? I heard a scream. Please sit back down. You need help getting up. We don't want you falling." The nurse stated as she rushed to the side of the bed.

"I've got to get out of here."

"Mia, you've been through a lot. You need to rest first."

"No, I need to get out of here."

"Mia, you need to lie back down. You have sutures in your stomach."

"Why am I here? I just want to go home."

I saw the young nurse leaned over and pushed the call button next to the bed. I was hot; it was burning up in here. I was beginning to feel dizzy. Another nurse rushed into the room.

"I need help. We're going to need to get her back in bed."

"Mia, you were injured in an accident; we're trying to help you. We need to get you back into bed," the second nurse explained.

"Why does everything hurt? Why are you spinning me?" I asked.

"Mia, you need to lie back down." The first nurse calmly stated.

The two nurses had me back in bed and covered with the covers. The room at least had quit spinning, but it was way too hot in here.

"She's running a fever." The second nurse said.

"I was afraid of that. Stay with her and make sure she stays in bed. I'll go get Dr. Blake."

~ Gretchen ~

Sunday afternoon, the waiting room was nearly full when Bailey, Collin, Natasha, and Quinn walked in. I looked up when the door opened. I was waiting for Trevor to come back. My eyes burned and I knew they were blood shot and had dark circles under them due to lack of sleep. I had my hair pulled back in a ponytail to keep it out of the way. I really needed to take a shower and get some sleep, but I just hadn't been able to make myself leave the hospital for long. Mia's friends walked over and sat across from me.

"Hi, guys," I greeted them.

"How's Mia today?" Bailey asked.

"She's running a fever now. They are worried about infection and fluid in her lungs."

"Oh, no. I thought she was doing better since she woke up yesterday," Natasha stated.

"She's a fighter. She's going to be fine," Quinn added.

"Yes, she is. But it doesn't make the waiting any easier," I sighed.

"Is her memory any better today?" Collin questioned.

"No, she's not making any sense today. She's tossing and turning, calling out bizarre things. She recognized Trevor yesterday, knew her dad, but doesn't remember me? How can that happen?" Fresh tears slid from my eyes as I quickly brushed them aside. "I want to thank you all for everything you've done. Trevor said you guys were organizing a blood donation in honor of Mia. You guys are very special friends to Mia. She's lucky to have you for support."

"It's the least we could do. We've felt so helpless … we had to do something to help." Bailey replied.

"Bailey and I have to drive back to Las Vegas tonight. We've got class in the morning. We're dropping Natasha off at the airport so she can fly back to school. Quinn will be checking in and keeping us updated. But if you need anything, or if something happens and we need to drive back, let us know, and we'll be here as quickly as we can."

"Thanks, Collin. I really appreciate that. I'm sorry your Thanksgiving break was ruined."

"We're just glad Mia's alive and will be okay. I'll be flying back home for Christmas break; that's only a few weeks away," Natasha said.

"Collin and I will be back for part of Christmas break too. She should be feeling better by then."

"I'll be back tomorrow to see how she's doing. I don't have class tomorrow; I can stop by after work."

"Quinn, you really don't have to keep coming by. I can text you and keep you updated. I know you have a lot going on with school and work. Mia wouldn't want you to get behind on anything."

"It's okay. I'll stop by when I have a few minutes."

"Well, we better head out if we're going to get Natasha to the airport on time." Collin said.

I stood up and hugged each of Mia's friends tightly, whispering thank you to each of them as they left the room. The waiting was wearing on me, but I had to be strong for Mia. My daughter needed all the support she could get around her. I brushed aside my tears. I knew we'd get through this somehow, someway. Life had just dealt us a staggering blow, but even in the worst of times there had to be something good that would come out of it. When Trevor arrived, I was going home for a shower and some sleep. I knew Mia was going to be okay, she had to be.

CHAPTER
TEN

~ Dylan ~

Corey sat across the table from me in the ski patrol hut. The door to the hut was wide open. The sun glistened off the slushy snow. The weather had turned warm with no end in sight. It had been a week since Mia's accident, and I had visited the hospital several times. I just couldn't get her out of my mind. The other night she was still fighting a fever and still not in the clear yet. I hadn't been able to get Chelsea to let me back to see her again, but I wasn't giving up.

"Hey, are you listening to me?" Corey asked.

"Huh, what?"

"Dude, you've been totally out of it the last couple of days."

"Sorry, I've had things on my mind."

"Yeah, a cute little blonde with dark brown eyes."

I grinned, "Maybe you're just sorry you didn't get to her first."

"She probably won't even remember you. You are pretty forgettable," Corey teased back. "I asked if you had plans Saturday night. A group of us are headed down the mountain for dinner at a new steakhouse."

"Sure, I'm game. When are you guys driving down?"

"Sara is calling for a reservation at five o'clock. She just needs to know how many of us are going."

"How many in the group are going?"

"I know of at least six of us including you; not sure if anyone else is coming."

"Sounds like fun. Are you and Sara getting serious?"

"Me? Getting serious? Doubtful, at least not right now. We're just friends. We're having fun hanging out."

"Does she know that? You know how the girls are always hanging all over you."

"Well, I am irresistible." He laughed.

"Whatever." I grinned as I stood up, grabbed my skis, and walked out the door.

<hr>

Saturday night after dinner with my friends I was driving home. The radio blasted classic rock as I maneuvered my jeep onto the freeway. Corey had tried to get me to go to the movies after dinner at the steakhouse, but I had passed. It had been a couple of days since I'd stopped in at the hospital and I decided I'd make a quick stop before I drove back up the mountain.

I pulled into the hospital parking lot and got lucky with a spot right up front. Visiting hours were almost over and I quickly navigated the hallways to the waiting room I'd spent a number of hours in during the past week. Corey was probably right. I was crazy. I didn't even know this girl who had invaded my daily thoughts. She probably even had a boyfriend. Yet, here I was again when I could have been at the movies with the rest of my friends.

Reaching the waiting room I found it empty. Every time I'd stopped by this week there had always been several of Mia's family and friends in the room. I didn't remember all their names, but I did recognize them. I left the room and walked quickly down to the ICU nurses' station. Maybe Chelsea was working tonight. She'd been off the past couple of days.

When I got to the ICU nurse's station Chelsea sat behind a computer, talking on the phone. She glanced up as I approached and held up a finger, letting me know she was almost done. I casually leaned against the desk and looked down the hall toward Mia's room. I still hadn't run into any of Mia's family, which was unusual.

"Hey, Dylan. I've been seeing a lot of you lately," Chelsea teased.

"Yeah, I've been checking in to see how Mia's doing."

"She's not here anymore."

"What? What do you mean she's not here anymore? What happened to her? Is she okay?"

"They moved her to a different unit. That's all I can tell you. Go back down to the main lobby and ask for her room number from the reception desk. They should be able to give you more information."

"Thanks, Chelsea."

Worried, I walked briskly back to the main entry. An elderly couple stood at the reception desk. I stood behind them and waited impatiently. I was running out of time. There was less than thirty minutes left for visiting hours.

The couple, finally got the information they needed and then slowly walked towards the bank of elevators off the lobby.

"One moment please, I'll be right with you."

I stepped up to the desk. I shifted my weight restlessly from one foot to the other as I waited until the young man finished whatever he was preoccupied with.

"Sorry, our computer system just went down, and I'm trying to reboot it. What can I help you with tonight?"

My luck was headed downhill quickly. Really? The entire computer system? Great, just great, I thought to myself.

"I'm looking for Mia Kinney. She's been in ICU this past week. One of the nurses there said she has been moved to a different unit and that you could help me."

"Give me a few minutes. Hopefully my computer will reboot. It's been having issues all day."

"Is there someone else who could help me?"

"Not at this hour. It seems to be coming up okay this time. Give me a minute."

"Okay, thanks."

I watched the elderly couple step into the elevator. The waiting room behind the desk was practically empty. There was a small group clustered together over in a corner. Janitorial staff was beginning the evening cleaning, and it looked like the gift shop was starting their preparation to close for the night.

"Okay, it's up. Who are you looking for again?"

"Mia Kinney."

"Here she is. Let me write her room number down for you. Take the elevators to the eighth floor. Turn left when you exit. Follow the hall until you get to the nurses' station. They can help you from there. Visiting hours are almost over so you won't be able to stay long."

"Thanks."

I took the paper he handed me. I walked quickly to the elevators, reaching them just as they opened. I stepped into the elevator and pushed the button for the eighth floor. Music played quietly in the background. Finally the doors opened with a crisp digital voice announcing "eighth floor." I followed the hallway and reached the nurses' station. An older, heavyset nurse looked up as I approached.

"Can I help you?"

"I was told Mia Kinney had been moved to this unit from the ICU."

"And you are?"

"A friend."

"Name please."

"Dylan Blackburn."

"Give me a minute, Dylan. Mia's mom is with her right now. I'll let her know you are here."

"Thanks."

The nurse got up and walked down the hall and into a nearby room. Left standing at the counter, I felt nervous. What was I doing here? Mia's mom probably wouldn't even remember my name. Maybe I should just turn and leave. But I knew deep down I couldn't. Something pulled me to Mia, and I didn't understand it.

A few minutes later the nurse stepped out of the room, and Mia's mom followed. As she reached me she pulled me into a hug, which surprised me. I guess she did remember me. I awkwardly hugged her back.

"Dylan, I'm glad you stopped by. I meant to get your number the last time I saw you, but by the time I remembered you'd already left."

"How's Mia?"

"She's doing much better. She finally beat the fever, and they got her infection under control. She's calmer now, more like herself, which is a huge relief, and she finally remembered me the other day."

"That's great Mrs. Kinney. I'm glad she's doing better. Do they know how long she'll have to stay in the hospital?"

"They haven't said yet, but they said to expect at least another couple of weeks if she continues to get better. Would you like to see her? I'm sure she'd like to see you again."

"Yeah, I'd like that."

"Follow me, I'll take you back."

~ *Mia* ~

I shifted slightly in bed. I'd finally been able to get somewhat cleaned up. I yearned for a hot shower, but had been told I needed to wait a few more days. Washing my hair out of a small tub of water was difficult, but at least my hair wasn't greasy anymore, and my mom had finally been able to get the last of the tangles out. My mom had braided it to help keep it out of my way and prevent future tangles. I was starting to feel human again. No longer did my teeth feel furry, and my throat was no longer scratchy, but it still burned like I had a bad sore throat.

My new room was a bit smaller than the previous room, but I had a better view out of the window. I'd been able to watch the sun set, which had caused bright crimson and oranges to streak across the few clouds that spotted the sky. The TV mounted to the wall across from my bed was finishing a rerun. The volume was so low I could only make out a few words.

My mom had left the room saying she'd be right back. I was so tired all the time now. I felt like all I did was sleep. I leaned my head back against the pillow and shut my eyes, just for a minute. I awoke to my mom's voice.

"Mia, there's someone here to see you."

My eyes flew open and caught the green eyes that had haunted my sleep staring back at me. I remembered him talking to me after the accident. His eyes were more vivid green than I remembered. Immediately I felt self-conscious about how awful I must look. I pulled the lightweight covers up a bit further.

"Hi, Mia. I'm Dylan Blackburn from the ski patrol. Do you remember me?"

"Yes, but I'm not sure how much was real. A lot of that day is all mixed up in a fog."

"I'll leave the two of you alone. There's not much time before they're going to shoo us out of here for the night." My mom walked over to the bed and leaned down to kiss me on the forehead. "I love you, sweetheart. Dad and I will be back in the morning."

"I love you too, Mom. See you in the morning."

"Dylan, I hope to see you again soon. Thanks again for all of your help and support. I'll always been indebted to you."

"It wasn't just me. The ski patrol works as a team. We're all crucial. There were several team members that helped with Mia that day."

"And I owe each and every one of them for helping to save my daughter's life. Okay, I'm really going this time. Night, Mia. Try to get some sleep."

"Night. Oh, and Mom? How about you get some sleep tonight too."

"I just might be able to now that you're doing better."

I watched as my mom turned and left the room. My eyes focused back to the handsome stranger standing at the end of my bed. I knew I looked awful, but was thankful at least I'd been able to clean up a little bit. His brown hair was streaked with blond and slightly spiky and framed his face perfectly. His southern accent was just as I remembered, as it had drifted through my dreams a number of times. I couldn't break eye contact with him as he walked to the chair that was next to the bed. He smiled and I felt my cheeks flush. He was gorgeous, way better looking than the broken memories that floated through my head of him. I glanced down at my hands as they tightened around the blanket. I took a deep breath to calm myself and then looked back up.

"You gave us all a pretty good scare. How are you feeling?"

"I'm still really sore. I don't remember much from the last few days. The last thing I really remember is arriving at the emergency room. I remember you though; you kept talking to me all the way to the helicopter. I think I even dreamed about you. Wow, I'm sorry, I can't believe I just said that out loud."

"That's okay, I'm flattered." Dylan smiled.

"It must be your accent. I kept hearing it in my head; it calmed me. I remember trying to focus on it."

"You were really lucky, Mia. If you'd landed further up or down the mountain Corey and I may not have heard you, and it would have taken us longer to get to you."

"I don't even know what happened. I was in the chair one minute and the next minute I was in the snow. I remember falling what seemed like forever. It didn't seem real. It was like one of those dreams you have where you're falling but you wake up before you land. I kept thinking to myself I was just having a nightmare and that I needed to wake myself up."

"You've been through a lot, three surgeries, fever, infection. You're a fighter."

"Probably more like stubborn." I grinned.

"Maybe a bit of both was needed." he smirked.

A nurse interrupted them as she entered the room. "Five more minutes."

"Okay, thanks." Dylan replied.

"Dylan?" My voice so quiet I wasn't sure if he'd heard me.

"Yes."

"Thank you."

"You're very welcome. Well, I guess I better go before they come chase me out of here."

"Will you come back?"

"Would you like me to come back?"

"Yes, I really would." And I knew I did. I reached my hand and touched the top of his hand. The contact caused a shiver to race up my arm.

"Then I'd be happy to come back." Dylan took my hand as it lay on top of his and brought it to his mouth as he kissed it softly. "Sweet dreams, Mia."

The gesture was so sweet; I think I lost part of my heart at that moment. He pushed the chair back and stood up. His bright emerald eyes searched mine as he gently placed my hand back on the top of the covers.

"I'm glad you're okay." He turned and his tall broad frame walked to the door. I wished he could stay longer.

"Dylan?"

He turned back to look at me "Yes?"

"Do you have a girlfriend?" It came out of my mouth before I could really think about it but I had to know. I held my breath waiting for his answer.

"No."

I grinned and I actually wanted to jump up and down. Excitement raced through me and I was finally beginning to feel like myself.

"Mia?"

"Yes?"

"Do you have a boyfriend?"

"No."

Dylan smiled, and his green eyes sparkled. "I'll see you later. I work tomorrow so I might not make it down until the next day, but I will be back."

"I'll be waiting." I knew I was smiling so big, but I didn't care. I watched him turn and leave the room and I couldn't wait until he'd come back.

CHAPTER
ELEVEN

~ *Quinn* ~

I reached for my phone as a text came through from Collin.

> *Collin:*
> *Bailey just heard from Mia*
> *she's out of ICU*

> *Quinn:*
> *Really? That's great I'll try to*
> *stop by and see her*

> *Collin:*
> *I'll let Bailey know, she*
> *keeps wanting to drive*
> *back, I told her we'd be*
> *there in just a couple*
> *weeks.*

> *Quinn:*
> *You know how those girls are*
> *lol*

> *Collin:*
> *I know!*

A HEALING SPIRIT

I set my phone back on my desk and tried to focus on the paper I was finishing for finals. After thirty minutes and not getting any further I gave up and decided to go see how Mia was doing. While I had waited for hours at the hospital during Mia's surgeries, I realized that I had feelings that I'd never even known were there. I guess when you recognize you might never get a chance to talk to someone again you re-evaluate everything that you may have wanted to say. It was probably nothing more than the same type of protectiveness I felt for my younger sister Natasha.

"Yeah, right." I mumbled to myself.

My emotions had been on a roller coaster ever since the accident, and I hated the ups and down, but I wasn't sure how to get things back on even, calm ground. I saved my document, shut down my computer, left my room, and was on my way to the hospital. Less than twenty minutes later I was nearly jogging through the halls to Mia's new room. I spotted Mia's dad and brother as they exited her room.

"Hello, Quinn."

"Hi, Mr. Kinney. Hey, Zach, how's it going?"

"Good, they let me see Mia today!" Zachary was an excited ten-year-old boy again, not the solemn boy he'd last seen in the waiting room.

"That's great. I bet she was excited to see you."

"That's what she said. She doesn't look so good though."

"Zach, give your sister a break. She's been through a lot," Mia's dad quietly reprimanded.

"I know, Dad. I'm just being honest. Isn't that what you always tell us?"

He laughed as he ruffled his son's hair. "Yes. Quinn, you're welcome to go in. We're just leaving. There's no one in there right now."

"Thanks."

"We'll see you around. Come on Zach, we've got to pick up lunch for your mom."

"Bye, Quinn." Zachary followed his dad full of excited energy.

I reached the door of Mia's room and pushed it open. Mia lay in the bed, her eyes shut; her face lacked any color. Her hair was pulled back and a braid hung over her right shoulder. I felt like someone had just punched me in the stomach. She looked so fragile. I couldn't understand all the new emotions that consumed me. I pushed them deep inside as I continued to walk to the bed. Balloons and flowers filled the small counter located along the side of the room.

~ *Mia* ~

"Hey, Mia."

The familiar voice made me smile as I opened my eyes and Quinn walked to the end of the bed. "Hey, Quinn."

"To quote your brother, you don't look so good," he said with a grin.

"Ha, ha. Thanks a lot! You're supposed to be my friend," I teased back.

"I am, that's why I can't lie."

"Here, sit. I texted Tasha earlier but haven't heard back from her."

"She's probably at work. I'm sure she'll text you back as soon as she can. You scared us all pretty good."

"Yeah, well, it's not something I planned to do. I missed the whole Thanksgiving break with everyone."

"At least you're still here with us, and everyone will be back in a few weeks. We can hang out then."

"Excuse me, Mia, we need to get you up and start walking." A dark-haired nurse in navy scrubs briskly entered the room.

"Okay, well, I better go then, Mia."

"No, Quinn, wait. You can stay with me. He can stay right?"

"Sure, the doctor just wants you to start moving. The sooner you get up and around, the faster you're going to get better. Your friend can help you, if you'd like."

"What do you need me to help with?"

"She's going to be weak, and she needs to keep the IV stand with her. Just walk along with her. You can push the IV stand. We'd like to get her to the end of the hall and back this first trip and continue to expand the frequency and duration."

"I can do that."

"Mia, I have some socks for you that have some grip to the bottom. These will help keep you from slipping."

The nurse moved to the side of the bed next to where Quinn stood and pulled the covers back. My hospital gown reached just to my knees. The rest of my legs were bare, and I needed to shave. I hoped Quinn wouldn't be able to tell. I pulled the second gown tightly around me like a robe. I hated how exposed the hospital gowns made me feel. My toenails were painted with my favorite hot pink glitter polish that sparkled under the lights. At least something was bright and colorful. The hospital socks felt slightly scratchy as the nurse slid them over my feet.

"Okay, Mia, we're going to try to get you to stand. What's your friend's name again?"

"Quinn." I answered as I looked up at him.

"Quinn, I'm going to have you stand on her right, next to the IV stand and I'll be on her left to make sure she's stable.

"Mia, I need you to roll to your side, carefully swing your legs to the side of the bed and use your arm to help push yourself to a sitting position. The weight of your legs will help as well."

"That sounds easy enough." I sat up slowly, pain flashed through my stomach as my abdominal muscles flexed. I pushed back a wave of light headiness "Ow, maybe not so easy."

"Take your time. We'll do this slowly, in steps."

I reached a sitting position, using my arm as my legs swung over the side of the bed where they dangled. Looking up I caught Quinn's gaze, his deep brown eyes searched mine, intense, different than I'd ever noticed before

"Take a minute. How are you doing?" The nurse asked.

"Okay. It's not burning so bad right now."

"Good, let's try to get you standing. Easy to your feet." She instructed.

I grabbed the side of the bed tight. I slid the last few inches off the bed so that my feet finally touched the ground. I looked down at my feet as I carefully tested my weight as I tried to stand.

"Take my hand, and let go of the bed. Good. Now, let's see how far you can go. Quinn, follow right behind us with the IV stand. Mia, take it slow, one step at a time, don't hesitate to rest okay."

"Okay, let's do this." I stated.

The three of us made it slowly to the door of the room and into the hallway.

"You're doing great Mia. How do you feel?"

"Tired."

"Do you think you can make it to the end of the hall and back?"

"I'll try."

"Good girl. Let's see how you do by yourself. I'm going to let you go."

The end of the hallway felt like it was at least a mile away. Pushing aside my doubts I was determined to get to the end and back; after all, how hard could it really be? One footstep after the next, no problem. Right.

"You're doing great. Keep it up. Quinn, stay right next to her. Mia, I want you to walk right next to the side of the hallway. If you need to stop and grab the rails, that's fine, I'll be waiting here."

I glanced up at Quinn as I smiled. "I feel like a child learning how to walk again."

"Trust me, you don't look like a child."

"Thanks for being here, Quinn."

"That's what friends are for right?"

"This feels above and beyond right now. Let's do this."

I reached the end of the hall and began the long journey back. I felt like I'd just run a marathon. My breathing was quick, and my legs were starting to shake under me. The nurse was just a few more feet ahead of me when my legs gave out and I stumbled. Quinn's quick reflexes caught me tightly around my waist before I hit the floor. My stomach burned, causing sharp pains to slice through me that radiated up and down my body. I hated being so weak—it completely sucked.

"Easy, I've got you." Quinn stated as he held me tightly.

His arm held me firm as I leaned against him for strength. I was surprised by how solid he felt. His light cologne tingled my senses as goose bumps ran up my arms.

"Come on, let's get you back." Quinn stated without letting go of me.

The nurse reached us in just a few quick steps. "Mia, you did really good for your first time up. Let's get you back to your bed. We'll try it again later. A little more each time and you'll start feeling stronger soon."

I carefully slid my arm around Quinn's waist as he helped me back into my room. I leaned into Quinn's warmth and strength. My stomach fluttered as I tried to keep my emotions in check. I was baffled by the feelings running through me. This was Quinn, one of my best friend's brothers. He was like another brother to me–a good friend–that was it. But now, I wasn't so sure and it was confusing. Maybe I did hit my head when I fell. We finally reached my bed and I slid back into the crisp sheets. Exhaustion overwhelmed me and I unsuccessfully tried to stifle a yawn.

"Thanks, Quinn. I almost landed on my face out there."

"You've got to stop doing that! Glad I could be of assistance. You look worn-out. I'll let you rest now. I'll come back another time."

"Okay, yeah, I am pretty tired. I feel like all I do is sleep."

"That's good. It means your body is healing."

"I guess so. I just want to get out of here and get home."

"I'm sure it won't be long. You are a pretty determined girl."

Quinn stood at the edge of the bed. He leaned over and quickly brushed his lips against my forehead in a quick kiss. "See you soon."

I lay in stunned silence after Quinn's kiss. His lips were soft against my warm forehead. Quinn was almost out the door before I finally pulled myself together enough to respond in a quiet whisper. "Bye, Quinn."

I was losing it; I had to be. Quinn had never shown any type of affection towards me before. We had a teasing brother-sister relationship. Fatigue overcame me before I could fully analyze the situation, and I fell into a troubled sleep.

~ Quinn ~

I was confused by my reaction to Mia, much less the impulse to kiss her forehead. I'd almost kissed her on the lips and reined myself in just in time. That would have been a disaster. I was sure Natasha would hear about it and would probably tease me mercilessly with just a quick kiss on her forehead. I didn't have any regrets though, and smiled at the thought. Maybe I did have feelings for Mia. Maybe they'd always been there buried beneath the surface, and it had taken almost losing her to bust them loose. Pursuing a more romantic relationship was a bit frightening though as she might not feel the same way. I didn't want to lose her friendship. We'd been friends for years, practically growing up together. Confused, I drove back to my house to finish my paper.

CHAPTER TWELVE

~ Dylan~

$\mathcal{I}$ was heating up dinner while I flipped through the TV channels. The holiday season was in full swing with Christmas movies, advertisements, and special sales. My small one-bedroom cabin was warm and homey. I loved it; the main living space was an A-frame vaulted space with large rough-hewn timber beams. There was an old, black freestanding fire stove in the corner of that sat on a brick hearth. Large picture windows looked down into a small valley. Most of the snow from the storm the previous week had melted leaving a few small piles still visible under the trees and on the shady side of the slopes.

It was still early evening and my thoughts drifted to my visit with Mia the previous night. I'd been relieved when she had asked me to come back and visit her. I'd planned to visit her tomorrow on my day off, but I'd gotten off a little early today. I didn't have any specific plans for tonight. If I left right now there'd still be almost two hours left of visiting hours.

~ Mia ~

I was bored. Completely bored out of my mind. I was tired of lying in bed, tired of sleeping, tired of watching TV, tired of being connected to the IV. I was fed up with my fingers and toes being swollen from all the fluids they kept pumping in me. Was sick of being prodded and pricked by the nurses. I was frustrated I couldn't take a real shower. Irritated that I had to call the nurse if I wanted to get up, and it had only been my first full day awake and in my new room.

The doctor had told me I would probably be here at least another week. I was already itching to escape. I was beginning to think insanity would ensue before I was allowed to leave. I wanted to go home, to sleep in my own bed, to eat real food. I still wasn't sure exactly what I'd had for dinner; I'd been so hungry though I ate it all.

My nurses were persistent in getting me up and moving. My strength was growing, and I had now been able to walk the length of the hall twice on my own without assistance. I wasn't out of breath as much, and my legs weren't shaking anymore.

My mom had brought my cell phone early in the morning when she'd come to visit. I finally had a lifeline to the outside world. There were several text messages and my voicemail was full of messages from friends and relatives all wanting to make sure I was okay. It felt good to finally have contact with them again. I reached over and disconnected my phone from the charger and flipped through my emails. I was beginning to text Bailey when the door opened. I groaned to myself. I thought it was the nurse again. It was probably time for more pain medication and to get me up again, but instead a deep, soothing, voice brought me to full attention.

"Hey, you're looking better."

I dropped my phone in my lap, forgotten. I was immediately lost in deep emerald green, sparkling eyes. "Hey Dylan, I thought you were working today."

"I did, I got off a little early and thought I'd come down to visit." Dylan crossed the room and sat in the chair next to the bed, never breaking eye contact.

My stomach quivered as I watched him walk to the side of the bed. His dark charcoal gray sweater emphasized his broad shoulders; a white t-shirt was slightly visible at the V-neck.

"I'm glad you came. I'm so bored. I can't wait to get out of here. I really think I'm going to go crazy before they let me out."

His laugh was a deep rumble. "You've been unconscious for over a week, and less than twenty-four hours after you wake up you're already ready to get out of here?"

"Yeah, don't laugh. I'm serious."

"I'm sure you are. You are a stubborn one, aren't you?"

I grinned at him. "Maybe."

"So, do you go to school? Work?"

"Both. Right now I'm getting my general education classes done at Riverview community college. I'm not sure what I want to do yet. I work part-time as a receptionist at a hair salon and sometimes babysit. Right now, I'm hoping my instructors will let me make up my assignments and finals. I don't want to have to take the whole semester over again."

"I'm sure they will understand and let you make things up. Sounds like you keep pretty busy."

"Yeah, I guess I've always been one who couldn't sit still. I get the feeling you know a lot more about me than I know about you. It's my turn to ask some questions."

"Fire away."

"Where are you from originally. I love your accent." I grinned.

"A little town in South Carolina, near Myrtle Beach."

"Family?"

"My mom lives up in Snow Ridge, not far from me. We've lived there for about five years. No brothers or sisters."

"Are you close to your mom?"

"Yes, she has a new boyfriend now. His name is Elliot; he's been good for her. They've been seeing each other now for a little over a year."

"And your dad?"

"I don't have any contact with him."

"Oh." I was a little taken back but his abrupt answer.

"It's okay, no loss."

I noticed the hardness that came over his face when the topic of his dad had come up. I was curious but didn't know how far to push. I wanted to know more about this handsome stranger who had helped save my life.

"I'm sorry. You don't have to talk about him if you don't want to."

"No, it's okay. The memories are not good ones, and I've tried to move on and forget about it."

"Maybe you can tell me another time if you want. How long have you been a part of the ski patrol?"

Dylan smiled. "A little over two years. I started college not really knowing what I wanted to do. During the winter of my second year I decided to try the ski patrol. I loved it and have been working there full-time since. During the summer they have other activities at the resort that I help with. I've been starting to get involved in a search-and-rescue team as well."

"Really? That's cool."

"There are several of us who are part of the search-and-rescue team and are also members of the ski patrol. My partner, Corey, helped with you when you fell. He's part of the search-and-rescue group with me."

I heard the noise of a cart being pushed into my room. "Ugh." I groaned.

"What's wrong?"

"They're coming to poke or medicate me again."

"It's for your own good." He laughed.

"That's all I've heard all day."

"Sorry to interrupt. Mia, we need to check your vitals, and it's time for your pain medication," the nurse stated as she entered the room.

"Do I need to leave?" Dylan asked.

"No, this will only take a minute. Mia, we also need to try to get you to walk one more time tonight."

"Maybe I should leave."

"No. Stay. You can walk with me."

I reached over and grasped Dylan's hand. It was warm—and strong. Tingles shot up my arm, and I let go almost immediately. I must be hypersensitive right now I thought to myself. First Quinn, now Dylan; what was going on with me?

The nurse checked my wristband and then handed me a small paper cup with pills and a glass of water. After I washed down the pills I handed the paper cup back to the nurse and waited while she checked my vital signs.

"Looks good. Okay, let's get you up."

Sitting up was the hardest part. My abdominal and back muscles still groaned in protest. My incisions from my surgeries were still very tender. It was easier to stand up and walk though then it had been earlier in the morning. I moved to the edge of the bed and glanced up into the clear green eyes that watched me intently. My breathing quickened as I struggled to get my thoughts in order.

"Dylan, can you grab the IV stand? It's easier if someone else pushes that while I walk."

"Sure. After you." Dylan gestured toward the door.

Dylan's right hand pulled the IV stand while I stood to his left. His hand lightly touching the slight arch of my lower back as we slowly walked out of the hospital room and down the hall.

The light touch of Dylan's hand against my back was distracting. This walk down the hall was much more difficult than the previous ones I'd taken. My focus was on the handsome guy next to me, instead of concentrating on the task of putting one foot in front of the next. I stumbled a couple of times, almost losing my balance, but was caught by Dylan's strong arm that gave me stability and support. Each touch though made my stomach plummet to my feet. As we entered my room on the return walk I let out a nervous giggle.

"What's so funny?" Dylan asked.

"Hmm…what?"

"You giggled. What's so funny?"

I glanced up into the warmth of his gaze. Dark, thick eyebrows framed his intense green eyes. His face was narrow and tapered gently to his strong jaw. He had a slight cleft in the center of his chin, with a coating of dark stubble that covered his face. At the bottom of his jaw–slightly off center of the cleft–I could see a faint white line where no hair grew. Without thinking I reached my fingers up and traced the scar.

"What happened here?" my fingers brushed along the edge of his scar. I felt his jaw tighten.

"An accident a few years ago. I fell and busted open my chin. They had to stitch it up."

"Oh, that must have hurt." My hand dropped to my side. I couldn't believe my boldness to reach out and touch him. It was like my hand had a mind of it's own.

"A little, not like what you've been through lately though."

Dylan's left hand reached up and brushed away pieces of hair from my eyes that had managed to escape my braid. His touch lightly followed down the profile of my cheek. Blood rushed to my face where his fingers touched. I broke his gaze and stared down at my sock-covered feet. Carefully his fingers reached my chin and with a slight pressure he lifted my gaze upward from the floor. I could feel tension as it radiated from him.

"What's wrong?" he asked.

"Nothing."

"Something's bothering you. I can see it written all over your face."

"You make me nervous. I look horrible in this ugly hospital gown and these scratchy hospital socks. And you have no idea what I'd do for a real shower." The words spilled from me before I could even think about what I was saying. I had a habit of doing that and I knew one day that was going to get me into trouble.

His emerald eyes sparkled. "Honesty, I like that."

Dylan's fingertips moved to brush my lips softly. My legs felt like they had just lost any strength I had left. His hand moved to the side of my face and gently his lips touched mine in a quick kiss. I sagged against his hand. He pulled away slowly and I lost myself in his eyes.

"I've been wanting to do that for awhile now. You're beautiful Mia. Hospital gown and socks included." He grinned. "You should probably get back in the bed before you're too tired."

Tired? I thought to myself, highly doubtful, my entire body felt like it had been energized. I wondered how I was going to be able to go to sleep now. Carefully I turned and slid into the bed, pulling the sheets over myself.

Dylan had barely sat back down in the chair next to me after pushing my IV cart up to the head of the bed when the nurse came back in.

"Sorry, visiting hours are over. Mia, you've made some great improvements today. Tomorrow we'll start increasing the distance."

"Okay." I whispered as the nurse turned and left the room, my eyes shifted back to Dylan.

"I see someone brought your cell phone. What's your number?"

I rattled off my number as I picked up my discarded phone and added Dylan to my contact list.

"One last question. Well, maybe two last questions. What's your favorite color and favorite food?" He asked.

"Well, I have a few favorite colors. Purple is usually the one I lean toward the most." I flipped my phone over revealing a purple case and smiled. "Food, hmm… Mexican probably, and any type of dessert. Why?"

"No reason, just curious." He grinned back at her as he stood up from the chair.

Before I could even prepare myself, Dylan had leaned over brushing his lips against mine. I kissed him back, my hand found the side of his face and the light stubble brushed against my palm. He deepened the kiss then pulled back leaving me yearning for more. My body tingled, my heart quickened, I sighed as I opened my eyes to stare into the handsome face looking back at me.

"I'll see you soon Mia."

"Okay, I'll be here. Guess I'm not going anywhere anytime soon."

"Then I won't have a hard time finding you. Good night Mia, sweet dreams."

"Night, Dylan."

Lying against the upright pillows as Dylan left my room I was sure I wasn't going to ever be able to fall asleep. Today had been by far one of the most confusing days of my life. My medication helped calm me and not long after Dylan left I fell into a deep sleep, resting without nightmares or the restlessness that had been present for well over a week.

CHAPTER THIRTEEN

~ Mia ~

I pulled off my new super-soft purple slipper socks that Dylan had bought me. They were so much better than those scratchy white hospital socks! I felt like I'd been living in a florist's shop the past week with the daily deliveries of colored flower bouquets and get-well balloons. Besides my family, both Quinn and Dylan had been constant visitors bringing me real food, keeping me company on my walks, and making me laugh.

It was finally time to go home, and I couldn't get out of there fast enough. I was dressed and waiting for the final release from the doctor. Christmas was a little over a week away. This year I'd gotten ahead on my Christmas shopping. Since I had been stuck in the hospital, online shopping had become my best friend. Bailey and Natasha would be back in town by the end of the week, and I couldn't wait to see them. Most of all I couldn't wait to spend time with Dylan outside of the hospital. He'd come to visit me almost every day, and if he didn't visit in person he would text or called me on the phone.

Dylan was still a mystery. I loved spending time with him. I felt like I'd known him my entire life, but there were times I felt like I'd hit a wall. He didn't talk much about his childhood or past beyond the last couple of years. When the topic would come up his answers were vague, and he'd change the subject. I wondered if I'd ever be able to chip away at the barriers or would that be a part of him he would never share with me. Whatever had happened to him had hurt him deeply, and I might never know what the cause of that pain had been.

I knew I was falling for Dylan, his voice calmed me, his deep green eyes that seemed to know what I was thinking before I did. I thought a lot about the day of the accident. If I'd never fallen from that lift would I ever have crossed paths with him? What if he hadn't been working that day, or at that particular station when I fell? I wondered, maybe sometimes the most difficult times in a person's life become the most beautiful.

Bailey had been through a life-shattering event a few years back, losing her entire family in a car accident. When Bailey had moved to Riverview to live with her aunt and uncle, she was so quiet, living in a constant nightmare. She was always questioning why she was the one who had survived. Natasha and I had befriended her, but it had been Collin that had finally turned her life upside down and helped bring happiness back into her life. The two of them had been good for each other, and I had gotten one more great friend as well.

I couldn't help feeling that maybe this whole experience was more than meeting Dylan. I wondered how many others had fallen from chairlifts like I had. I felt like I had survived this accident for a reason. There must be something I could do to prevent others from going through what I had the past few weeks.

I sat bundled up on the couch. I'd been home for two days now, and it felt incredible to start getting back to a normal routine. I'd been trying to catch up with my schoolwork. My teachers had been very supportive and were working with me so that I wouldn't have to take my fall semester classes all over again. It was still overwhelming though, and I wondered if I'd be able to get caught up before the next semester started.

To make matters worse I couldn't seem to focus on my schoolwork. Every time I got my laptop out I found myself scanning through the Internet researching chairlift accidents. I couldn't believe how many people each ski season fell off chairlifts. I was lucky, very lucky, as many of them didn't survive the fall. My heart broke every time I read about someone's child falling, their life abruptly stolen from them during a fun family activity.

I knew skiing and snowboarding were hazardous sports, but I was more aware of broken bones and other injuries, like hitting trees or other obstacles. I'd never really thought about falling from a chairlift. My parents had been taking me and Zachary skiing since we were little. We'd practically grown up on the slopes. While we were taught to be careful on the lifts I didn't realize before how children especially were at risk when they rode up on those lifts. Their shorter legs and proportions of their bodies put them in a position inherently more prone for falling than an adult.

What was even more amazing to me was that there were states that required safety restraint bars on the chairs; I'd never seen one before. What shocked me was that out of all the states that have ski slopes only two states required these bars—Vermont and New York.

While these bars wouldn't stop all falls, they had been shown effective to deter injuries. Even if it saved one person wouldn't it be worth it? I felt like there had to be something I could do, some way to bring better awareness to the benefits of restraint bars, and chair lift safety in general.

CHAPTER FOURTEEN

The room was pitch black. A scream had ripped Dylan awake from a sound sleep. He sat up listening when he heard something shatter. A muffled groan, and then he heard it, his mother's pleading. Dylan pushed back the covers and leaped from his bed, running towards the agonizing sounds.

His dad's rages were escalating, becoming more frequent, and more violent. Would it ever end? He'd begged his mom to leave. His dad had threatened he'd kill her if she tried to leave him. She'd told Dylan the risk was too great; she worried he'd track her down and that Dylan would be the one to suffer. What she didn't realize was that he was already suffering.

Dylan wasn't a child anymore. The past year he'd shot up in height and strength, and he wondered how much more of this he could take. Bursting into the living room his eyes swept across the room. His mom was pushed backward on the couch, her right eye was already swollen, and her arms were up over her head. The glass mason jar full of roses from his mom's garden was shattered on the floor. The coffee table had been overturned.

"STOP!" Dylan shouted.

"Dylan, no." His mom whimpered from the couch.

"Boy, stay out of this. Go back to your room." His dad turned to glare at him.

"No Dad, leave Mom alone."

Shoving past his mom on the couch his dad turned to him. His dad's face was flushed with fury, his eyes dark and cold. Dylan braced himself. He'd never been on the receiving end of his dad's violence. His verbal attacks yes, but so far he'd never endured the physical abuse that he'd seen his mom suffer through as he grew up.

"Go back to your room. NOW!" His dad yelled at him.

His dad's breath confirmed what Dylan had suspected. He'd been drinking, and from the slight stagger as he'd crossed the room, it appeared he'd had quite a lot to drink. His father was strong, and alcohol made him even more unpredictable and deadly. He stood almost six and a half feet tall. He was a construction worker, and that kept his muscles toned and strong. He was a force to be reckoned with, especially when intoxicated.

"Leave Mom alone. Why don't you just leave?"

"You want some too?" He grabbed Dylan's shirt pushing him against the wall.

Dylan could see his mom struggling to get on her feet. "Randy, no, leave him alone. Please," she begged.

"He had his chance. Disobedient little brat needs to learn a lesson."

Dylan pushed hard against his dad, causing his dad to lose his balance. He got one punch in, that landed hard against his dad's stomach. Randy laughed, mocking him. "Is that all you've got boy? Such a weakling. You're an embarrassment."

Randy swung his fist, catching Dylan under the ribs. Dylan felt the crack and the instant pain shoot through his chest, knocking the wind out of his lungs, as he gasped for air. He watched his mom stagger behind his dad.

"Randy, stop. He's your son. Leave him alone."

"He hit me first, Jolene."

Dylan staggered to stand back up, just in time for the blow to the side of his face knocking him backwards, his body twisting slightly as he fell. He landed on the stone fireplace hearth, his chin took the brunt force and split open. Dylan felt a warm stickiness pool across his mouth and tasted the rusty saltiness of his blood. He heard his mom scream and then nothing but blackness.

~ *Dylan* ~

I sat up, my mouth dry, sweat dripped across my forehead, and my sheets were damp. I felt my chin where my scar was a daily reminder of the nightmare I'd lived through. It had been a long time since I'd dreamt of that awful night and I wondered if I'd ever be able to totally put it behind me. It was only four a.m., I knew I'd never be able to go back to sleep. I might as well get ready for the day. I hoped it would go fast and the weather would cooperate so that I could get down the mountain after work to visit Mia.

I followed the GPS instructions to Mia's house. Driving down the mountain had been treacherous and took me twice as long as usual. The fog had rolled in and the weather report was calling for another storm that could last over the weekend. I was tired, and had to be even more careful navigating the curvy roads. The nightmare I'd woken up to that morning had left me restless, but there was no way I was canceling on Mia tonight. This was the first time I'd be seeing Mia outside of the hospital, and I wondered if things would be different.

I'd been at ease with her from the very beginning. There was something about her that enticed me. I liked how Mia's emotions were open for anyone to see, it was like reading a book. She was honest and wasn't trying to hide things. Her brown eyes had light golden flecks along the edge making them appear like they sparkled when she smiled or laughed. She had a perfect smile that brought out the cutest dimples deep in the sides of her cheeks. And when she smiled it lit up her entire face. The little time I'd been able to spend with her I knew that she didn't hold anything back. She tackled life head on and full of spirit and I found that incredibly attractive.

I felt myself letting down my guard around her and that frightened me. There had only been two serious girlfriends in my past and both times I'd opened my heart to them, they had ripped it out and stomped all over it. The past couple of years I had kept my relationships on my terms and never let them totally into my heart. I swore to myself that I'd never go through that type of heartache again. So far, it had worked out just fine, but I wondered if I'd be able to keep Mia at a distance. She was different, and I felt some of my walls crumble the more time I spent with her.

Zachary was the one who opened the door for me when I finally arrived at Mia's house.

"Hey, Dylan. Come on in."

"Hi, Zach. Are you on Christmas break yet?"

"Yep, today we only had a half day, I'm out until after New Year's. Mia's in the family room. It's this way."

I followed Zachary to the back of the house. I noticed there were family pictures that lined the staircase leading to the second floor. Smiling I spotted one of Mia when she must have been two or three—she was cute even then. Her contagious smile was even more adorable with a few missing teeth. I entered the family room. It was an open plan that connected to the kitchen. Mia sat on a sage green couch, facing the entry, with a cream blanket covering her. She glanced up at us as we entered the room. Her face lit up with a smile, her dimples flashed.

"Hey, there. Here come sit next to me. I already have the movie loaded."

I couldn't believe how different Mia looked out of the hospital. Her face had more color in it. She wore a cream-colored sweatshirt and her hair curled just below her shoulders. It was the first time I'd ever seen it loose. She was stunning.

"You're looking much better." I said as I sat on her left, propping my feet next to hers on the ottoman.

"Thanks. You look the same, well almost. You shaved, no stubble today." She reached up and ran her fingers over his cheeks. "It's so smooth, like a baby's butt." Mia giggled.

I snagged her fingers from my face, brought them to my lips and kissed them. "Hmm…I'm not sure I like my face being compared to a butt," he teased.

"That's not what I meant. I like it; it just took me by surprise. You've always had stubble on your face when I've seen you."

"I'm just teasing, Mia. You can compare my face to whatever you'd like. Well, maybe anything, but only when you aren't upset with me."

Retaining her left hand I intertwined my fingers with hers. I laid our interlocked hands on top of the blanket that covered her legs.

"Okay what are we watching?"

"A classic from when my parents were younger. They made me watch it, and I loved it. Have you ever seen *Some Kind of Wonderful?*"

"Can't say I have. Let me guess it's a romance?"

Mia's face flushed. "Well yeah, but it's a good one, I hope you like it. It's one of my favorites."

"Get it started, let's see. I was hoping for some action adventure movie. You know fast cars and stuff like that." he teased.

"Typical; this is better trust me."

Mia rested her head on my shoulder and settled in. I let go of her hand and wrapped my arm around her shoulder pulling her even closer. She fit perfect against my side. My fingers twisted in her silky hair and brushed against her shoulder. I didn't even care what we were watching. I just enjoyed being with her.

The movie was near the end when Mia pulled her head slightly away from my shoulder.

"My favorite part is coming up, best scene ever." She sighed. "Are you liking the movie so far?"

"Actually, yeah. Not a bad pick. What's the best scene ever?" he asked.

"Just wait, you'll see." Mia nestled back against my side as we watched as the main characters, Watts, who was a tomboy in love with her best friend Keith, teased him that he was unprepared to go on a date with the pretty Amanda Jones. Standing in the garage that he worked in she convinced him to pretend she was Amanda and to practice his kissing on her, just to make sure he was passable. Keith agreed but it was Watts who pushed away, unable to take the intensity, confirming that yes he did know how to kiss. By the end of the movie Keith realizes that it's not the pretty Amanda that he's in love with, but Watts, his best friend.

With the credits rolling, Mia found the remote that had fallen into the couch and flipped the TV off.

"Well, did you like it?"

"I did, but next time I get to pick."

"Pick one of your favorites. I'm anxious to see what you choose, 'cause I know mine will be better," she teased.

"We'll see. You might actually be surprised." I wasn't sure yet what I would select, but I'd find something good.

"On a different note. I wanted to ask you something."

"Sure, what? You sound serious."

"I've been doing a lot of thinking and research lately about chairlift safety. Have you ever heard of or seen a safety restraint bar?"

"I've heard about them. They aren't very common around here. Why do you ask?"

"Why don't all ski resorts use them? I didn't realize how many people, especially children, fall off lifts every season, most of them don't survive."

"I'm not sure why they aren't used. I think it's a cost issue, or the resorts feel like the actual accidents are such a small percent in relationship to the number of skiers that use the lifts that the cost to install the restraints isn't worth it."

"Did you know that only two states even require that chairlifts have restraint bars?"

"That's it? No, I didn't realize that."

"I don't understand. If they know it can help keep people safer, why they don't use them?"

"I'm not sure."

"Dylan, I can't seem to let this go. I can't explain it. I just feel like I need to do something, to try to bring more awareness to the skiers and snowboarders who use the chairlifts."

"Mia, I think it's great that you want to get involved. As ski patrol we're taught techniques for proper loading and sitting on lifts, but you're right, there are so many who come up to enjoy the snow who may not be as informed."

"Would you help me?"

"Of course. What would you like me to do?"

"I'm not sure yet. I guess I just wanted to know what you thought about the whole thing, to tell me that I'm not crazy."

I shifted on the couch to face Mia, my hands lightly touched each side of her face. "No, I don't think you're crazy. I think you've got an unwavering amount of courage and determination to meet and battle any challenge."

"Thanks. I can't tell you how much your support means to me."

I pulled her closer as I leaned over and brushed my lips to hers. Mia's hands moved to the back of my neck, her fingers running through my hair. Desire heated every muscle in my body. She smelled amazing, her lips so soft, her mouth so warm. I deepened the kiss, our tongues touched. Hers was timid at first and then more insistent. Zachary broke the moment when he ran down the stairs startling us.

"Yuck, are you guys seriously kissing on the couch?"

"Yes, now go back upstairs Zach." Mia twisted out of my embrace to scold her brother.

"Mom said I could get ice cream." Zachary said as he ignored Mia and continued into the kitchen.

"It's okay." I whispered to Mia. "I should probably be going anyways. You need your rest, and I need to get back up the mountain before the roads get worse and I get stuck down here."

"That would be okay, you could stay here. The couch is free." Mia grinned.

"Tempting, but I have work in the morning."

"Okay, let me walk you out."

I stood up first. I pulled the blanket off of Mia and gently helped her up. Hand in hand, our fingers twisted together we walked to the door and out to the front porch. Mia closed the door behind us for a few moments of privacy. She turned and reached her arms around my neck. I wrapped my arms around her waist, my hands sat at her lower back, our lips picked up where we had left off. Ending the kiss far too soon I wished I could keep her in my arms, but I knew it was late and I needed to get going. I pulled her tight against me. Her head shifted against my chest and I settled my chin on top of her head.

"I need to go," he whispered.

"I know, but I like being held by you."

"Good, cause I like holding you. A lot. Get back inside before you get cold, I'll call you later."

"Okay. Text me when you get home so I know you got there safely."

"I will." I kissed her one last time, before I finally pulled away. "Good night, Mia." I said as I brushed her hair out of her face.

"Night, Dylan. Drive safe."

"I always do."

I walked down the sidewalk to my jeep. She stood on the porch, her arms wrapped around herself as I opened my door. I waved to her as I pulled away and drove into the dark, moonless night.

CHAPTER FIFTEEN

~ *Quinn* ~

Thoughts of Mia were constant since that awful day of the accident. Finals were a nightmare, and work had been crazy with everyone trying to finish up deadlines before taking off for the holidays. Every time I'd tried to get over to see Mia something came up. Natasha would be home for break in a couple of days, and I wanted a chance to see Mia before my sister and Bailey monopolized all her time.

Walking to my car after work I pulled my phone out and texted Mia.

Quinn:
Hey Mia are you busy tonight?

Mia:
Do you consider playing
board games with Zach
busy?

Quinn:
Lol, no, how'd he rope you into
that?

A HEALING SPIRIT

Less than twenty minutes later I was climbing out of my lifted Chevy truck, a two-liter Mountain Dew and half gallon of mint chocolate chip ice cream in hand. Tonight felt different. I wasn't sure why, but I planned to explore some of the new feelings that had emerged for Mia. I was curious to see where things would go.

The wind had picked up, and a burst of cold air chilled me as I reached the front door. I rang the doorbell and then waited for it to open. I watched several of the neighbor's houses light up with Christmas lights. The door opened, and Mia's dad stepped aside for me to enter.

"Evening Quinn, come on in."

"Thanks, Mr. Kinney. Smells good in here."

"Gretchen's been baking for the past few days. I'm not sure what all she's making. All I know is that I can't see the countertops anymore, it's full of pans of treats. I don't even know what she's going to do with all of it."

"My mom rarely has time for baking. At holiday dinners we're lucky if we get a homemade pie. It's usually from some restaurant."

"I'll have Mia pack you up some treats then. We've got plenty."

"Thanks, that would be great."

"Hey, Mia, look who I found at the front door. Looks like he's bringing you your favorites. Mountain Dew and ice cream."

Mia looked up from the kitchen table where Zachary had already spread out Monopoly.

"Oooohhh, ice cream too? Really? I only requested the Mountain Dew, what type of ice cream?"

"Mint chocolate chip; isn't that you're favorite?"

"It is. How'd you know that?"

"How many times have you and Natasha had sleepovers at the house?"

Mia laughed as she stood up, relieving me of my precious cargo. "Yeah, I guess you're right. I didn't know you ever paid attention to us little girls though."

"Your mom has been baking. Wow, look at all these treats."

"Yeah, you name it, she's made it. She's been running around for days, decorating the tree, wrapping presents, now all this baking. You'd think we were having an army over here during the holidays." Pulling out glasses and bowls Mia turned from the cabinet as I leaned against the kitchen island. "You want some of this deliciousness you brought?"

"Sure, just a little of the ice cream though, I'm eyeing these brownies, with the caramel and chocolate drizzle and what looks like crushed pretzels?"

"Some new recipe she had to try. They are actually pretty good. I wasn't too sure when she was making them."

I stood there watching Mia as she dished up the ice cream. I could honestly say that I wasn't thinking sisterly thoughts. I wanted to brush aside her blonde hair as it curled around her face and kiss her. If she didn't return my feelings I knew I was in for some serious heartbreak. Such a mess I thought to myself. How'd I get to this point with my sister's best friend? Maybe I was crazy and I should just leave it alone. But then lots of relationships started out as just friendships. I'd kick myself later if I didn't at least try.

I watched Mia move through the kitchen. She was almost back to normal. It was hard to believe that just a few weeks ago she had been fighting for her life in a hospital bed. Mia caught me watching her. I stood my ground and kept eye contact and smiled. She giggled as she turned back to dishing up the ice cream. A giggle? That was not the reaction I was looking for. I looked down at my sweater; did I have something on it?

"What's so funny?" I finally asked.

Shaking her head, she kept her attention on the ice cream. "Nothing, just thinking."

"About?"

Zachary entered into the kitchen in his typical energetic way. That boy was always moving. It was exhausting sometimes just watching him.

"Quinn! Are you staying?" he asked.

"For a while, why?"

"Cool, you can play Monopoly with us. It's even better with more than two players." Zachary plopped into the bar stool next to where I stood.

"I can't believe you like that game. It takes forever. Don't you have anything else you'd rather play?"

"Nope, no one ever plays with me, and I finally got Mia to agree. She's not backing out now. Hey, is that ice cream you've got there?"

"Quinn brought it. Do you want some?" Mia asked.

"Yes, a big bowl!"

"Not surprised." Mia chuckled as she opened the cabinet and pulled out another bowl.

~ *Mia* ~

Three hours later, Zachary had amassed a fortune, and laid claim to almost all the important properties, loaded with hotels. I reviewed my paltry few dollars left and my worthless properties that I still owned.

"This is why I hate this game," I mumbled.

"Ah, come on Mia, it's not that bad," Quinn chided.

"Really, Quinn? You're not much better off than me; Zach's kicking our butts."

"Maybe I just let him win?"

"Let me win? No way! I beat you guys fair."

"Okay, I surrender." Quinn stated.

"You don't surrender in this game. You go bankrupt," Zachary corrected.

"Then I'm completely bankrupt. You win, Zach."

"And winners have to clean it all up and put it away," I grinned.

"Ah, come on, Mia," Zachary groaned.

"Nope, I'm done. You can put it away."

"Fine."

"I should be going anyways, you probably need your rest. Buying and selling property for hours has taken its toll on you," Quinn teased.

"More like getting stomped by a ten-year old. Did you want some of those brownies? I can wrap up a plate of goodies. There's cookies, and fudge. I don't even know what all is in these containers."

"Sure, load me up. I'll take whatever you want to give me. My dad will be in heaven."

I searched through the lower cabinets finally finding a free container. Zachary started sorting through the play money and putting the game away. Quinn sat on one of the barstools at the island as I filled a large square container full of treats. I felt Quinn's gaze and I looked up and caught his deep brown eyes as they watched me. The intensity I felt was different than ever before. His hair was dark brown, almost black like Natasha's. It was cut short, his eyebrows were thick, his face covered with a dark stubble. His black, long sleeve sweater was snug against his broad shoulders. He was handsome, in a way I'd never noticed before. His gaze made me nervous. I'd never seen him look at me so intently before. I sealed the container and handed it to Quinn as he got up from the barstool.

"Thanks."

"Thanks for stopping by. Getting beat in Monopoly was more enjoyable with someone else to share my pain."

"Anytime."

Zachary glanced up from putting away the game as Quinn and I left the kitchen. "Bye, Quinn, see you later."

"Later, Zach."

Quinn followed me to the front door. With his free hand he lightly touched my arm, stopping me before I reached the door. I turned towards him, my stomach was nervous. Something was wrong, I could feel it.

Quinn lifted his free hand to my face, lightly touching the side. He tilted my chin up to face him. He was going to kiss me, I was sure of it, and panic flooded me. I had to stop him.

"Quinn, wait." I reached up to cover his hand and gently pulled his hand down from my face.

"Mia, I'm not sure what's happening. All I know is that sitting in that emergency room waiting to see if you were going to live or die, shook me. I realized maybe we could be more than just friends."

I sagged against him, my heart breaking. What could I say to him? One of my closest friends, I'd practically grown up with him. I could always count on Quinn if I ever needed anything. Maybe if Dylan hadn't come crashing into my life things would be different. What a mess. I didn't want to lose my friendship with Quinn.

"Oh, Quinn. I don't know what to say." I sighed.

"You don't have to say anything right now. Just think about it. I know it's a shock."

"It's not that. I just don't have those types of feelings for you Quinn. You're like an older brother to me, one of my best friends."

"And friends can become more."

"Quinn, please. I don't want to hurt you."

"Just give it some time, I can wait." Quinn leaned over and brushed my forehead with a kiss and opened the door. He turned as he reached the edge of the front porch. "Good night, Mia. I'll see you later. Just think about it okay? Give it a chance."

I watched, stunned as Quinn climbed into his truck. He waved goodbye and pulled away from the curb. I shut and locked the door, turning I leaned my back against it. Part of me wanted to cry. My phone vibrated in my front pocket. I pulled it out and I read a text from Dylan.

Dylan:
Thinking about you, I'll see you soon.

What in the world was I supposed to do now? How did my life get so complicated, so quickly?

CHAPTER SIXTEEN

~ *Mia* ~

The next few days I spent in relative isolation. My emotions fluctuated from excitement every time I talked to Dylan, to confusion and sadness when I thought about Quinn. Dylan hadn't been able to get back down the mountain because of two massive snowstorms that had landed on top of each other. I missed him, a lot, more than I cared to admit.

I had used the days of uninterrupted time to finish all my school projects and finals. A huge weight had finally been lifted off my shoulders and I would be able to now enjoy the rest of my holiday break.

Outside the rain pounded the already-soaked ground, it was early evening and already dark outside. The wind was brisk and the temperature was dropping quickly. The weather reports had warned of hail and maybe even a light dusting of snow, which was highly unusual for Riverview. The wind carried the rain horizontally as it slammed against the windows. The gloomy weather fit my mood perfectly.

I sat on the couch with my feet propped up, as I flipped through the TV channels, while the storm raged outside. Bailey and Natasha had just gotten home for the Christmas break and were on their way over. I desperately needed to sit down with them and have a talk. I knew they would be able to help me sort through this mess I had found myself in.

The doorbell rang, and I practically flew to the door to greet my best friends. I flung the door open. Bailey and Natasha stood there soaking wet. I didn't care, I wrapped them both in my arms. As we hugged each other my mom came down the stairs.

"It's freezing out there! Come in and dry off before you all get sick!"

The three of us separated, and Bailey and Natasha stepped into the house as I shut the door behind them. They shrugged off their wet jackets, and I tossed them on the hooks that were placed near the front door.

"Mia, you're looking really good. How do you feel?" Bailey asked.

"Not too bad. I almost feel like myself again. Let's go up to my room; we need to talk."

Bailey and Natasha shared a glance and shrugged their shoulders.

⁓◞◟◞⁓

I sat propped up on my pillows as they leaned against the headboard of my bed. Bailey and Natasha sat cross-legged facing me as I ran through the recent events with Dylan and Quinn.

"What am I going to do? I don't want to hurt Quinn."

"I just still can't believe it. Quinn? Really? He hasn't said a word."

"I doubt he wanted to say anything, Tasha."

"I'm sure he'll get over it." Bailey added. "We were all in shock after the accident. Maybe he's just misreading his brotherly feelings into more than they really are? Quinn's always been protective of you."

"Maybe, oh I hope so. I don't want things to get weird. We always hang out and do things together when you guys are in town. I don't want to give that up, and I don't want to lose him as a friend."

"I'm sure he'll come around. Did you tell him about Dylan?" Natasha asked.

"No, I never really had the chance. I was standing there in total shock. I didn't know what to say."

"You're going to have to tell him sometime about Dylan." Bailey added.

"I know. I'm just not sure what to even tell him. It's not like Dylan and I are official or anything. We've been talking a lot and hanging out, but he hasn't asked me to be his girlfriend."

"Well, if he asked you, would you say yes?" Natasha asked her eyes sparkling. "He was pretty cute as I remember, and that accent, I could get lost in that for days."

I laughed as I grabbed a nearby pillow and threw it at Natasha. "Of course I'd say yes. I'm really falling for him. He's all I can think about. But he's been hurt in the past. He's built some pretty big walls that I can't seem to break down. Will just knowing a part of him be enough?"

"Give it time. Sometimes it's hard to let your guard down completely. You keep waiting for the next bad thing to happen, because that's how life has treated you. It's what you know, what has become familiar. Trust me, I know.

"When Collin came into my life I felt like I knew him my whole life. It was the first time in forever that I started to feel alive again. Even though I knew we were connecting and things were going good. That fear was still there, buried deep, it was hard to let go. And FYI it's often very irrational as well. It festers and makes you only see the negative and you're just waiting for things to fall apart," Bailey explained.

"Yeah, I remember all of that. Especially at Collin's graduation, when I gave him a piece of my mind." I laughed at the memory.

"Collin's never forgotten that. Anytime we get in an argument, even if it's a little one, he often will make some remark asking if I'm going to have you call him." Bailey smiled. "Sometimes it's worked to my advantage."

"So, what are your plans, Mia? For the rest of the holiday break?" Natasha asked.

"Well, if the storms clear this weekend and if we can get up the mountain, I think I'd really like to go up to the resort. I'd like to say thank you in person to everyone who helped me."

"I think that's a great idea. Bailey and I can go with you if you'd like."

"Yes, I'd like that. Collin and Quinn can come too if they want."

"Oh, I'm sure Quinn will be up for it, based on this recent turn of events. I can't wait to see this in person," Natasha added.

"Give him a break, Tasha, don't make this worse on him," Bailey added with sympathy.

"We'll see. After the years of teasing he's given me, he deserves a little of his own medicine."

"In any event, Mia, you really are looking good. You seemed to have recovered pretty quickly," Bailey stated.

"The first couple of weeks were the worst. A lot of the time in the hospital was such a blur. Some of it I don't even know if it was real or if I was dreaming."

"Well, I just have to say for the record that I'm tired of spending Thanksgiving day in the hospital. Two years in a row guys! I mean, seriously?" Natasha stated.

"Oh, yeah. I totally forgot about last year with my appendix," Bailey replied.

"You guys better not have jinxed me for next year. I'm done with spending time in hospital waiting rooms! When you add Collin's little car accident in the mix. I'd think we were magnets for accidents!"

"I agree! I hope none of us spend any more time in that place. I couldn't get out of there fast enough!" I stated.

"Well, think of it this way, if you'd never fallen you would have never met Dylan."

"I know Tasha, I've thought about that a lot. Besides meeting Dylan, and all of that excitement, I wanted to talk to you about something else that's been bugging me. After I got home from the hospital I started doing some research online about chairlift accidents. Did you know there's such a thing as a safety restraint bar? It comes down over your lap to help prevent people from falling out of chairlifts."

"Really? I've never seen one; is it new?" Bailey asked.

"No, that's the thing, they've been out for a while. There are two states that even require resorts to have them by law, but that's it, only two states. I feel like I need to do something. There's got to be a way to bring more attention to this safety option. If the option is out there and has been developed, why not use it? Dylan said he'd help me, but I'm not sure where to even start."

"Mia, I think that's a great cause. There's got to be somewhere you can start. Maybe local politicians, or is there some sort of local ski association or governing body?"

"I hadn't thought about the politicians. What would they be able to do?"

"I'm not sure, but if other states already have laws in place then I'd think that some of that footwork has already been done. Maybe you could help get some sort of regulation in place for our state too."

"We're just glad you're here with us. You are so strong and energetic, Mia, I think you can make a difference."

"Thanks guys, I knew I could count on you both."

"Always, that's what we're here for. You both have always been there for me during all my ups and downs. It's my turn to help support you." Bailey reached over and hugged me.

CHAPTER SEVENTEEN

~ *Mia* ~

Snow dusted the ground and rooftops when I woke up early Sunday morning. I knew it wouldn't last long, and would probably melt within the hour. The view out my window was beautiful, yet a bit odd to see palm trees frosted with snow. I slid my window open to breathe in the cold, crisp air.

My friends would be by to pick me up soon, so we could drive up to the resort. I was tense. I couldn't stop the anxiety of returning to the slopes where my accident had occurred. I turned away from the window and walked into my bathroom to get ready for the day.

As I had predicted, by the time my friends had arrived the dusting of snow on the ground had melted. I grabbed my jacket, said goodbye to my mom, and climbed into the back seat of Quinn's truck next to Bailey and Collin. My stomach was in knots, and I tried to calm my racing heart. My friends' excited chatter was nonstop, but I had no idea what they were talking about. I focused on watching the blur of trees as we steadily climbed the mountain road. My thoughts drifted back to the last time I had traveled this same road just a few short weeks ago. Bailey's hand grasped mine and snapped me out of my trance.

"It's going to be fine."

"I know. I didn't realize how hard it might be to drive this road again. It's not like we're going snowboarding today. I don't understand why I'm so freaked out."

"Fear is rarely rational, Mia. It just is. But you're safe and you'll get over it, I promise. It just takes time."

"Thanks, Bailey."

"And you'll get to see Dylan soon too right?" Bailey whispered.

"Yeah, it's been awhile. I am looking forward to that."

"Hey, what are you too whispering about back there?" Quinn asked.

Bailey and I both started laughing. Natasha turned in the passenger seat to look at us. "Nothing." We both replied together.

The tension was broken, and the mood in the truck stayed lighthearted as we continued the climb up the mountain.

~ *Dylan* ~

I shifted in my chair, I was restless. I glanced up at the clock in the ski patrol hut for what must have been the hundredth time in the past few minutes.

"Relax, dude. You can't make the clock move any faster." Corey jabbed.

"I am relaxed. I'm just anxious to see Mia. This trip has got to bring back all types of memories for her, probably not too many pleasant ones."

"I don't think I've ever seen you so spun up over a girl before."

"I'm not spun up."

"Whatever. Then what do you call it? You've been practically a ghost at all the activities we've been doing lately. I don't even know how many times you've driven up and down the mountain in the past few weeks. I'm not saying it's bad, I'm just saying I've never seen you like this."

"Mia's different. There's just something about her. I feel like I've known her forever, Corey."

"Well, that's a good thing, right?"

"I guess. It's just got me a bit off balance. I wasn't expecting to find a relationship this intense right now."

"Relationships rarely are expected. They usually just come crashing down on us. In your case it was a bit more literal." Corey grinned.

"Nice you can joke about it. She almost died, Corey."

"Maybe she just really needed to get your attention. It worked right?"

"You better not say things like that to her. I mean it. She's been through hell and back."

"Easy, I'm just teasing you. I know how serious things were. I was there that day too, remember? I'm just trying to lighten the mood. I think she's been good for you, Dylan. I've seen a side of you I don't think I've ever seen before."

"And what's that supposed to mean?"

"When I do see you, you're more relaxed. Just happier I guess."

My phone vibrated on the table between us. Picking it up I read Mia's text. "It's Mia. They are in the parking lot."

I tucked my phone in my pocket, and I pushed back my chair so quickly it almost crashed to the floor. I grabbed my skis at the door and was snapping them on as Corey shut the door to the patrol hut and followed me down the slope.

~ *Quinn* ~

Mia walked from the parking lot to the resort with Bailey and Natasha on each side of her. Collin and I walked a bit behind them. I could tell Mia had been stressed on the drive up, and my heart ached for her. She'd said very little to me after the night we had played Monopoly. Even today she seemed distant, and I didn't know how to reach her. I hoped she just needed some time to realize that we would be good together. So far Natasha hadn't said anything to me directly, but I knew they had talked. Those three girls talked about everything together.

"She seems frightened," I stated.

"Well, the last time she was here she was in some severe pain. Just being here in the same place has got to bring all of that back," Collin replied, as he looked at me closely. "What's up with you, Quinn? You've seemed a bit off the last couple of days."

"I don't know. Ever since we were waiting in the emergency room it's brought up feelings for Mia I didn't know I had."

"You mean like more than a sister?"

"Yeah."

"Have you told her?"

"The other night, I let her know. But she's been distant since then."

"What did she say when you told her?"

"Not much. Just that she thinks of me as a brother, a best friend."

"Well, that's how you guys have been for as long as I've known you. Are you sure your feelings are more?"

"Seriously, Collin? I don't want to kiss my sister, but that's all I can think about when I'm around Mia. So, yes, I'm sure my feelings are more than just brotherly."

"Wow, okay. Maybe she just needs some time. She's been through a lot."

"I know. I'm not trying to push anything."

"Well I'm here for you. I think you guys would be great together."

"Thanks, buddy."

We reached the open deck of the resort that looked out onto the snow-covered slopes. Bright-colored dots speckled the hills. Mia stood looking up at the chairlift nearby as it climbed slowly up the hill. She reached out and grabbed Bailey and Natasha's hands and held them tight. I stayed back a bit and watched. I wanted to be here for Mia, to support her in whatever she needed. But I was also afraid to move too fast. Especially after how she'd reacted that night we played Monopoly.

A HEALING SPIRIT

~ *Mia* ~

I noticed the bright red jackets of ski patrollers as they raced down the slope toward the deck. My heart quickened. I knew it was Dylan.

"There's Dylan," I whispered to my friends.

"Yeah, as cute as I remember." Natasha grinned.

"Behave, Tasha." I shoved my friend slightly, as I laughed.

I walked closer to the edge of the deck tugging my friends along. Dylan and one other ski patroller reached the bottom, stopping with a slight dusting of snow. They popped their skis and anchored them upright in the snow next to their poles. Dylan pulled his goggles over his head and removed his helmet as he walked toward me.

"Hey, Baby." Dylan said as he was just steps away from me, his arms outstretched. I, dropped my friend's hands walked quickly into his open embrace. His jacket was still cool to the touch from the cold wind. It cooled my cheeks as I laid my head against his strong chest.

"I've missed you," I whispered against his chest.

"I've missed you, too. How are you doing?"

"Okay now that I'm in your arms."

Dylan laughed as he kissed the top of my head. We stood there for just a minute more before I reluctantly pulled away. I loved the warmth, strength, and peace I found when I was in Dylan's embrace. I wished I could stay there forever.

I stepped to the side of Dylan. His arm was anchored around my waist as I turned back to my

"

friends. "Guys, this is Dylan. He was one of the ski patrollers who helped save my life."

"I remember you all from the emergency room, and Mia's always talking about you. It's Bailey, Natasha, Collin, and Quinn right?"

"Good memory." Collin stepped forward to shake Dylan's hand. "Good to see you again." He stepped back next to Bailey as he lightly placed his hand against her lower back.

Quinn stepped forward and shook Dylan's hand. His eyes searched mine and I saw hurt flicker through his eyes My heart ached for him, but I didn't know what to do to make it better.

"Dylan."

"Quinn."

"Mia, do you remember Corey? He was there that day with me." Dylan asked.

"A bit, there was another person too, wasn't there?"

"Yes, Justin. He was the one that brought the toboggan that took you down the hill. He's at the top of the mountain today. He'll be down in a little bit so you can meet him, too."

I stepped over to Corey, taking him by surprise when I reached up to hug him. "Thank you. I know you were just as important in saving my life as Dylan was."

Corey awkwardly hugged me back. "Umm… you're welcome. I was just doing my job."

I stepped back and looked up at Corey, "I know, but I'm still thankful."

"Let's head over to the ski patrol office. There are more people there for you to meet." Dylan grasped my hand, leading me across the deck. My friends and Corey followed behind.

CHAPTER EIGHTEEN

~ *Mia* ~

Several hours later I was relaxing in the Lodge, near the fireplace sipping hot chocolate with my friends. Dylan and Corey had returned to the slopes to finish their shift and would be joining us again when they were off. The anxiety and tension that I had felt earlier in the morning had finally lessened, and I had been able to enjoy the afternoon.

I'd shed a few tears while I was introduced to the members of the ski patrol who had assisted me after my accident. I was overwhelmed with their genuine concern and their interest in how my recovery was coming. I'd even asked them about the restraint bars and was shocked to learn that most of them were aware of the bars but that most ski resorts hadn't implemented them due to the cost. I was even more determined to gather more information and bring better awareness to the public about the safety of the chairlifts. Not only the restraint bars, but proper seating on the lift. Similar to the recent shift in skiers and snowboarders wearing helmets as more awareness was made about preventing head injuries. Anything that helped prevent injury and death was worthwhile, no matter what the cost. My thoughts were interrupted when Dylan and Corey arrived. They pulled up extra chairs to the table. Dylan's arm draped casually across the back of my chair, and I leaned against it.

"Are you guys off now?" I asked.

"I am. Corey has an extended break but will have to come back to do the night-skiing shift. We had someone call in sick. Are you all headed back down the mountain now?"

"That's the plan." Quinn answered.

"Do you need to get back home right away, Mia?" Dylan asked.

"I don't think so, why?"

"I can take you home later. I thought I'd take you to my mom's so she could finally meet you."

"Oh, okay. Yeah sure, I'd like to meet her too."

"Mia, I'm sure you're exhausted. You shouldn't overdo it," Quinn stated a bit harshly.

I had felt Quinn's uneasiness all afternoon. I watched as his jaw twitched. I knew he was agitated. It was my worst fear coming to life. I felt my friend slipping away, and I didn't know if things would be the same between us again. "I'm fine Quinn, really. I'll just text my parents. Dylan can bring me home."

"Whatever, well, I have to get back. Are the rest of you coming?" Quinn got up almost knocking his chair over in his hurry to get out the door.

"Yeah, we're coming." Collin stood, offering his hand to Bailey as she got up.

"We'll see you later, Mia. Good to see you again, Dylan."

Bailey and Collin turned to follow Quinn who was already at the exit doors.

"Sorry about Quinn. He's not been himself all day." Natasha apologized. "Bye Mia, Dylan."

"Well, that just got awkward. I think I'll take off, too." Corey stated as he got up from the table. "I'll see you later Mia. Dylan, I'll catch up with you tomorrow."

"Quinn's not usually so rude." I looked up at Dylan getting lost in his vivid green eyes. It was like he could see straight to my soul.

"What is your relationship with Quinn? I sense there's a lot more there than just friendship."

"We're just friends, Dylan, really. He's always been like an older brother. Tasha and I practically grew up together. I spent a lot of time at their house. Quinn was always there. As we got older he was always protective of me like he was Tasha. After Bailey moved to town and she started hanging out with us Quinn wasn't around as much. Collin and he became friends, and then when Bailey and Collin started seeing each other, we all just started hanging out and doing things together. This past fall when everyone left for college it was just Quinn and I left and we'd grab coffee and lunch. Stuff like that, but it's always just been as friends, there's never been anything more."

"Something's changed then because when he looks at you he's not looking at you like a sister or just a friend–trust me."

I broke the gaze as I looked down at my lap. "I know," I whispered.

"Mia, tell me. Did something happen between the two of you?" Dylan carefully turned my head up so he could see my face. His voice was tense.

"Nothing happened, Dylan, really. The other night he stopped by and Zach coerced him into playing

Monopoly with us. When he was leaving he told me that when he was in the waiting room after my accident not knowing if I would live or not he realized he had deeper feelings for me."

"And, what did you tell him?"

"I told him I didn't feel like that about him. That I didn't want to lose his friendship, but that he was like a brother to me and that was all."

"Well, it doesn't seem to have sunk in."

"I haven't really seen or talked to him since that night. I just thought it would pass."

"Are you sure you don't have deeper feelings for him?" Dylan's voice was edgy.

"He's just a friend, Dylan." I reached out to touch Dylan's face. My fingers brushed lightly over his stubble that ran across his strong cheekbones. "You're the only one I have deep feelings for. You're the one I think about all the time. The girls asked me the other night if we were official. I didn't know what to tell them. We've never discussed it."

"Is that what you want? To be official? There's a lot about me Mia that I'm not sure I can ever completely let go or talk about from my past."

"I would hope you could eventually let me completely in Dylan. But I know that I'm happy when I'm with you. I feel safe, like I'm at home. I don't want to be with anyone else."

"I don't want you to be with anyone else either. I've fallen for you. You are all I think about when I go to bed at night, when I wake up in the morning. While my heart breaks for all the pain you've been through recently, I can't help but be thankful that you landed near my hut that day and came crashing into my life."

"I've had the same thoughts Dylan. I think it was meant to be."

My hand shifted from his cheek to around his neck as I pulled him closer. My fingers ran through his dark hair as it brushed against the stiff collar of his jacket. My lips touched his, starting the kiss. His lips deepened it, he possessed my mouth as his arms pulled me tightly to him.

⁓⸱⸺⸱⸺⸱⸽

~ Quinn~

My focus was on the road as I drove my sister and friends back down the mountain after leaving Mia with Dylan. But my mind was working overtime as my emotions were raging. I'd been stewing all afternoon, from the moment we met the ski patrol at the resort my afternoon was in the toilet. Watching Mia fling herself into Dylan's arm's about killed me. My heart felt like it had just been ripped from my chest and had been crushed into the cold snow. I had absolutely no idea she'd had contact with him. It had completely blindsided me.

I think what killed me the most was that I'd never seen Mia so happy before. Her eyes sparkled with excitement and happiness I'd never seen before. I knew her and deep down I knew her heart already belonged to another. I wanted her to be happy I really did, but I had thought she'd find that happiness with me. The chance I thought I'd had with her had slipped away.

The truck was quiet most of the way home. Natasha kept looking at me and I knew she wanted to say something. But thankfully she kept her thoughts to herself. I was in no mood for teasing. Collin and Bailey whispered in the backseat, and I was sure that I was the main topic of their conversation, but as long as I didn't have to hear it I didn't care. I was miserable enough, and my friends knew me well enough that they let me be.

~ Mia ~

Dylan helped me out of his jeep, always the gentleman.

"Are you ready to meet my mom?"

"A little nervous, but yes."

We walked hand in hand as he guided me to the front door.

"Why are you nervous? She's really easygoing. I promise she won't bite." He grinned.

Dylan turned the key in the lock and opened the door. He stepped aside as I entered the warm, cozy cottage.

"Mom?"

"In the kitchen, Dylan. Come on back."

"Come on, it's this way." Dylan led me to the back of the house. His mom was at the kitchen sink loading dishes when we entered. "Mom, this is Mia."

Dylan's mom turned from the sink her hands were dripping with water. "Oh, Mia. What a surprise. I didn't realize that Dylan was bringing you here tonight. I've heard so much about you." She quickly dried her hands and briskly walked across the kitchen and hugged me.

"Mom, you're going to scare her off."

"Nonsense. I'm just happy to finally meet her."

"It's very nice to meet you, too."

"Have y'all had dinner yet?"

"No. Mia came up to the resort to meet everyone that helped her the day of the accident. I just got off work and decided to bring her here before I took her home."

"I have plenty of leftovers from the other night. I'll heat some up for you. Please sit, while I get everything out."

"Thanks Mrs. Blackburn. Is there anything I can help with?"

"Jolene, please. There's no need to be formal. Relax you're a guest. I can get it, but thank you, for the offer." She smiled as she turned from the counter to the refrigerator as Dylan and I sat at the counter on the barstools.

"How are you feeling, Mia? Dylan told me about your accident and all your surgeries. You're looking really good."

"I'm doing much better. It was rough there for a while, but I'm feeling more like myself every day."

"It's amazing how quickly you've recovered. You had quite the fall. Dylan said you fell a little over thirty feet."

"That's what they say. A lot of that day is blurry. I remember certain things, but not other things. Dylan's steady, calming voice was something I remembered even when I first woke up in the hospital."

Jolene looked over at her son, as he sat with his arm around me. "Yes, Dylan's very calm when under pressure. He's always been that way, very protective too. The ski patrol has been a good fit for him."

"Dylan is pretty amazing." I grinned.

"Eat, then we'll go relax in the living room so I can get to know you a bit better."

After dinner Jolene shared several stories about a young and crazy Dylan. She even brought out some old albums of Dylan as a baby. I flipped through the pages of Dylan's childhood laughing at several of them. Dylan cringed next to me every time the page turned to reveal an embarrassing photo.

I noticed through all the photos there wasn't one photo of his dad. Several, I noticed, had been cut. I could feel the tension in the room when I turned to one of those. I was curious, wanting to ask questions, but I knew that the subject of Dylan's dad was a sore one and I didn't want to ruin the evening. I'd have to wait until Dylan was ready to talk about it.

It was late and Dylan had finally shuffled me out the door to start the trip down the mountain. I didn't realize how tired I was until we started the drive. Dylan held my hand across the console as I blinked and yawned trying to keep myself awake. My body finally gave up.

~ *Dylan*~

I felt Mia's hand go lax in mine as she nodded off. Her head rested against the passenger window. She looked so peaceful while she slept. I turned my attention back to the curvy road. Quinn's reaction today worried me a bit. They had a long history, just friends or not. I really hoped that Mia meant what she'd said today.

I had known for a while that I was completely under her spell. We had a chemistry that I'd never had with anyone else before. My mom had even commented on it when we left, whispering in my ear that I better not mess this one up. That she was the one. I knew that my mom was right. If I was honest with myself I'd known it almost from the beginning. Mia was special. I would do anything to protect her, to keep her safe. She had already broken down several of my walls and found a place inside my heart and I knew I'd never be the same again.

CHAPTER NINETEEN

~ *Mia* ~

After several dead ends looking for ways I could become active in chairlift safety a local news reporter had contacted me to do a feature story on the local blood bank. I knew that a significant amount of donated blood and blood products had saved my life. My friends had organized blood donations in my honor while I was in the hospital. I'd heard all about it after I was recovering. What I hadn't realized was that the local blood bank had never had such a large outpouring of community support in honor of one person before and the reporter wanted to follow up on the story.

The reporter had called me to talk about my accident, and the next thing I knew they had introduced me to a reporter from one of the larger networks. The larger network wanted to do a personal interest story. I'd talk about what I'd been through, and that I'd also be able to talk about what I'd researched about chairlift safety. It was my first open door, and I was excited to be doing something, but scared at the same time.

The blood bank had also approached me and asked if I'd be one of their spokespersons. I had accepted immediately. I wanted to do anything I could to give back to the organization that had been crucial in saving my life. It was a good start to my crusade. I didn't know yet exactly how far I'd get but I had to start somewhere.

It was Christmas Eve, and I sat on the couch in my family room. I was leaning against Dylan's solid chest, my ear was nestled over his heart, while his arm rested across my shoulders. The pre-recorded segment on my accident and my crusade to implement better safety on chairlifts had just finished on the local TV channel.

"Well? What did you guys think? Did I look as nervous as I felt?"

"Sweetheart, you did amazing! I couldn't be more proud of you," my mom responded.

"I didn't have any doubts in you, honey. You're going to make a difference I know it," my dad added.

"My sister's famous now!" Zachary chimed in.

Dylan chuckled, his fingers traced lightly over my shoulder. I shivered with his touch. "Are you cold?"

I lifted my head from Dylan's chest, as I looked up into his emerald eyes. "Umm, quite the opposite actually. Thanks again for going with me today. I had no idea that they'd interview you as well."

"Yeah, that took me a bit by surprise."

"Zach, it's late. You better get into bed or Santa won't come tonight." My mom pushed him lightly off the couch.

"Oh geez, Mom. You know I haven't believed in Santa for years now, right?" Zachary's eyes rolled as he pushed himself off the couch and dragged himself across the room.

"Okay kids we're off to bed as well. Mia, if I find you out of your bedroom before morning you're in big trouble. Dylan, Mia will help you pull the bed out of the couch. Downstairs is your area. No funny business between you too under my roof. Got it?"

"Come on, Dad, you're embarrassing me." I groaned.

"Trevor, they are both adults and responsible." My mom lightly pulled on my dad's arm as they left the room.

"No worries, Mr. Kinney. Thanks for letting me stay here tonight."

"Can I crawl under a blanket and die now?" I sighed.

"He's just trying to protect you. He's being a good dad."

"Ugh, I'm nineteen. He's got to let go sometime."

"I doubt he'll ever totally let go. You'll always be his little girl Mia, and that's not a bad thing. At least he's here for you, he loves and protects you."

"That reminds me. I meant to ask you the other day. Why don't you have any pictures of your dad? I noticed that when your mom was flipping through the albums. It looked like some of them had even been cut." I lifted myself off of Dylan's chest so I could look at him, shifting my body so I sat sideways on the couch, my legs rested across his lap. Dylan's cheek twitched as I studied his features.

"Mia, I'm not sure I want to talk about this right now."

"Why? It can't be that bad."

"My dad wasn't like yours. I've put all that behind me. I don't want to bring it all up again."

"I don't understand why you won't tell me."

"Mia, I'm asking you to please drop it, okay? He's not a part of my life anymore. He hasn't been for years, and that's the way it will stay."

I felt Dylan tighten under my touch. His face hardened, his green eyes, which normally sparkled, were cold. I'd never seen him look so heartless before, or even how quickly his mood had flipped. I tried to brush it off, but I was hurt that he wouldn't trust me enough to tell me about his dad. I pulled my feet from his lap as I stood up. "Okay, whatever, that's fine." His hand reached for mine. I quickly wrenched from his grasp and walked briskly away.

"Where are you going?" Dylan's voice was edged with anger.

"To get you a pillow and blanket. Unless you'd rather sleep without them." My voice was harsher than I had intended. I was fighting back tears and emotions that I was having difficulty reining in.

Grabbing the pillow and blankets from the linen closet downstairs I tried to calm myself down. I knew Dylan wasn't trying to hurt me on purpose, but it hurt nonetheless and deeper than I wanted to admit.

I returned to the living room and placed the bedding on the couch next to Dylan and turned to leave. "Night." I whispered, but before I could get two steps away Dylan reached me, and hauled me into his arms.

"Please don't be mad at me." His hand was behind my head, as I turned to lay my head against his chest and listen to his beat strong underneath me. He kissed the top of my head. As he leaned back slightly against the back of the couch, his hands held the sides of my face so that he could look at me. "Just give me some time, okay? It's really hard for me to talk about."

My eyes swam with tears, and the dam was about to burst. I couldn't keep the tears back, and one escaped and slid down my face. His thumb caught it and gently brushed it aside.

"Please don't cry, Mia. You're breaking my heart here."

"I just don't understand why you don't trust me."

"It's not about trust, Mia. I do trust you, with all my heart. But my past, there's darkness there and I don't want to burden you with it. It took me a long time to bury it, and I'm not sure I can unbury it."

"But it's a part of you, Dylan, and I want to know everything about you. It's not going to be a burden to me."

"Can you give me some time?"

"Sure."

"Thank you."

"Dylan?"

"Yes, Baby."

My arms reached around Dylan's neck. My tears brushed aside I tugged him closer to me and looked into the face that I knew I loved, completely and unconditionally. "Umm…I think I'm falling in love with you."

"I think that's the best Christmas present I could ask for."

"That's it? That's all you have to say?" I tilted my head back slightly, my eyes searched the depths of his. I was a little upset that was all he had to say when I noticed that the corners of his mouth turned up just slightly as he grinned down at me.

"How about, I don't think I'm falling in love with you, but that I know I'm in love with you, Mia."

His lips took possession of mine as I sighed, opening to let him have full access. Our tongues touched, the jolt of energy that I felt radiated throughout my body, down to my toes. All I knew at that moment was Dylan. His hands held the side of my face, as they kept me tight to him. I breathed in the crisp, clean smell of his cologne. My heart was pounding so hard when he finally pulled away. His gaze scorched me and was my complete undoing. How could one look send all rational thoughts flying completely out of my head?

"I love you, Mia. Maybe from the moment I laid eyes on you, as you lay there in the snow. I'm not sure how to explain it. There was something there that drew me to you."

"Sometimes there is no explanation. It just is."

"You're amazing, do you know that?"

"You're the one with the huge heart. I know you try to hide it, but I see it when you talk about your mom, and how you act with her. You're kind, and gentle, and I'm so very lucky to have you in my life."

"I wish you didn't have to go upstairs to bed."

"I know me, too. But if my dad catches me down here I'm toast."

"I know, but I can still wish, right? It is after all the season for miracles." Dylan teased.

"You're going to get me in trouble. Maybe I should take back what I just said, maybe you aren't so good for me." I said laughing. "Here, let me help put your bed together before we both get in trouble."

I lay in my bed staring at the ceiling as sleep eluded me. My brain was racing a mile a minute and knowing Dylan was downstairs was driving me to complete distraction. I longed to lay in his strong arms, maybe then I could sleep. For the past several hours I conjured up all kinds of possible stories about Dylan's past. With each scenario that I imagined I knew that no matter how bad it might be, I knew I wouldn't care. How bad could it really be? And why would it matter now after all this time? Why was he so resistant to tell me? I worried that maybe he'd never tell me what had happened, would I be able to let it go if he never did tell me?

I flipped onto my side, my brightly lit clock blazed two a.m. Frustrated, I reached for my water bottle only to discover it was empty. "Great, just great." I mumbled to myself. I tossed back the covers, grabbed the bottle, and headed downstairs to refill it from the fridge.

The hall light cast a shadow into the family room where Dylan slept. I padded quietly across the floor to the kitchen where I filled my water bottle. As I was screwing the lid back on, Dylan turned over on the sofa bed and caught my attention. I couldn't resist watching him sleep and silently walked closer to the couch. His groan startled me, and as I looked closer I realized he was sweating, his hands clutched the sheet. He had to be having a nightmare, his face was full of tension.

I carefully sat on the edge of the thin mattress, and lightly ran my fingers across the side of his face. "Dylan, babe, wake up."

My touch startled him, his hand shot up in a defensive position, as if to block a blow to the head. His eyes were glassy as if he wasn't seeing me. It startled me, it was like he was looking through me.

"Dylan, it's me, Mia. You're okay." His hand grabbed my wrist pulling it away from his face. "Dylan, take it easy. Wake up, babe." I was getting scared, I'd never seen anyone this deep in a nightmare before. Finally, Dylan's grasp on my wrist lightened, his eyes came into focus.

"Mia? What are you doing here?" Dylan pushed himself up into a sitting position.

"I came down to get water. You were having a nightmare, I was trying to wake you up."

"I'm sorry. Did I hurt you?"

"No. Why would you say that?"

"No reason."

"Do you have nightmares often?"

"Sometimes. Not as often as before. It's gotten better over the years."

"Oh, Dylan. I'm so sorry. Why haven't you ever said anything?"

"Seriously? Come on Mia, yeah that's a great topic to discuss. How does that topic come up? Oh by the way, I have these nightmares that I've dealt with for years? Yeah that's a great conversation starter. It's just something I have to deal with. It's no big deal okay?"

"I'm sorry, Dylan. Is there anything I can do?"

He grinned, his face back to the easygoing Dylan I was used to seeing as he pulled me down next to him. "Maybe."

"Dylan!"

"Shhh....You're going to wake up your parents. Just lay here by me for just a couple minutes and then you can go back upstairs."

"You are bad. You're going to get me into trouble." I giggled as I slid next to Dylan. He pulled me tight to his side, his arm draped over my stomach, I grasped his hand, twisting my fingers into his.

"Mmm…you fit perfect next to me." He whispered into my ear.

"Yeah. I better be careful or I'm going to fall asleep like this, and we might not live to see another Christmas if my dad finds us like this."

"Just a couple more minutes."

"Okay."

I lay there thinking about anything I could to keep myself awake, but Dylan's warmth was intoxicating and was making me drowsy. It felt so good to lay there in his arms. His breathing shifted and deepened and I realized he'd fallen back asleep. It took all the willpower I possessed to easy myself out from under his heavy arm so that I didn't wake him. I picked up my water bottle as I quietly ascended the stairs, avoiding the two steps that typically creaked.

I climbed back into my bed, and nestled into my covers. Within minutes I was asleep, fatigue finally consumed me. My last thought was of Dylan's strong arms wrapped around my waist as I had lain next to him. The two of us did fit together perfect–like we had been made for each other.

Randy Blackburn sat at a beat-up bar nursing his beer. The air was stuffy and rank, smelling of spilled alcohol with occasional whiffs of urine and vomit. The barstool appeared to have been a red vinyl at one time, but it had darkened with age and had several rips where the off-white stuffing was visible. He could care less, he was just happy to finally be out of his prison cell. Years of confinement had his temper boiling. The burning need for vengeance was the only thing that kept him from going insane in the tiny box he had called home for too many years.

The TV above the bar was quiet. Christmas specials and Christmas commercials that saturated the screen made him sick. The feel-good stories about hope and good will, families coming together supporting each other, it was all just a bunch of trash. His so-called family put him behind bars.

He had been on a wild goose chase the past months in search for his ex-wife and son. They couldn't have just disappeared, but so far he'd had little luck in tracing them. The last lead had sent him to Southern California, but so far he hadn't been able to turn anything up of significance.

Randy wasn't giving up though; they had to be somewhere. Fed up for the day he tossed some cash on the bar for his drinks, swallowed the last of his now warm beer and pushed back his chair. An interview on the TV stopped him cold in his tracks.

It couldn't be, he thought to himself. There was no way he was that lucky. He yelled out for the bartender to turn up the volume he leaned closer to the TV. It was a human-interest story on ski accidents. The reporter was interviewing a pretty blonde girl, and there beside her, holding her hand was his son, the worthless piece of trash.

It had been five years since he had last seen Dylan, as he had sat in the courtroom when he testified against his own father. Dylan had filled out, he'd changed, grown up from the little runt he'd been, but Randy knew it was him, even before they gave his name on the special report.

Randy smirked, his mood now upbeat. He tossed down an extra five-dollar bill and left the bar. A good night's sleep was what he needed now. The news report had been so kind to even give the name of the resort where the ski accident had occurred as well as the information that Dylan was employed as part of the ski patrol. If Dylan was there in Snow Ridge, then he knew his good-for-nothing ex-wife wouldn't be far away and he'd finally have his revenge. Maybe Christmas was indeed full of miracles, because one had just landed in his lap.

CHAPTER TWENTY

~ Dylan ~

The smell of bacon frying and cinnamon rolls as they baked in the oven woke me. I folded my blankets and neatly stacked them on the edge of the couch after I pushed the pull out bed back into the sofa.

"Morning, Dylan, did you sleep well?" Mia's mom asked as she flipped the bacon.

"Yes, thanks again for letting me stay last night."

"No need for you to have to make that long drive, just to come all the way back down the hill today. There's extra towels in the downstairs bathroom if you'd like to take a shower."

"Thanks, that would be great. Where would you like the blankets and pillow?"

"You can just leave them there."

I enjoyed being around Mia's family. They were open and welcoming, very different from the tense, often violent home life I'd grown up with. After my dad was put in jail my mom finally pulled herself together, filed for divorce and moved us as far away as she could. Over the past five years she had tried so hard to make things easier for me. I loved my mom and worried about her. I was relieved she'd finally broken away and had moved on with her life. She was more confident now, and not as frightened every waking minute of the day like she'd been. Those first years after she had left my dad had been difficult for her as she tried to find her own way through life. She deserved to be happy after spending so many years in hell. She never complained to me. Her only comment when I'd get her to talk about it was that out of everything she had me, and that I was worth it all.

~ *Mia* ~

I was woken up out of a sound sleep when Zachary jumped on my bed.

"Ugh, Zach, get out of here. Leave me alone." I rolled over and buried my face under my pillow.

"Come on, Mia, everyone else is already up and downstairs. Mom won't let me eat until you get up."

"It's too early, just let me sleep five more minutes."

"Miiiiaaa. GET UP!"

"Fine, get out of here then so I can get dressed."

"Hurry up, don't be taking an hour like you usually do. I'm starving and there's lots of presents downstairs to open!"

I lay in my comfortable bed as I tried to remember what I'd been dreaming about before Zachary had rudely woken me up. Whatever it had been it was gone now and not likely that I was going to be able to pull it back into my memory. I tossed back the covers and dragged myself out of bed to get ready.

After my shower and getting dressed, I toweled off my hair and left it down to air dry. I knew if I didn't get downstairs soon Zachary would be back upstairs harassing me.

Laughter greeted me as I entered the kitchen. Dylan noticed me first, his bright smile lighted up my morning. His hair was still slightly damp from a shower and he looked as cute as ever.

"Morning, Mia." His voice, caused shivers to run up my spine. With just a few words he could cause me to melt. I loved his accent; there was something very sexy about it.

"About time, we're starving down here." Zachary grumbled. "Can I eat now Mom?"

"Grab a plate and dish up." My mom finished dishing up a large plate and placed it in front of my dad. "Dylan what can I get you?"

"I can get it, thank you, though." Dylan moved from the kitchen table to follow Zachary as he filled his plate. "How on earth do you plan to eat all of that?" he asked Zachary.

"Sleeping beauty over there took forever and I'm starving."

"You must have a hollow leg or something. I'm not sure I can even eat that much."

I joined the procession as I slid next to Dylan, my hip bumping slightly against his. "Morning." I whispered in his ear. "Miss me?"

"Yeah, you slipped away while I was sleeping."

"Trust me, it wasn't easy. Your arm is like a lead weight."

Dylan chuckled. "Next time you might not be able to escape so easily."

"Next time huh? So sure of yourself." I teased back.

"You bet."

~ Dylan ~

Christmas morning flew by in a blur of food, presents, wrapping paper, and ribbon. Shortly before noon Mia and I were driving over to Bailey's aunt and uncle's house, before driving up the mountain to spend the rest of the day with my mom and her boyfriend.

Bailey greeted us at the door. She hugged us and wished us a Merry Christmas as we stepped inside. "Come in everyone's already here. There's plenty of drinks and snacks."

"We can't stay long. We promised Dylan's mom we'd be at her house a little after lunch."

"Okay, everyone's just coming and going anyways. I'm just glad you guys were able to stop by."

"Hey, Riley. Come see who's here." Bailey called out.

"Riley's here?" Mia asked.

"Yes, Eileen and Riley stopped in. They're getting ready to leave soon though, you just caught them."

I watched as a cute, brown-haired little boy, with big brown eyes came tearing around the corner. Mia bent down to her knees and caught him in her arms picking him up while she gave him a big hug.

"Hey, Riley. Man, you've gotten so big since I last saw you."

"And I'm four now. You missed my party."

"Yeah, I'm sorry, buddy. I was in the hospital."

"My mom said you were really sick."

"I was. I've missed you, though. Maybe I'll come take you to the park next week. Would you like that?"

"Yes!"

Mia set Riley back on the ground. "I'd like you to meet someone. This is my friend Dylan. Dylan, this is Riley. I sometimes babysit him now that Bailey's moved away."

"Hi, Riley. It's nice to meet you."

Riley stood at Mia's leg as he looked up at me. His big brown eyes wide. He hesitated for only a second before accepting the hand that I had placed in front of him.

"Hi. Do you have any little brothers or sisters?" Riley asked.

"No, I don't. It's just me."

"Oh. Collin does, he has a little sister we used to play together a lot. But she moved away and we don't play very often anymore. And sometimes when Mia comes over Zach plays with me too."

"That must be fun."

"Come on Mia, we're playing a game." Riley grabbed Mia's hand in his and pulled her toward the noise coming from the back of the house.

"Well, I think my girlfriend just got swiped from me, by a four year old," I mumbled as Bailey laughed.

"Riley's a very social and fun kid. Come on, Dylan, I'll introduce you to my family."

~ Quinn ~

I had been in a lousy mood since the trip to the ski resort. Mia hadn't called or texted me and I hadn't been able to bring myself to do either after seeing her with Dylan. I knew I either needed to fight for her or let her go. Natasha had told me to leave it alone, that Mia seemed happy and that was the most important part. While I knew she was probably right it didn't make me feel any better.

Collin sat next to me on the floor with a board game in front of us. Riley had conned us into playing, but at least it had helped take my mind off of Mia–at least a little bit. From the current layout of the board the four-year old was winning. Riley came running back in the room with Mia in tow. My eyes caught Mia's as Riley tugged her to the floor next to me. She looked beautiful in her red sweater and snug jeans. Black boots reached her knees, and her hair was loose around her shoulders. My breath caught and I knew getting over her was not going to be easy. Especially when I kept running into her. At least Dylan wasn't with her–that was a plus. Maybe I'd be able to spend some time alone with her. I needed to know what was going on, and if there was any hope for us.

My plan was crushed minutes later when Bailey walked into the room with Dylan by her side. Bailey was introducing Dylan to the rest of her family as she moved through the kitchen. Riley was talking nonstop to Mia about all his recent adventures. Though Mia was sitting just inches from me she kept her focus on Riley. I felt a barrier grow between us that we'd never had before.

After thirty minutes and Riley winning the game we'd been playing. I felt like the room was closing in on me. I couldn't watch Dylan touching Mia any more. I knew I was at my limit. Dylan and Mia were sitting next to each other on the love-seat whispering to each other. I had moved to the kitchen as I tried to stay away from them. Standing at the island I was slapping dip on my plate when Natasha came up beside me.

"Easy, Quinn. It's Christmas, and you're throwing daggers with your eyes."

"Stay out of this, Tasha."

"Come on, Quinn. Let it go. It's not like you guys were even seeing each other."

"Just leave me alone."

"Fine, be that way." She turned on her heel and left the kitchen.

I noticed Dylan as he walked toward the front of the house by himself. Scraping the dip I'd just scooped onto my plate into the trash, I placed the dish in the sink and caught up to Dylan in the front living room. I came up from behind him and grabbed his arm. Dylan turned, and we were face to face.

"If you hurt her, I swear, I'll make you regret you ever came into her life." I hissed.

"Let go of my arm." Dylan was strong and he didn't back down an inch.

"I mean it. I've known her way longer than you. You think you can just walk into her life and steal her away from me?"

"Really, Quinn? From what Mia says, you guys were just friends. She thinks of you like a brother. I didn't steal her away. She was never yours to begin with."

My face was on fire with rage, Dylan's words sank in. I knew that what he said was true—which just pissed me off even more. "Mia doesn't deserve to be hurt."

"Who said I'm out to hurt her? Regardless of what you may think about me, I know how special she is. I have no intention of hurting her or letting anything or anyone hurt her."

"Whatever. I'm watching you, one wrong move and you'll regret it."

I couldn't stay in the house another minute. I pushed past him and left the house, slamming the front door in my wake.

CHAPTER TWENTY-ONE

~ *Dylan* ~

Brushing off the snow on my red ski patrol jacket while I walked toward the resort lodge I was anxious to get inside. My shift was over for the day, and I knew that Mia would be waiting for me. The slopes were crowded today, and my day had been busy. Holidays usually were action-packed and today had been no different. My walk across the lodge was brisk as I located Mia lounging near the large fireplace at the edge of the dining area. Her boots rested on an ottoman, a mug in her hands. My breath caught as I watched her. I still had trouble believing how lucky I'd been that she'd crashed into my life.

I walked up behind her, leaned over and kissed the top of her head. "Hey, Baby. Are you ready to get out of here?"

Mia tilted her head back as she leaned into me. "I sure am."

She placed her mug on the side table, grabbed her purse, and stood up. I immediately pulled her into my arms as I kissed her gently. I couldn't believe how much I missed her when we were apart.

"Let's go. What adventures do you have planned for us tonight?" Mia asked.

"Nothing super exciting. A quiet evening with just me."

"That sounds perfect."

I wrapped my arm around her waist and guided her through the crowded lodge. As we reached the glass double doors a group of kids passed us, chattering nonstop and not paying attention to where they were going. I shifted my weight pulling Mia to the side to let the group pass. As I reached for the door, movement in the in the corner of the room drew my attention. I couldn't see the man's features clearly, but there was something vaguely familiar about his stance.

"Dylan? What's wrong?"

"Nothing."

"What are you looking at?"

"It's nothing." My heart skipped a beat and pounded in my chest. A shiver ran up my spine as the hair on the back of my neck tingled. It couldn't be; there was no way my dad could be here. *I must be seeing things,* but a sick feeling shook me to the core, bringing back memories, dark memories I'd fought so hard to bury. I shrugged it off as I turned back to Mia and forced a smile. "Let's go. After you."

<hr>

Randy had been waiting, and finally his patience paid off. Three days of sitting around the ski lodge had about driven him insane. Thankfully, they had alcohol and the food wasn't awful, but today he'd hit payday. He knew the moment Dylan walked into the lodge, sensing his presence. Dylan had packed on weight, no doubt muscle, and added height to his frame, but there was no mistaking his son. It was almost like he was looking in the mirror at his past self. Randy skirted along the edge of the lodge. He stayed in the background watching as Dylan moved through the room and stopped at the blonde-haired girl who had been featured on the news report.

He watched as the two of them walked to the exit doors. He moved along the edge of the room as he followed the couple. Randy came to an abrupt halt as Dylan glanced his direction. Randy thought he saw recognition in Dylan's face, but he was too far away to be sure.

Randy worried that the game was up before it had even begun. He turned slightly so only the side of his face was visible, and he risked one more glance at the front door just in time to see the two of them exit the building. He placed his empty bottle on a nearby table then hurried out the door after them.

~ *Mia* ~

Dylan steered his jeep into the gravel driveway and pulled under the carport attached to the small mountain cabin.

"I love it, Dylan. It's so pretty up here."

"It's quiet, that's for sure, and small, but it works for me."

I followed Dylan up the steps to a small covered porch as he unlocked the front door and entered the cabin. I immediately fell in love with the cabin. The living area was vaulted with exposed heavy timber wood trusses. Floor to ceiling windows framed the dense forest that surrounded the cabin. A stone fireplace anchored the corner of the living room and was flanked on either side with skinny windows. The living area was open to a small dining space next to a small "U"-shaped kitchen. Sliding doors off the family room opened into a bedroom. A ladder in the center accessed a partial loft area. The cabin was clean, no clutter, only the basics. A large sofa with two end tables sat facing the fireplace with a flat-screen TV mounted above the wooden mantle.

I stood in the middle of the open living room and turned gently in a circle as I took in the view of the room. "Wow, Dylan, this is amazing. It's a beautiful cabin. How long have you been here?"

"A little over a year. I'm renting it from a co-worker of my mom's. He used to rent it out for tourists. When he found out I was looking for a place he offered it. I couldn't pass it up. Rent is reasonable, and it's just the right size for me."

"I love the openness, and the vaulted space. Can you see down the mountain or just the forest?"

"The trees are pretty dense, and we're not quite high enough to get the view out over the valley."

"What's up the ladder? A loft?"

"Yes, it's a small area that can be used as an office space or a guest room. I have a desk up there but that's about it, I use it mostly for storage. Are you hungry? I have some leftover pasta in the fridge."

"Sure. That sounds good."

Dylan walked to the small kitchen and pulled out plates and containers from the small fridge. "I hope you like it. I'm not the best cook in the world, but I make do."

"I'm sure I'll love it. Can I help with anything?"

"Sure, grab whatever you'd like to drink, the cups are over in the cupboard next to the sink. I'll heat the plates up."

When everything was ready I followed Dylan over to the couch. "Are you ready for tonight's movie attraction?" Dylan asked.

"Of course, what did you pick?"

"*Fast and Furious*. Have you seen any of them?"

"Umm…nope. There's more than one?"

"There's several of them, you haven't seen any of them? Not even the first one?"

"No, not even the first one."

"Well, I think it's time for a marathon then. We'll start with the first one. It's got fast cars and lots of action, but there's a bit of a love story in there as well. I think you'll like it."

Dylan grinned as he picked up the remote from the side table and flipped on the movie. I snuggled closer to Dylan as I sat next to him on the couch. I balanced my plate of food on my lap and settled in to enjoy the evening.

I was enjoying the movie just as Dylan had predicted. I was relaxed and felt at home spending quiet time with Dylan. I knew I'd fallen for him hard and fast, but it felt right. My feet were propped up on the small ottoman, next to Dylan's. My head was nestled on Dylan's shoulder while my fingers were intertwined with his.

The movie was almost at the end, and I wasn't sure what to expect after. My heart raced. I'd dated through high school, but I'd never had a real serious relationship before. My experience was limited and I'd never slept with anyone. There were times when I felt like I was out of my league with Dylan. He was older and sexy as hell. If he wanted to go further tonight, was I ready? I knew I loved him; it was like nothing I'd ever felt before. Maybe I was just getting ahead of myself, but I struggled with my emotions. I had waited knowing that I wanted my first time to be with the right person. Someone that I loved and cared deeply about and I knew with all my heart it was Dylan.

The credits rolled and my stomach was tied in knots wondering where things might go from here. Dylan flipped off the TV and DVD and turned to me with a huge grin.

"Well? Did you like it?"

"I did. Really. Can we see the rest of them?"

"Of course! I can keep you locked up here for hours then."

He tucked a strand of loose hair behind my ear. His eyes were intense as I lost all train of rational thought. His hand shifted to the back of my neck as he gently pulled me closer to him. His warm lips were salty from our dinner as they took possession of mine. Our tongues touched and searched each other. I wrapped my arms around his neck, my fingers trailing through his short hair as I pulled him closer to me.

In a swift movement he had picked me up and I was now sitting on his lap my legs straddling him. His fingers traced down my side as they slipped under my sweater and cupped my breast. Shock and tingles burst through my body. My thoughts were scrambled as new sensations I'd never felt before surged through me. I broke the kiss and slightly pulled back. I rested one hand on his chest.

"Mia?"

"Everything is moving so fast." My eyes searched his for understanding.

"It's okay. No pressure. You've been through a lot in the last few weeks."

He traced the side of my face his fingers settling on my lips as I hunted for the right words. I kissed his fingertips as he pulled his hand away and rested it on my hip.

"It's not just that. Umm…I've never been with anyone before." I waited for his response. My stomach felt like it had dropped to the floor.

"Really? Never?"

I shook my head.

"Wow. That's a massive turn-on. I like–no–actually, I love that you've never been with anyone." His hand cupped the end of my chin as he tilted my face up slightly.

"I want it to be with you. But I'm not sure if I'm ready," I whispered.

"Oh, baby. I can't tell you how happy that makes me. We'll take it slow."

"Okay. I love you. Dylan."

"I love you too, Mia."

My lips were once again held captive by his when the ringing of his phone brought us back to reality. Dylan leaned over to check it and sent it to voicemail.

"It's just my mom. I'll call her back."

"It's okay if you need to get it."

"No, it's fine; she'll leave a message. I can call her later."

Dylan set the phone back on the table when it started ringing again.

"Dylan, maybe you should answer it."

"I'm sure it's nothing. She didn't leave a message the first time so it's probably not that important."

The ringing stopped, but within seconds it was ringing again. Sighing Dylan picked up the phone. "Guess she's not going to stop until I answer it."

"It's okay." I smiled, a little distraction right now helped me pull my thoughts together.

"Hi, Mom. Wait, slow down, Mom, I can't understand a word you're saying. Take a deep breath and start again."

I sat up and watched Dylan as emotions flickered across his face, as I listened to the one-sided conversation.

"Where are you? Are you in your safe room? I'm sure you just accidentally forgot to lock the door. Is anything missing?"

Dylan paused as his mom continued the conversation. I noticed his body tense up, the muscle in his cheek twitched, and his usually bright green eyes had darkened, edged with concern. I knew without a doubt something was seriously wrong. *Safe room?* I thought to myself what was that?

"Okay, Mom. I'll be right there. Stay where you're at." Dylan hung up the phone as he turned to me. "We've got to head over to my mom's. I'm sorry."

"It's okay; what happened? Is she all right?"

"She's fine, but she's got herself in a complete panic. She came home, and the front door was cracked open. I'm sure she just forgot to lock it. I need to go make sure she's okay and see if I can calm her down. I'm sorry to ruin our evening."

"The evening isn't ruined. Let's go. Your mom is more important."

"Thanks, Mia."

Ten minutes later we arrived at Dylan's mom's cabin.

"Stay with me. I need to check the outside." Dylan explained as we got out of the car.

Carefully Dylan walked the perimeter of the cabin, before we climbed the steps of Jolene's front porch. We passed through the small entry vestibule and walked through the short hall to where it opened up to the living and dining area. Dylan continued a pattern throughout the main level of the house as he searched each room.

When we finished the main level he opened a door that lead to a basement level that I didn't even know existed. I followed behind silent, as I watched Dylan. I felt the tension radiating through him. He was calm and completely in control.

In the basement Dylan again searched each room until he reached the last door and he knocked on the door in a specific pattern. I stood behind him and waited. After a few seconds I heard the click of a lock and the door slowly open. Jolene exited the small closet and flung herself in Dylan's arms. Her eyes were red and she looked shook up. She held her phone and what looked like a photo album tight to her chest.

"Mom? Are you okay?"

Jolene looked far younger, almost childlike, her face was white as a sheet, her eyes big and dilated. She finally pulled out of Dylan's embrace. "Oh, Dylan. It's him. I know it's him, he's come back."

Dylan wrapped his arm around his mom.

"Let's go upstairs okay. I've already searched, there's no one in the house."

Dylan helped his mom up the stairs as I followed quietly behind. There was something more significant going on than just leaving the door unlocked. Dylan guided his mom to the couch in the living room and sat next to her while I sat in a chair opposite them.

"What are you talking about Mom? Tell me exactly what happened."

I watched mother and son as they talked. I wasn't sure what I should do. Dylan's mom was a mess. It was like she was a completely different person from the happy, confident person I had met just a few short weeks ago.

"I came home from the grocery store. I was carrying a bag of groceries, my keys were in my hand. I always have them ready when I get out of the car. I came in the side door by the kitchen, and the house felt cold. I set the bag down on the table and walked over to check the thermostat. That's when I realized the front door was cracked open. Dylan, I didn't use the front door today. I only used the side door."

"Maybe you just didn't have it shut all the way and a gust of wind pushed it open. It was kinda windy today."

"Come on, Dylan. You know I always check all the doors. Every time I leave and every time I get home. It's a ritual. I never forget. It was shut and locked when I left; I know it was."

"What about Elliot, does he have a key? Maybe he stopped in and he forgot to lock it."

"Elliot's been in L.A. for the past two days. He doesn't get home until tomorrow."

"Okay, does anyone else have a key?"

"Just you. Dylan, he was in the house."

"Who was in the house Mom?"

"Your father."

"That's impossible Mom. He's locked up, and there's no way for him to find us here."

Dylan glanced over at me. His face had lost color. Was this what he didn't want to talk about?

"He was here, Dylan. Look."

Dylan's mom placed the album she'd been clutching in her arms and placed it on the coffee table that sat in front of the couch. She opened it to a page in the middle. Once it was open I recognized it as one of the albums we'd been looking at the night Dylan brought me over here to meet his mom. I looked where his mom was pointing. On the center coffee table lay one of the photo albums that we had looked at the night I was here.

"No, it can't be," Dylan whispered.

I watched as the rest of the color drained from Dylan's face as both he and Jolene were focused on a photo album that sat in front of them. The angle of the book concealed the actual photo that had spooked them though so I had no idea what had caused Dylan to panic.

"He wants me to know he's here. He wants me to be scared, to not know when he'll be back. He left this on the kitchen island. Open to this page. Right next to the phone!"

"How can this be? How could he have found us? I thought he wasn't supposed to be out for another couple of years."

"I don't know Dylan, but they let people out early all the time."

"Why didn't anyone contact us?"

"I haven't really kept in contact with the police back there. I thought it was better if we just kind of vanished."

"With today's technology Mom, it's really not that hard to find people, but we were careful. We need to contact the police right away. We're not messing around with this. Who knows what he's capable of now."

"Okay." Jolene slumped against Dylan's shoulder. "I'm so sorry, Dylan."

"Why are you sorry, Mom? You didn't do anything wrong."

"I'm sorry I couldn't protect you from this."

"Mom, I'm old enough to take care of myself, and you as well." Dylan pulled out his phone and quickly dialed 911.

I sat in stunned silence as I listened. This must be what Dylan had been keeping quiet. My heart broke for Dylan and Jolene. I didn't know the whole story, but something pretty significant must have happened for Jolene to be so afraid, and for Dylan's father to have spent time in prison.

Less than ten minutes passed before the doorbell rang. Dylan got up to answer it. I stood up from my chair and sat in the spot Dylan had just vacated. I took Jolene's cold hands in my own.

"It's going to be okay. Dylan will take care of it. He's not going to let anybody hurt you."

"Oh Mia, I'm so sorry to drag you into this. Dylan's very lucky to have you by his side. I had hoped this would have stayed in the past, but it doesn't look as if we're going to be that lucky."

"We'll figure it out."

I wasn't quite sure yet what exactly we were going to figure out or what we were dealing with, but I knew with all my heart that we would find a solution. I knew that there was no way that Dylan would let anything happen to his mom. His love and concern for her was obvious.

Dylan stepped back into the room with two policemen that followed close behind. The two officers were the complete opposites of each other. One was tall and skinny, with dark hair, the other was short, stocky, with blond hair.

"Mom, this is Officer Jones and Officer Tracy. They have some questions for us."

I slid over on the couch so Dylan could sit next to his mom, while the two officers sat in the adjacent chairs. I reached for Dylan's hand to let him know that I was there for him. He took it and held it tightly. His body was rigid; his jaw twitched.

I listened as Dylan's mom answered the officers' questions. They asked her to walk through each step from when she came home and found the front door open. They promised they would add some additional patrol units in the area, and advised that Jolene alert her neighbors to be on the lookout for anything unusual. After their short interview, they informed her that they would contact her after they researched Dylan's dad's prison records. At this time there wasn't anything else they could do. The officers stood to leave, and Dylan walked them out.

Jolene sighed as they left. "Typical, they're never any help. I don't know why we bother."

My concern increased as I watched Dylan's mom sink against the back of the couch completely defeated. I was at a loss. I'd grown up with a loving family. This type of drama was foreign to me. I'd heard enough to know that something serious had happened. I wished that Dylan would open up to me and let me completely in. I felt like an outsider, and I didn't like it.

Dylan returned to the couch. He placed two business cards on the table in front of the couch as he sat back down.

"I'll stay here with you until Elliot gets back into town. Do you think he'd come stay with you until we get to the bottom of this?" Dylan's voice was strained, but focused.

"Yes."

"Good. Mia, would your parents be okay with you staying here tonight? I'd rather not leave right at this moment."

"I'm sure it will be fine. I am nineteen; they really can't say no."

"I know, but you're still living under their roof. I don't want to make things difficult for you at home."

"I'll call them."

I was touched that Dylan was concerned about my parents. It was yet one more testament to his strong character and respect for others. And one more thing that I loved about him.

CHAPTER TWENTY-TWO

~Dylan~

This was not how I expected or wanted the evening to end. I had watched Mia's face as my mom had revealed pieces of my past. Thankfully she was easy to read and I at least had some hope that she wouldn't go running for the hills. But the fear still raged inside. The thought of her leaving was gut-wrenching.

My mom had been upset, and she had been rambling. The photo album had been open to a page where previously had been a photo of my mom smiling in a field of flowers. That photo was missing and had been replaced with a wedding picture of my parents.

My mom had destroyed every picture that had my dad in it. Either cutting him out of the photo or throwing them away. That photo hadn't been in this house before tonight.

I knew now that I was going to have to tell Mia the whole story. I tried to push down my rising panic and the memory of the figure in the lodge earlier in the day flooded my memory. There was no way I could keep it from her with the possibility that my dad was out there lurking.

We sat with our feet propped up on the ottoman in my mom's living room. My mom had finally calmed down enough that she had left the two of us alone as she headed to her room to try to get some sleep. The living room was dark, only the glow of the table lamp that sat next to the couch casted light inside. The moon was full and the light sparkled off the snow, visible through the large picture windows. I wrapped my arm around Mia, she leaned her head on my shoulder. I didn't know what to say or even where to begin.

"I'm so sorry to drag you into this," I finally whispered.

"Into what Dylan? What exactly do you think you're dragging me into? You haven't done anything wrong."

"I thought he was out of my life. I never wanted to see, or think about him again."

"Why haven't you ever said anything about him?" Mia shifted so she could look up into my face. Her deep brown eyes searched mine for answers.

"I didn't want to chance losing you," I sighed quietly.

"Losing me? Why would you lose me?"

I broke Mia's gaze and focused on the snow-covered trees beyond the warmth of the cabin. I leaned my head back against the couch and closed my eyes. I was struggling. The last time I'd opened up about my past and my dad to a girl that I loved, or at least thought I'd loved, she had turned on me. It had been a huge blow. A heart-wrenching lesson that I'd learned the hard way, not once, but twice. It was one I didn't want to repeat again. Even though every bone in my body told me that Mia wouldn't react the same. I knew she was different, but I was still afraid. Afraid of even the possibility of losing her when I'd just found her.

"I don't even know where to start."

"At the beginning. Please just talk to me." Mia reached her hand to my cheek applying just enough pressure for me to turn my head back towards her. "Dylan, I love you. There's nothing you could tell me that will change that. I promise."

Torment and fear trickled up my spine. Words I'd heard before. "Don't promise something that you might not be able to keep."

"Dylan, I know you. I know it's only been a short time, but it's like we've always been together. I feel like you are a part of me. Nothing from your past is going to change that feeling."

Leaning down I caught her lips in a kiss. My hands twisted in her hair as I pulled her closer to me. I clung to her warmth, and her love. I hoped that she would still look at me the same after she knew everything. I reluctantly ended the kiss and pulled back. I rested my forehead against hers and closed my eyes.

"I hope so, I really hope so."

I leaned back, and took a deep breath, losing myself in Mia's calming brown eyes. I committed her tender look to memory in case I never saw that look on her face again. After a minute of silence I dug deep into my memories, the one's I'd tried so hard to forget over the years, and searched for the right words to say.

"My dad was never like yours. He's always been a drunk, and he's mean when he's drinking. When I was little it wasn't quite as bad, or maybe it was and I just didn't know or don't remember. But as I got older it got worse.

"He was often verbally abusive to me. If I spilled milk, he'd curse at me, tell me I was a good-for-nothing little shit. Usually the next day after something like that would happen he'd come home and bring me a new toy and say that he was sorry for yelling at me. Other times my mom would try to cover for me and with her he wasn't just verbally abusive, but physically abusive. There were times her bruises were so bad she could barely move. He never marked her face though; it was always in areas that were hidden.

"My mom was an only child, and her parents had died shortly after I was born. She didn't have any family nearby and my dad knew that she had nowhere to go. After a violent outburst, he'd bring her flowers, candy, and other special gifts. He'd tell her he was sorry and that he'd never hurt her again that he loved her and couldn't live without her. She loved him and she wanted to believe that things would be different. She'd forgive him and things would be good for a while and then something would trigger another outburst and the whole cycle would repeat.

As I got older I could see the cycle, almost predict it coming. I knew if things were calm and going really good for too long that a big blow up was not far away. I begged my mom to leave, but she couldn't break away. She'd tell me all about all the good things he'd done for her and that he really did love us. She would tell me that when he got angry it was because she did something wrong or something to make him mad. She put the blame on herself, she really believed that it wasn't his fault but hers and if she could just be a better wife then he wouldn't get mad."

I paused and watched the emotions flicker across Mia's face. She had had wrapped her hands tightly in mine, giving me strength to continue my story.

"One night, when I was sixteen, it was late, and I was in my bed sleeping when I woke up to them fighting. It was horrible, this time it had gotten so out of hand that my mom's eye was already swollen shut when I entered the room. I'm not sure exactly how many times he'd hit her. There was glass all over. I remember that, flowers from my mom's garden were strewn all over the coffee table, water dripped over the edge.

It was the first time I tried to break up a fight. I stepped in trying to get my dad off my mom. I still wasn't as tall or as big as he was. He worked construction so he was strong and solid. I wasn't any match for him, but I was sixteen, and I thought he was going to kill my mom. I knew I had to do something.

He was drunk, very drunk. I remember him staggering over to me, he was telling me to leave, to go back to my room. I didn't, instead I got one punch in that only served to rile him up even more. He swung at me, and it knocked the wind out of me. I staggered upright only to receive a blow to my head that spun me backwards and it sent me crashing to the floor. I hit the corner of the fireplace hearth.

This scar on my chin is a forever reminder of that night. When I came to, I was in a hospital bed, with a mild concussion, and three broken ribs. They told me that I was lucky that it didn't puncture my lung."

"Oh Dylan, how horrible. I can't even imagine living through something like that." Mia lightly ran her fingers over the faint scar. "This doesn't change anything Dylan, it was all out of your control; you can't blame yourself."

"That's not the end of the story. Seeing me in the hospital was the last straw for my mom, and I wasn't about to let her back down again. I was old enough now and I testified against my dad. He was sent to prison.

"I had a girlfriend at the time. Her name was Dakota, we'd been together for over a year, we were close, but I never brought her to my house. She met my mom once, but when we hung out I went to her house. She was from a stable, normal family, they ate dinner together, they were close. I felt safe there. I never told her about my dad or what happened in my house.

"When everything happened and all the ugliness about my family came out in the papers, and my dad being sent to prison, she broke it off. She said she just couldn't handle it. I was heartbroken–shattered–actually. I thought she'd stand by me, but when things got rough, and I needed someone to help me through, she split.

"Now, when I look back, I'm glad I found out her real nature before things got even more serious, but at the time it was horrible. I was already shaken up from everything that had happened, and then to lose one of the two people I thought I could actually count on was a huge blow. A few months later my mom decided she wanted a fresh start, and we moved here. I finished high school and started college.

"My first year of college I started dating an older girl. Her name was Kacy, she was fun to be with, always joking and it was a nice change for me. I started to let my guard down, and began to enjoy life. She had dealt with drama in her family, which she'd been very open about, but she didn't let it get her down or bother her. At least that's what I had thought.

"Her uncle had been an alcoholic. He had three daughters, and for years he had molested the oldest until she had finally broken down one day and told Kacy everything. Kacy's family stepped in and took in the three girls. It gave me hope that there really were people out there that cared and helped those that needed it.

"We'd been going out almost nine months when I finally got the courage to tell her about my dad and everything that had happened. Her reaction was not what I expected. Instead of understanding and supporting me, she turned on me. She told me that there was no way she could be involved with anyone that came from a 'tainted family background.'"

Mia's eyes widened.

"'Those were her exact words 'tainted family.' She said that she'd seen and witnessed too much in her own family and she was done with the drama. That she wanted to find someone who had a normal, loving background and family. That she was sorry but that she couldn't see me anymore.

"I finished out that semester and I came back to Snow Ridge and started the ski patrol. From that moment I swore I'd never tell anyone about my past again. I'd already suffered through the actual events, but then to have two girlfriends, who I thought cared about me, leave because of it, was too much. I was never going through that again.

"And here I am, opening up that old wound again—baring it all—risking yet another heartbreak." I looked away, my eyes had misted, and I refused to shed one tear in Mia's presence.

"Dylan, look at me."

"It's okay, I understand, really I do. You are amazing Mia, and you don't deserve to have to deal with this type of drama. I'll take you home as soon as I can in the morning."

Mia shifted so that she was straddling my legs. She practically was sitting in my lap as she faced me. Her hands touched each side of my face, she gently turned it so I was looking at her.

"I'm not those girls. They are the ones that lost out. It's going to take a lot more than that to push me out of your life. You can't be held responsible for what someone else did. You are the victim, not the villain. You are not your father, Dylan, and you never will be. You are caring, loving, sensitive, and considerate. I'm lucky to have you, and I'm not letting you go. I am here for you. No matter what."

I stared into Mia's deep brown eyes, and within them I saw nothing but unwavering love. Something I'd never even dared to hope for. I gently lifted my hand to her face. She leaned into my palm turning slightly as she kissed it.

"Mia, I'm the lucky one. I don't deserve you."

I pulled her tightly against my chest, her head tucked securely under my chin. Her arms wrapped under my arms and locked together behind my back. I breathed in the scent of her shampoo and I relaxed. For the first time in years I felt a huge burden lift from my shoulders.

I released her after a few minutes as I shifted on the couch. I swung my legs from the ottoman and stretched out lengthwise on the couch. I leaned against an armrest as I pulled Mia in front of me. Her body was situated between my legs with her back lying against his chest. It felt amazing to hold her and my heart was bursting with love for this beautiful, vivacious, girl that I had fallen into my life.

"Kick off your shoes. Just lay here with me."

"Hmm…this feels good, comfortable." Mia laced her fingers through mine as I held her loosely around her stomach.

"Are you still sore or tender where your incisions were?"

"They've mostly healed up, but sometimes I'll twist or move wrong and they ache a bit."

"Tell me if I bump them."

"You're fine."

We lay there with only the ticking of a clock in the kitchen audible. The breeze was picking up outside, tossing the snow in flurries. The tree branches swayed slightly, visible in the bright moonlight.

I broke the silence first, fear running through me. "Mia, if my dad was here, and knows where we are, it's not good. He's dangerous, probably even more so now. You could be in immediate danger just being with me. I'm not sure I could handle it if anything else happened to you, and especially if it was because of me."

"We'll be careful. We can't live with what-ifs. That's one thing I learned first hand with my accident. We have to live each day to the fullest. We never know what's going to happen, and worrying about it every second isn't going to prevent anything from happening. All it's going to do is make you miserable with the stress, and then he wins. If he comes here, we'll deal with it together okay?" She tilted her head back so she could look at me.

"Have I told you how much I love you?"

"Not in the last few minutes, you haven't." She grinned.

"Well, I do." I squeezed her tightly and within minutes we were both asleep wrapped in each other's arms.

Randy sat in the living area of the cabin he'd been able to rent after finding his ex-wife. He couldn't believe how lucky he'd been. The cabin sat a few streets above hers. Though the access came in from a different street, the view out the back of his cabin looked right down the hill towards hers.

With a set of binoculars, he had the perfect line of sight to the front of her cabin. If he was careful he could traverse through the forest to her cabin and no one would even notice.

He was giddy with excitement for his new cat-and-mouse game. He'd been spying on the house when Dylan and his girlfriend arrived. He knew that Jolene had found his little gift. Not long after Dylan had arrived he had seen the cops show up at the door. Randy wasn't worried, though he knew they'd find wouldn't find anything. He'd been careful and used gloves.

It had been so easy to get into her cabin. It was a last-minute decision that had him leaving the front door cracked open. He thought it would be a nice touch. He wished he could have seen her reaction though. Knowing she'd been rattled enough to call Dylan and the cops was going to have to be enough for now.

He knew one thing for sure; the lack of security and the relative seclusion of the mountain town were going to make his job a whole lot easier than if she'd been in a larger city.

CHAPTER TWENTY-THREE

~Dylan~

$\mathcal{I}$ woke to a stiff neck and a heater that seemed to be set to inferno across my chest. Mia's blonde hair tickled my nose. She had shifted during the night and was lying on her side between my legs. Her arm bent under her head that rested on my chest. Heat radiated off of her. I carefully swept her hair from her forehead. I was immediately concerned, she was too warm and she felt feverish. Trying not to wake her I shifted slightly so I could look at her face, it was flushed, and her cheeks were pink. I picked up her hand that wasn't tucked under her head and it was warm, too warm.

"Mia, wake up, Baby."

"Hmm."

I brushed my fingers lightly over her forehead, "I know it's early, how are you feeling?"

Mia withdrew her arm from under her head. She winced as she flexed her fingers. "I'm really tired, and my arm's asleep. I can't keep my eyes open."

"Mia, you feel really warm, like you are fevering."

"It's just hot in here. I'm okay, just tired."

"Babe, it's not really hot in here. In fact it's a bit chilly. You're the one that's hot. Can you sit up for a minute?"

Mia dragged herself up to a sitting position on the couch as I moved my body from under her so I could look at her closer.

"Mia, does anything hurt? Do you ache anywhere?" I noted the glassiness in her eyes. Her cheeks were almost rosy in color when I looked at her straight on. I didn't like what I was seeing. I knew although she was recovering amazingly quickly from her injuries, her body was still weak.

"Dylan, I'm fine. I'm just tired. Can I just lie back down?"

"I'll be right back, give me a minute."

Walking into the bathroom I opened cabinets as I searched for a thermometer. I knew my mom had one somewhere, but I wasn't having any luck finding it. I left the bathroom and I stood at my mom's door debating if I should wake her. I decided it was better to let her sleep. I really didn't need a thermometer to tell me that Mia was fevering.

I went back to the bathroom and soaked a washcloth with cold water. I stopped at the hall closet and snagged a pillow and blanket. As I reached the couch Mia had already curled up and fallen back to sleep.

Pushing the ottoman closer to the couch I sat down next to her. I propped my feet up on the ottoman. I placed the pillow in my lap and gently pulled her over so her head lay on the pillow. Taking the blanket I covered her and folded the wet washcloth so it rested on her forehead.

"Brr, that's cold." Mia mumbled.

"Shhh, just go back to sleep okay."

"Okay."

I brushed back the blonde strands that stuck to the wetness of the washcloth. I watched her sleep and worried. The previous night's events with my mom and the possibility of my dad being out of jail were bad enough, but the thought of Mia getting sick right now was even more stressful. Or even worse what if she was having a complication with her injuries? Fevers could mean any number of things. I'd had enough first aid training to know something could be seriously wrong.

I flipped the TV on low as I searched through the early morning shows and infomercials while Mia slept. When the washcloth warmed I refolded it and placed the cooler portion on her forehead. She didn't seem to be getting hotter, but neither was she cooling down.

Sunlight streaks filtered through the snow-laden trees when Mia began shaking and moaning slightly in her sleep. I dabbed her forehead with the washcloth in an attempt to cool her. My mom staggered into the room, her hair was tousled and her eyes were streaked with red indicating she hadn't been able to sleep well.

"Morning, Dylan. What's wrong?"

"Something's wrong with Mia. She's burning up with a fever. I woke up a few hours ago and she was hot."

"It's probably just a virus, honey. The flu has been going around. I'll see if I can find the thermometer."

"I hope that's all it is."

Mia's face looked relaxed though while she slept. She was so beautiful, not only on the outside, but inside as well. She was considerate, caring, and concerned about everyone else around her. As I watched her sleep, memories of her lying so still in the hospital rushed back. I hated the feeling of being completely helpless to do anything more than sit by her side. My mom returned with an ear thermometer and handed it to me as she stood next to the couch.

"Did you tell her everything last night?" she asked.

"Yeah."

"And? How'd she take it?"

"She said none of it matters. That it doesn't change how she feels about me."

"Good. I'm glad. I knew she was different from the other ones. I know you didn't want to dig up the past again, but she had a right to know Dylan."

"Deep down I knew that. I just didn't want to risk it again. She's special, Mom. I don't want to lose her."

My mom leaned down to kiss the top of my head. "I think this one is going to stick around, honey. Now, check her temp."

I positioned the thermometer in Mia's exposed ear and waited for the beep. Reading the digital numbers my heart sank. "Shit." I sighed. "102.4"

"That's not good, Dylan. We need to wake her and try to get it dropped. Then you need to get her home, in case something goes wrong, or she gets worse she'll at least be closer to the hospital."

I ran my hand lightly down Mia's arm. "Mia, you need to wake up."

"I'm cold Dylan. It's freezing in here."

"You're fevering. You're running a temp of 102.4. We need to get you cooled down."

"No, I'm already cold. Please, can you get me another blanket?"

"I'll get one Dylan." My mom turned and quickly left the room. She returned with another blanket, a glass of water, and a bottle of Tylenol. "Here she needs to get some fluids in her too, and this should help bring down the fever."

"Mia, here sit up just a bit, drink some water. Can you take Tylenol?"

"Yes, Tylenol is okay." Mia said as her teeth chattered. Her body was shaking as she took the glass and swallowed the Tylenol. She handed the glass back to me. I placed it on the adjacent side table and pulled her tightly against me. I wrapped my arms around her blanketed body, and held her, as her body shook next to mine.

"Mom, when's Elliot getting here?"

"I talked to him last night. He was leaving his seminars early this morning and was coming straight here. I expect him maybe in an hour or two."

"Can you call him, make sure he's on his way? I don't want to leave you before he gets here."

"Dylan, Mia's more important. You need to get her down the mountain."

"Mom. Please, just call Elliot." My voice was stern as I glanced over the top of Mia's head to look at my mom, leaving no room for argument.

"Okay."

"I'm fine. You guys don't need to talk about me like I'm not here." Mia mumbled against my chest. "I'm sure it's just a little cold."

"Well, I'm not taking any chances. Your body is still recovering from the fall."

Mia nestled her head back against my chest. I rubbed up and down her back, as I talked to my mom. I felt Mia relax and her breathing deepened as she fell back asleep.

~*Mia*~

Hushed voices nearby filtered through my subconscious. I rolled on my side and realized I was alone on the couch. Blankets were pulled up under my chin. There was something stuck to my forehead. The pillow under my head was soaked, and I was on fire. My whole body ached and my head was throbbing.

I threw back the blankets and the cooler air against me was a relief. I pealed the nearly dry washcloth off my forehead and set it on the table. I slowly sat up. The voices that had woken me sounded like they were coming from the kitchen. I swung my legs over the edge of the couch and stood up. Lightheaded, I held onto the edge of the couch while I gained my balance and found my way to the bathroom.

As I finished in the bathroom and splashed cold water on my face I heard Dylan calling for me. I toweled off my face and opened the bathroom door. Still not completely stable on my feet I swayed slightly as Dylan reached me.

"Are you okay?" he asked.

"I'm a bit dizzy, and now I'm super-hot. I feel really weak."

Before I even had a moment to think Dylan swept me up in his arms. I wrapped my arms around his neck as he carried me back to the living room. I had never been picked up and carried before but I loved the feeling of being in Dylan's arms.

"I'm going to break your back." I whispered against his chest.

"Nah, you barely weigh anything." Dylan said as he placed me gently back on the couch. "The Tylenol should have kicked in by now." He picked up the thermometer from where it sat on the table and handed it to me.

Dylan sat next to me as I checked my temp holding it in front of me after it beeped. My eyes widened slightly as I handed it to Dylan.

"103.9" I whispered.

"Mia, it should be going down by now not up. We need to get you home. Elliot just got here so I can leave Mom. I've already given him the background and the cards of the cops that came by last night."

"It's just a fever, Dylan. Probably just the flu. It's going to be fine."

"Yes, you're going to be okay. I'm not going to let anything happen to you. Stay here, I'll go say goodbye to my mom and Elliot and then we'll get going."

"Okay."

I felt horrible, not just physically, but mentally. Dylan had been there for me during my accident, it was my turn to support him. But instead here he was once again taking care of me. I knew I was causing him even more worry, which was the last thing he needed right now.

Dylan carried me bundled in a blanket to his jeep, while I complained. "I can walk Dylan, this is crazy. You don't have to keep carrying me." I mumbled against his chest. His strength soothed me and I felt safe in his arms, but I also felt ridiculous being carried to the car.

"Just let me take care of you, okay?"

"I don't seem to have a say in it, do I?" I teased back.

He cracked a smile as he looked down into my eyes. "Not really."

Dylan's mom followed behind with Elliot by her side. As they reached the jeep Elliot pulled the passenger door open. Dylan deposited me on the seat and allowed me to settle the blanket around myself. He walked around the jeep as his mom handed me my jacket and purse. Then she leaned over and kissed my forehead.

"You take it easy." She instructed.

"I will. I hope I didn't infect your house."

"It's fine, don't worry about it. You're more important."

"Thanks Jolene. Be careful too."

"I will. I've got Elliot here." She looped her arm through Elliot's and stepped back as Dylan got into the driver's seat. "Drive safe, Dylan."

"I will, Mom. Make sure to call me if anything happens. Elliot, don't let her leave your sight until we get more information."

"I won't. I took a couple days off. I'll make sure she's safe."

"Thanks."

Elliot shut my door as Dylan started the jeep and we backed out of the driveway.

Halfway down the mountain I was focused on the road in front of me. Not only did my body ache everywhere, but now my stomach was cramping and my mouth began to water. I tried to swallow the saliva that was building up faster in my mouth than I could get rid of. I knew I was in trouble. I reached for Dylan's hand as it rested on the gearshift. He looked at me and I could see panic flash through his eyes.

"Mia, what's wrong?"

"Can you pull over? Like right now?"

My hand tightened on his. He glanced in his rear view mirror as he found an area where the road was wide enough and pulled the jeep to a screeching halt. Dust flew up behind us as I grabbed the door and flung it open. I stumbled out the door and fell to my knees. Almost instantly everything that had been in her stomach was expelled onto the cold dirt.

Dylan raced around the front of the jeep. Reaching me he crouched behind me as he pulled my hair back away from my face.

"I'm completely embarrassed." I moaned.

"Why?"

"This isn't the most attractive thing to see."

I rested my hands on my knees focused on the dirt and gravel in front of me. My stomach cramped suddenly, and I leaned over as more bile was forced from my body.

"It's okay. I'm sorry you're feeling horrible."

While Dylan held my hair in one hand, his other gently rubbed my back. He was so tender with me, and so calm. My heart swelled, I still couldn't believe how lucky I'd gotten with him. After a few minutes my stomach felt better. My shoulders relaxed as Dylan rubbed them.

"I think I'm okay now." I felt Dylan's hand tighten on my upper arm as he helped pull me up. "I just had a deja-vu moment." I tried to smile. "When we came up the day of the accident Bailey got carsick and we had to stop along the side of the road for her. Collin had gotten out and helped her just like you did for me right now."

"That doesn't sound like much fun."

"I guess it was a clue to how the day was going to go. It didn't get much better after that."

"Well, you did get to meet me, so maybe not all bad?" He smiled as he leaned into the jeep and pulled a bottle of water from the cup holder. "Here, easy with the water. You might just want to wash your mouth out right now. Let your stomach settle for a bit before you try to swallow any. And then take it in small sips."

I took the bottle from him and noticed how badly my hands were shaking. I washed my mouth out spitting the water on the ground. I kept telling myself it was just the flu, but deep down there was this small buried fear that maybe it was more than just the flu. I shoved the fear away and told myself I was going to stay positive.

Dylan helped me back into the jeep and jumped back in the driver's seat. He looked over at me. Concern was written all over his face as he studied me.

"I'm okay, really." My voice was feeble and I knew I didn't look fine. I hated people worrying about me. Hadn't I caused those that cared about me enough sleepless nights and worry over the past weeks?

"If you need to stop again, just let me know." He took my hand back in his, and rested it against the gearshift as he maneuvered back onto the road and down the mountain.

It was midmorning when we reached my house. Dylan lifted me back in his arms and carried me to the front door.

"Seriously, Dylan. I'm perfectly capable of walking."

"I'm sure you are, but maybe I like carrying you." He grinned down at me.

"Please. I feel like a child."

Dylan reached the front door and rang the doorbell. It wasn't long before My mom opened the door.

"What in the world. What's wrong?" Panic sliced through her voice as she stepped back to let Dylan enter still holding me tightly in his arms.

"She's running a fever and threw up on the way home."

"I can talk you know." I tried to interject.

"Dylan, bring her into the family room and put her on the couch."

"I can walk too. Really, you guys are over reacting. Dylan you can put me down now."

Dylan ignored me as he walked to the back of the house and carefully set me down on the couch. My mom leaned over brushing her hand against my forehead.

"Mia, you're burning up."

"It's probably just the flu, Mom. I'll be fine. I'm just tired." I leaned back against the couch as I toed off my shoes and folded my feet under me.

"When did this start?" My mom asked as she hurried to the kitchen.

"Early this morning. She just woke up with a fever. She took some Tylenol, but it didn't seem to help."

"I'm serious you guys. You don't have to talk like I'm not here." I sighed.

My mom filled up a glass of water and removed a large mixing bowl from the cupboard. Dylan sat down next to me as my mom handed him the bowl and placed the cup on the table next to the couch.

"I'll be right back with the thermometer."

I leaned my head against Dylan's shoulder as he put his arm around me. "You know if it is the flu you're probably going to get it next." I stated.

"Maybe. If I do, oh well. Then you can return the favor and take care of me."

"Oh no, give me the bowl, quick."

Dylan yanked the bowl from the floor and set it in my lap just in time. I rinsed my mouth again and spit the water back in the bowl. I was scared to drink anything else.

"Yeah, that was super lady like." I groaned.

My mom returned with the thermometer, and handed it to me. In return I handed the bowl back to her so that she could rinse it out.

"Mia, what's your temp?" My mom asked from the kitchen.

"It's still 103.9."

"I'm calling the doctor."

"Come on, Mom. It's not that serious."

"I'm not taking any chances, Mia." She grabbed the phone off the counter and dialed the doctor's office.

CHAPTER
TWENTY-FOUR

~Dylan~

Mia slept on the couch for the rest of the day. I refused to leave her until I knew she was okay. Per the doctor's instructions we were watching Mia to see how she did. Any changes in her condition and we were to bring her in immediately, but at the present time the doctor was pretty sure that it was just the flu. Mia didn't seem to be showing any other signs that would indicate otherwise, which had been a huge relief.

I sat at the end of the couch with Mia's feet propped up on my lap while she slept. Zach fluttered in and out, often with a reprimand from his mom to keep the noise down. So far Mia hadn't thrown up any more and had been able to keep some water and Gatorade down. Which were all good signs that it was probably just the stomach flu.

A movie played quietly in the background as I absently rubbed Mia's feet. Most of the day I'd spent keeping cool clothes on her forehead and helping her mom where I could. Mia's dad called several times from work to check on her. The love and support that Mia's family had for each other was something I'd longed for while I grew up. I knew my mom cared and did her best, but it was nice to see a family that came together. They had opened their home to me as well–with no reservations–and treated me like one of their own. Even in the short amount of time I'd been around them.

My mom had texted me hours earlier asking for an update on Mia. I was relieved that my mom liked Mia, but then she was so easy to like it didn't surprise me. I knew firsthand how easy she had infiltrated my heart.

My mom's life had just been turned upside down, but instead of worrying about herself she was more focused on Mia. She'd done the same thing when I was little. She always put others first, which sometimes put her straight in harms way. I hoped that she'd keep focused and aware of her surroundings. If my dad lurked somewhere up in the mountains, I knew my mom wasn't safe.

Later in the day my mom sent a text that confirmed what we had already figured out. My dad was no longer in prison. He'd been out for over two months. I knew it was only a matter of time before I was going to have to come face to face with my past and confront it.

~Mia~

Late in the afternoon I finally stirred. Dylan's arms rested on my ankles at the opposite end of the couch. His head leaned against the back of the cushions as he slept. He was so calm, so gorgeous as I studied him. I pushed myself up into a sitting position, my feet slid slowly out from under his arms. The movement brought Dylan wide awake, his eyes focused on mine at the other end of the couch.

"Are you okay?" he asked.

"Yeah, I think so. My stomach isn't as upset, I just feel really weak."

"Can I get you anything?"

"Maybe some more Gatorade. I'm not sure I'm ready to attempt food yet. I hate being sick. Haven't I spent enough time lately resting? It's getting old, big time." I moaned as I leaned my head back against the couch. I picked my head up almost instantly after it touched the cushion as I looked over at Dylan. "Wait, weren't you supposed to be at work this afternoon?"

"I called in sick."

"You didn't have to stay here. I feel bad; all I've done is sleep all day."

"Trust me, I'd rather be here with you, even if you were just sleeping. Let me get you the Gatorade. I think your mom is still at the grocery store. She was going to make you chicken noodle soup."

"Mmm, she makes good chicken noodle soup. That actually sounds like something I might be able to eat."

Dylan returned from the kitchen with the Gatorade. He sat down next to me, and lifted my legs back into his lap. "Just relax. You're looking a bit better, your face isn't as pale as it was earlier."

"I feel gross. Like I need a shower in a big way."

Dylan laughed as he lightly ran his fingertips down my cheek. "You're still beautiful in my eyes."

"Maybe you're the one that had the fever and it fried a few brain cells." I teased.

"I'm just glad it seems to be passing."

"I hope you don't get it, or your mom. Have you heard from her? Is she okay?"

"Yes, she's texted a couple of times. She's been worried about you."

"About me? I don't want her to be worried about me. I feel terrible for her. She was really upset last night. She was like a whole different person."

"Yeah, it's been a long time since I've seen her that distressed. She has changed and grown so much stronger over the past couple of years. She's more confident in herself, and gained independence that she never had when she was with my dad. But last night I saw her as she was years ago. Hopefully, having Elliot there with her will give her the strength she needs to pull herself back together."

"What about your dad? Did the cops find out anything?"

"He's out of prison. He's been out for a few months."

I watched the change in Dylan's face. His jaw twitched slightly, his eyes lost their warmth. I reached for his hand as it sat over my thighs, my fingers interlaced with his. "Everything will be okay."

"I'm not so sure."

"He just got out of prison. He's probably already broken his probation by even being here in California. If he tries anything he's risking going back to prison."

"The problem is, I don't think that's a deal breaker for him. He lives by a different set of rules than most people."

"We'll figure something out. Maybe he changed while he was locked up, for the better. Maybe he just wants to say he's sorry."

Dylan grinned. "Very, very doubtful, but I do appreciate your optimism. That's actually one thing I really love about you. You always look for the good. The positive in life, in everyone, no matter how bad things get."

"If you're always negative and angry, looking for the bad, then the only person you're really hurting is yourself."

"Very true, but sometimes it's easier said than done."

"Maybe." I grinned. "I think my mom's home, sounds like the garage door is opening."

"I'll see if she needs help with the groceries." Dylan slid out from under my legs, and headed toward the garage. He reached it just as the door into the house opened.

"Dylan, goodness, you startled me. Is everything okay?"

"Yes, Mia just woke up. Do you need any help?"

"Sure, there's one more bag in the car you can bring in for me. Thank you."

"Hi, Sweetheart. How are you feeling?" My mom asked as she sat the bags of groceries on the counter.

"Better. Dylan said you're going to make chicken noodle soup for dinner."

"I thought that would be easier on your stomach, and I know how you love it. You need to get some food down."

"That sounds perfect. I think I'm going to go upstairs and get in the shower. I feel really gross."

"Do you need help up the stairs, or do you think you're okay?"

"I think I'll be fine. I'll yell down if I need something."

"Okay, be careful."

Cautiously I stood up from the couch. I moved steadily across the room towards the stairs as Dylan came in with the last bag.

"I'll be back in a few. I'm going to take a shower." I explained.

"You sure you're okay? I can help you up the stairs." Dylan grinned as he reached me.

"I'll be fine. I need to get back on my feet. The sooner I start moving, the sooner I'll be feeling better."

Dylan leaned over and brushed a chaste kiss on my forehead. "Okay, I'll help your mom with dinner."

The hot water cascaded down over my back. The steam billowed out above the shower door. I was beginning to feel human again. My thoughts raced back over the past twenty-four hours. A lot had happened and I was trying to wrap my brain around everything. I was relieved that Dylan had finally opened up to me about his past. I was worried about what his dad might be up to. I'd never had to deal with that type of violent drama in my life before. It was difficult for me to relate, but I wanted to be strong for Dylan.

My thoughts shifted to Dylan's previous girlfriends. I couldn't understand why they had been so superficial. Guys like Dylan were special; I knew it the moment I saw him. Or maybe it was his voice, that easy southern drawl that got into my head. I'd never forget how he'd soothed me after I fell, his calm voice as he talked to me on the ski slope and in the ambulance. He was always in control, confident, and even-tempered. His gorgeous looks were a bonus that came along with the big heart.

I shut off the water, wrapped a towel around my hair and another around my body. I picked up a hand towel and wiped the steam off the mirror as I stared at my reflection. Throwing up in front of Dylan had been humiliating; there was nothing worse than being so sick in front of him. He hadn't gone running for the hills though, he was so gentle while he took care of me. I tugged on my favorite yoga pants and a loose sweatshirt. After I brushed my teeth and knotted my hair in a messy bun, I felt almost normal and returned downstairs.

Dylan was chopping vegetables in the kitchen when I returned. Hiss gaze caught mine as I pulled a bar stool out and sat across from him.

"Looks like my mom put you to work."

"Actually I volunteered."

"I bet that just won you even more brownie points. Though I'm pretty sure she already adores you." I smiled as I watched him.

"You look like you're feeling better." Dylan commented.

"Yes, and I'm sure I smell better too." I grinned. "Where's my mom?"

"She's upstairs with Zach. He's got it now, he threw up outside. She's helping him get cleaned up, and then she said she'd be back down."

"Oh no! Then it is contagious. Dylan, you should run before you're exposed even more."

"Mia, I'm sure at this point if I'm going to get it there's not much I can do. I've been with you for the past twenty-four hours, and I'm okay so far."

"Yeah, you're probably right, but still I'm going to feel horrible if I infect you too."

Zachary entered the room first his face was pale. My mom right behind him, her hand on his shoulder as she guided him into the room.

"Zach, go lie down on the couch. I'll bring you a towel and a bowl."

"Thanks a lot, Mia. Now, I can't go to my friend's house tomorrow night for New Years Eve," Zachary grumbled.

"Aw, I'm sorry, buddy." I said affectionately. I ruffled his hair as he walked by. "If it makes you feel any better, I'm pretty sure my plans for tomorrow are messed up too. I doubt my friends are going to want to come over now and risk getting sick."

My mom tucked a blanket around Zachary, and placed a bowl and a glass of water within his reach.

"This sucks, Mom." Zachary groaned.

"I know, but it looks like it's pretty quick. Mia already looks better, so at least it won't last long, hopefully." She leaned over and touched Zachary's forehead. "It doesn't feel like you have a fever, so that's good."

"Are you still working tomorrow?" I asked Dylan.

"Yes, they have me on the morning shift, so I'll be done early. Well, I guess that's pending I don't get sick." He grinned.

"I promise to come take care of you if you do. It's the least I can do since you took such great care of me. I'll call Bailey and Tasha to see if we're still going to do anything. I'm not sure they'll want to risk getting exposed to this since they are both leaving town right after New Year's."

Dylan slid the diced vegetables into a bowl and handed it to Mia's mom as he placed the cutting board and knife in the sink.

"Thank you. Dylan, I really appreciate your help. Mia he's a keeper." She grinned at me, I knew my face was probably bright red.

"I know, Mom." I smiled at Dylan's grin as he finished washing his hands. "Told you." I whispered to him.

⌒⌒⌒

I stood wrapped in Dylan's arms, his hands rested on my hips, the crisp night air surrounded us on the front porch.

"I wish you didn't have to leave." I whispered into Dylan's chest.

"I know. I hate leaving you too. But I'll be back down after work tomorrow. We'll ring in the New Year together."

"Okay." I reluctantly pulled back from his warm, strong, chest. I ran my fingers lightly along the dark stubble that shadowed his face and finally interlocked them together behind his neck. "Text me when you get home." My eyes searched his vibrant green depths. I could get lost in them for days.

Dylan's grasp on my hips tightened as he tugged me closer. He captured my mouth with his own. He stepped back slightly his forehead touched mine "I love you, Mia."

"I love you too, Dylan. Thank you, for taking care of me."

His bright emerald green eyes studied my brown ones. "I'll always take care of you; you know that right? No matter what?"

"Yes."

"Okay, well, I better go while I still can. Good night, Mia. I'll text you when I get home."

I brushed my lips over his one last time, before I stepped back from his warm embrace. The cold air replaced the warmth I'd felt within Dylan's arms. "Night, drive safe."

Standing on my front porch I wrapped my arms around myself in an attempt to keep warm and waved, as Dylan backed out of the driveway and drove into the dark, winter night.

CHAPTER
TWENTY-FIVE

Randy sat at the back of his rental house with his binoculars. His patience was finally paying off. It appeared that his ex-wife was now alone most of the afternoons, though he'd yet to see her leave the house. Dylan still stopped by every day but had stayed shorter lengths of time. His anticipation was growing, it won't be long now and he'd be able to put his plan into action.

It was late morning when he noticed movement in the front yard of her house. Randy watched his ex-wife look cautiously up and down the street before she hurried to her car. This was the first time he'd laid eyes on her since the night he left the picture in her living room. By the time her car was backing out of the driveway he was in motion. It was time to put his plan into action.

~*Mia*~

I began the long windy drive up the mountain. Dylan's mom was helping me with a surprise dinner for Dylan. My stomach was in knots; even though I'd traveled this road several times since my accident, this was the first time I was driving it myself since that fateful day. The roads were clear, but there was a chance of a storm moving in overnight.

New Year's had been quiet; Dylan had somehow managed to escape the stomach flu that seemed to have attacked my entire family. Bailey and Collin had left a couple of days previous, driving back to Las Vegas as their classes were starting back up. Natasha had flown back to Oregon that morning, and Quinn was still keeping his distance. I hadn't seen or talked to him since Christmas. Natasha had told me to give him time, he'd come around, but I felt like somehow it was my fault that my friend was hurting.

Dylan had been edgy for the past couple of days. After the night he learned his dad had been released neither he nor his mom had seen, or heard anything else. Elliot was still staying with Dylan's mom but had returned to work during the day. While Dylan's mom seemed to have let it go and was moving back into her normal routine. Dylan wasn't so sure that was the end of things. He was waiting for something bad to happen and it was taking a huge toll on him. I was hoping that maybe a special evening would help calm him. I had one more week left of my winter break before my classes would start back up, and I was planning to try to spend as much time with Dylan as I could.

Snow began to appear in patches along the side of the road as I ascended the mountain. The higher the elevation, the more snow appeared, until everything was covered. A little over an hour later I parked my car in Jolene's driveway. I stepped out into the crisp mountain air, significantly colder than it had been at my house. I hurried to the front door and rang the doorbell.

Dylan's mom opened the door. She moved aside quickly to let me in. "Brr, it's cold out there. The wind has kicked up since this morning. How was the drive up?"

I stepped into the warmth of the cabin as Dylan's mom shut and locked the door behind her. "Not too bad, the roads were clear. Thanks for helping me with this Jolene. I wanted to do something special for Dylan."

"I think he's going to love it. He's been uptight lately. He really needs to relax. I keep telling him to stop worrying about me, but you know how he is. Let me grab his spare key and I'll follow you over to his cabin."

I followed Dylan's mom into the kitchen as she grabbed a spare set of keys from a drawer. "I'll be right back. I left my jacket in my bedroom."

I set my purse and keys on the counter, next to Jolene's. I sat on a bar stool and made myself comfortable while I waited for Jolene. A scream from at the back of the cabin startled me. My heart pounded, I yanked the bar stool out of my way and in my haste it tilted and landed on the floor behind her.

"Jolene? Are you okay?" I called out as I rushed toward the bedroom.

The bedroom door was cracked open when I reached it. "Jolene?" I called as I pushed the door open.

~*Dylan*~

The wind whipped around my face, the cold biting. I picked up speed as I continued to navigate down the ski slope. I pushed myself harder and harder in an attempt to release the uneasiness I'd been feeling for days. When I reached the ski patrol hut I slid to a quick stop that sent snow flying as my skies cut deep into the powder. Corey, not far behind me, came to a halt next to me.

"Dylan, what is wrong with you? You've been agitated for days now. I've never seen you like this." Corey asked.

"It's nothing. I'm fine." I pushed my goggles up as I clicked out of my ski bindings, and thrust my skis upright into the snow.

"Is everything okay with Mia?" Corey shoved his skis next to mine as he followed me into the patrol hut.

"Yes, things are good." I removed my helmet and gloves and tossed them on the nearby table as I walked across the room to start the coffee pot.

"Then what's up with you? Come on, you can tell me."

"It's nothing, Corey, really. I'm just dealing with stuff."

"What stuff? Is your mom okay?"

I turned and looked at my best friend. I could tell Corey was worried about me. Corey was always so carefree and joking around, but not today. He knew a little about my past but I'd never told him the whole story. I slid into one of the chairs at the table.

"My mom is okay, for now."

Corey sat in the chair across from me. "What do you mean 'for now'?" Corey's blue eyes were filled with concern as he watched me.

"My dad is somewhere nearby. He was released from prison a few months ago. He's found my mom. He was in her house the other night."

"Holy crap, Dylan. Why haven't you said anything?"

"Because I don't need to worry anyone else. This is my problem to deal with."

"Come on, we're friends, that's what friends are for. Is there anything I can do? Wait, how do you know he was in her house?"

"The front door was left open, he left a message for her. There was a photo album left on the coffee table. It was open to a page with a photo of them on their wedding day. My mom got rid of all the pictures she had with my dad in them. The picture that had been in that spot is gone."

"When did this happen?"

"A little over a week ago."

"Well that explains a lot."

"What's that supposed to mean?"

"Just your moods. You've been quiet, just not yourself. I thought something was going on with Mia."

"No, things are actually really good with Mia." I smiled.

"That's good. I'm happy for you Dylan. You deserve to find someone special. By the way, Sara and I are going to the movies tonight. Do you and Mia want to join us?"

"Sounds like fun; I'll text Mia."

~Quinn~

Sitting at my computer I stared at the screen while I tried to focus on the work I needed to finish. The conversation I'd had with Natasha on the way to the airport that morning kept nagging at me.

Maybe I was overreacting with Mia; we'd been friends for so long. Was I really willing to throw all that away? I'd never seen Mia so happy, and it looked like Dylan really did care about her.

Dylan didn't seem to be a bad guy. It just rubbed me the wrong way when I saw Mia in the arms of someone else. Everything that Dylan had told me on Christmas Day was true. There never had been anything going on between Mia and I besides friendship. I had no right to be so angry at either of them.

Faced with the cold, hard truth, I knew I needed to deal with it and quit being so grumpy; it was time to let go. Once my decision was made, I felt like a huge burden had been lifted off my shoulders. I picked up my phone and sent Mia a quick text.

~*Mia*~

I pushed the bedroom door open and expected to find Dylan's mom lying on the floor, but she wasn't there. I searched through the bedroom and walked quickly toward the bathroom. I called again out. Still nothing.

"What the heck?" I whispered to myself as I opened the bathroom door finding the bathroom empty as well.

The house was quiet and I was baffled. Where was Jolene? The hair on the back of my neck tingled and the floor behind me creaked. My heart raced, but before I could turn around I felt a sharp pain at the back of my skull and everything went black.

A HEALING SPIRIT

"Something's wrong, Corey. It's been almost three hours since I texted Mia, and she hasn't responded at all. If I call it just goes to voicemail. That's just not like her."

"Maybe she fell asleep. I'm sure everything is fine. Who knows with girls, it could be anything." Corey looked over at me as we walked together toward the parking lot after clocking out for the day.

"Yeah, you're probably right." I said cracking a slight smile.

"Sara and I will be headed down the mountain around five I think. If you hear from Mia before then and want to come with us just let me know."

My uneasiness wouldn't go away; it had been getting worse as the afternoon went on. I climbed into my jeep and exited the staff parking lot. The drive to my mom's was short. My plan was to run in quick, make sure everything was good and then drive back to my place.

I turned onto my mom's street and noticed Mia's car in the driveway, which brought a smile to my face. "Well, this is a pleasant surprise." I parked along the street, locked my jeep and let myself into my mom's cabin.

"Mom? Mia?" I called out as I walked through the entry. The house was eerily quiet something was wrong. When I reached the kitchen I noticed their purses on the counter. One of the bar stools lay overturned on the floor. Panic flooded through my body, my heart quickened. "Mia!? Mom!" I shouted.

I returned to the front entry and opened the coat closet. I grabbed the baseball bat that I knew my mom kept there. I gripped it tight as I moved into the living area. My eyes searched for anything out of place, but everything seemed to be where it was supposed to be. Slowly, I continued my search down the hallway. I checked the hall bathroom, the spare bedroom, the master bedroom, and the master bathroom, but there was no one in the house. I noticed that the sliding glass door in the master bedroom was unlocked. I rushed back into the living room and checked the double French doors and found them secure, as was the side door in the kitchen.

My gaze settled on the purses on the counter. I noticed my spare keys lay next to my mom's purse, and Mia's phone and keys lay next to her purse. I grabbed Mia's phone and realized that Mia had never seen my text, as it was still visible on her screen. There was also a text from Quinn that had come in almost an hour before mine that hadn't been read either–which meant they'd been missing for at least four hours. My heart was slamming against my chest as I dialed 911.

~*Mia*~

My head throbbed, and it was difficult for me to breathe. I was lying on my side, a cloth was stuffed into my mouth. The cold from the floor seeped through my body. Slowly I opened my eyes. It was dark and I could barely make out a shape in front of me. As I tried to sit up I realized my wrists were tied in front of me, and loosely connected to rope that wound around my ankles.

Sitting upright was almost impossible. The rope cut into my skin as I tried to move.

The shape in front of me moved slightly and let out a groan. I pushed myself closer, an inch at a time. I realized the shape was Jolene. I tried to roll Jolene over, and finally after several attempts I was successful. She was trussed up in a similar fashion as I was. I noticed dried blood was caked on her forehead and ran down the side of her face, as it trailed into her hairline. I had no idea how badly hurt she was.

At least Jolene was breathing, that had to be a good sign. I surveyed our surroundings as my eyes slowly adjusted to the dark. The room lacked windows, only a steep staircase in the opposite corner. The room was small. Empty shelves lined one side, a single light bulb with pull string hung from the ceiling, and a bucket sat in the corner. No blankets, no boxes, nothing else appeared to be on the cold concrete floor but the two of us.

Jolene groaned again, bringing my attention back to her. I felt for her hands, taking them into my own. Her eyelids fluttered, her eyes were glassy as they opened and stared at me. Her fingers tightened around my hand as we gazed at each other.

I let Jolene's fingers go as I pushed myself closer to her. I crawled close enough where I was able to reach her gag. After several tries my fingers finally touched the edge of the cloth. She leaned her head down, positioning the cloth so that it was closer to my grasp. Jolene pushed on the gag with her tongue as I pulled. The gag finally slid down her chin.

"Oh Mia, I'm so sorry," she whispered, her throat scratchy. "Here slide back down so I can reach you."

My gag finally slipped down around my neck, allowing me to finally breathe easier. "Are you okay, Jolene?"

"For the most part. I don't think anything is broken or hurt, besides the pounding in my head."

"Where are we? Do you know who did this?"

"It was Randy. He was in the bedroom waiting for me. I have no idea where we're at. How'd you get here?"

"I don't know. I just woke up here. I heard you scream, I ran into the bedroom but you weren't anywhere, then everything went black. What do you think he's going to do to us?" I whispered.

"Oh, honey. I have no idea."

"Dylan's going to be frantic."

"We'll figure something out. Randy might be crazy, but he lets his emotions and anger get the best of him. We need to try and stay calm and think."

~Dylan~

I paced the kitchen as I waited for the cops to show up. The operator had told me they would reach Officers Jones and Tracy and have them sent over immediately. My imagination worked overtime, every scenario worse than the previous one. My phone beeped on the counter, it was a text from Corey. I grabbed the phone and dialed his number.

"Hey, so are you guys coming with us tonight?"

"Mia and my mom are missing." I responded, my voice clipped.

"WHAT?!?" Corey practically screamed in my ear.

"I stopped by the house after we got off. Mia's car is in the driveway. Her keys, phone and purse are on the counter. My mom's purse and keys are here too. Both cars are here. The sliding door in my mom's room was unlocked. They aren't anywhere in the house. The police are on their way."

"I can't believe this. I'll be right there."

I clicked off my phone and knew I needed to call Mia's parents. I didn't know what I was going to say to them. I was pretty sure they were going to hate me for sure now. It was my fault that Mia was in danger and I'd never forgive myself if anything happened to her or my mom. I knew better, I knew that my dad wasn't going to give up so easily. I never should have let down my guard until they found my dad.

I picked up Mia's phone of the counter, and held it tight, knowing it was probably one of the last things she had touched. What was she doing up here anyways I wondered. I flipped through her text messages as I looked for answers. Quinn's text was short and a bit of a shock.

Quinn:
I'm sorry for being such a jerk.
I'm glad you're happy. I hope
we can still be friends.

Before I could think it completely through, I pulled Quinn's contact information up on Mia's phone and dialed. Quinn answered on the second ring.

"Hey, Mia."

"Quinn, it's Dylan."

"Oh. Where's Mia?"

"Have you talked to her at all today?"

"Umm. Why?"

"Quinn, Mia's missing. I'm trying to figure out how long she's been gone."

"MISSING? What do you mean missing? Where are you?"

"It's a long story. She drove to my mom's house. I stopped by after work, the house was empty. Their cars are both here, their purses, keys, phones, everything was left on the kitchen counter."

"Did you call the police? Where could they have gone?"

"The police are on their way. Look I'm sorry I called. I'm just trying to get as much information as I can. I saw your text on her phone. I didn't know if she'd talked to you earlier, if maybe she said anything."

"I haven't talked to her since Christmas."

"Oh, okay. I've got to go; I think the police just got here."

"Dylan, what's the address there? I'm coming up."

"There's not much you can do Quinn. I'll let you know as soon as I know anything else."

"Dylan, I'm coming up. She's my friend too, practically a sister. What's the address?"

"I'll text it to you. I've got to get the door."

"Okay, I'll be there as soon as I can."

Randy couldn't believe his luck. Not only had he managed to snag Jolene, but Mia as well. He'd only planned to take his ex-wife, but when Mia unexpectedly showed up he couldn't resist. The underground cellar he'd stumbled upon during one of his excursions was a perfect hiding place. He knew they'd never be able to escape. And the entrance to the cellar was concealed with brush and snow, which was perfect.

He'd just finished clearing out of the rental cabin and was moving his supplies to the small cabin near the cellar. He needed some time to let things cool down a bit before he tried to move again. Randy had waited a long time for this moment to come. A little more waiting was nothing to him.

It was dinnertime, and he was unusually hungry, with all the excitement he'd worked up an appetite. His only regret was not being able to see Dylan's face when he realized his precious mom and girlfriend were missing.

Yes, today was a good day, he thought to himself. He deserved a beer, and maybe not just one. It was time for a little celebrating.

CHAPTER TWENTY-SIX

~Dylan~

Calling Mia's parents had been excruciating. They'd already been through so much. To then tell them that their daughter was missing, and in the hands of a madman, was one of the hardest things I'd ever had to do. What was worse was that it wasn't just a stranger, but my own flesh and blood.

My mom's cabin swarmed with police. I continued to pace the kitchen, unable to sit or stand still. I had to do something. The waiting was killing me. Corey sat at the bar quietly watching me. The muscle in my cheek twitched as I kept grinding down on my teeth. I was a complete and utter wreck. I needed to pull myself together and think it through or I'd never be any help to Mia or my mom. I needed to take a deep breath and focus, to rely on my training for emergency situations and move one step at a time.

I glanced at the oven clock–5:04 p.m.–it had been over an hour since I had found the cabin empty. I knew we were racing against the clock, but we were racing it blind with absolutely no idea when time would run out. There had been no contact from my dad and so far the police had not turned up any clues as to where they might have gone. The doorbell rang and I left the kitchen in a hurry to answer it. Opening the door Quinn stood on the porch, I stepped aside to let him enter.

"Looks like you found it okay." I shut and locked the door as I motioned Quinn towards the kitchen.

"Have you heard anything?"

"Nothing."

"Did you call Mia's parents?"

"Of course I did. They're on their way up."

"Hopefully they left right away; the clouds are pushing in. It looks like that storm is going to hit after all."

"Corey, do you remember Quinn? He's one of Mia's friends."

"Hi, I remember you."

"You were one of the first ones that arrived on the scene when Mia fell right? We met you that day Mia came back up to the resort after her accident." Quinn stated.

"Yes, Dylan and I are partners. We work the local volunteer search and rescue team as well when needed."

Quinn sat at the table with Corey. I walked past the kitchen counter. and paused at the full height windows in the living room. I stared out into the forest. The wind was blowing, snow was beginning to fall. The sun had already been lost behind the thickening clouds, and it was getting dark.

I knew it was very possible both my mom and Mia were out in the cold, exposed, and if that was the case the chances of them surviving even through the night were slim. I felt completely helpless, something I hadn't felt in years. It was an emotion I swore I'd never feel again. I needed to focus, think things through. I would not let my dad ruin my life again.

⌘

Randy tossed the last of his twelve pack of beer in the trash, the familiar numbness took over his body. He felt invincible, like he could conquer anything. It was time to pay his good for nothing ex-wife a visit.

He snagged his jacket, a flashlight, and left the small cabin. He staggered slightly as he tripped down the last steps to the snow covered ground.

The wind had picked up and swirled snow in his face as he walked the short distance to the entrance of the cellar. The timing of the storm couldn't have been better. He knew it would make any type of search near impossible. It would also help cover any of his tracks. Randy arrived at the buried trap door, dusted off the new snow, reached for the lever and turned the key in the padlock.

⌘

~Mia~

"It's getting so cold. Do you think he just left us down here?" I asked, my teeth chattered. I bit down as I tried to stop the uncontrollable shaking.

"It's possible, but somehow I don't think he's done with us yet. Randy always enjoyed the chase, toying with me. I think he'll be back. When he does, we need to be ready. There's got to be something down here we can use to our advantage."

"I think it would be easier if we're sitting up. Maybe if we push ourselves over to the side there by the shelves we can use the wall for support?"

"It's worth a shot and better than just lying here. The shelf will help hide us a bit initially when he does return."

"I'm not sure that's going to be a good thing or a bad thing." I whispered as I slowly pushed myself over the dirty, rough concrete.

"Did you hear that?" Dylan's mom asked.

"Hear what?" I stopped moving to listen.

We both turned to the staircase as the door was flung open, cold air rushed in. The beam of a flashlight flooded the space. Large black boots were visible as they descended the steep stairs, then dark jeans, and then a large shadow of a man stood at the bottom. The flashlight beam turned and focused on us.

"Is it him?" I whispered.

Jolene turned her head to look behind her. As she turned her head back to me, a tear slipped down her cheek and she nodded, unable to speak. Fear sliced through me. This couldn't be good.

Dylan's dad crossed the small room, the smell of alcohol followed. I took my first real good look at the sperm donor for the love of my life. Because that's all he really was; he wasn't a dad in any real sense of the word. Dylan's dad didn't know one thing about love.

"Well, well, looks like you both woke up. I'd apologize for the accommodations, but you know, I'm not really sorry. You should be thanking me that you're out of the weather though. The storm is coming in and it's going to get even colder as the night goes on," he chuckled.

"Aren't you glad to see me Jolene? I know you missed me. I thought about you every day I was locked up in that tiny cell. Every day, you and Dylan were all I thought about. I knew I'd find you. I always told you I would find you if you left me. We're meant to be together. You can't leave me. But, I'll have to punish you for your disobedience."

Dylan's dad reached out with his hand pulling Dylan's mom up to a sitting position by her hair. She shut her eyes. I watched in horror as Dylan's dad slammed his fist into her jaw. Her head was thrown backwards with the force of the blow. Blood trickled down her mouth. I bit my lip as I stifled a scream.

"Nothing to say to me now, huh? You sure did a lot of talking in the courtroom. You just couldn't keep your mouth shut then." he sneered.

I couldn't keep my mouth shut. "Stop! Leave her alone!" I screamed as Jolene's head bobbed forward. I wasn't sure if she was even still conscious.

"No, Mia, please. Stay out of this," she whispered.

Dylan's dad dropped Jolene on the floor and his eyes blazed to me. He looked crazed, his eyes wild as he moved the flashlight beam focusing on my face, blinding me.

"What do you think you can do to stop me, little girl?" He hissed, as he stepped closer to me. "Maybe, I'll keep you around for a while. It might be fun to play with you. You're such a sweet, innocent little thing."

My blood ran cold, I refused to shrink away and held his gaze. Dylan hadn't been exaggerating when he told me the stories about his dad. My heart shattered for him and Jolene. I couldn't even fathom living in a house with someone so heartless and evil. My love for Dylan grew. How he'd managed to grow up and become such an amazingly tender, and loving person was a true testament to his character and how important his mom had been in his life.

My stomach churned as Dylan's dad ran his fingers down my face, down my throat, and brushed across my breasts. I was completely repulsed.

"Yes, I think it will be fun to teach you a lesson in respect."

The stench of alcohol rolled off his breath. His fingers moved back to my face and clenched my chin tightly as he pulled my face upright to look at him. I had the urge to gag, but kept it down. I refused to show him the fear that ran through my veins. I wouldn't give him that satisfaction.

"Respect? You don't know the first thing about respect," I shrieked.

The slap across my cheek snapped my head sideways. I refused to cry out and turned back to look at him straight in the eye. He stepped back and looked startled. He must not have expected that reaction from me. *Good* I thought. I would not give him the power he so desperately was seeking.

"You just wait, missy. You'll be sorry for that."

He turned back to Jolene and kicked her in the side, knocking the wind out of her as she fell hard onto the concrete. She was unable to move her hands out quick enough to break the fall.

"I'll be back. You can think things through in the dark and cold." He turned and climbed the stairs. The room was shrouded in darkness once again as the door slammed shut.

"Jolene, are you okay?" I pushed myself in her direction.

"I'll be okay. I've taken worse hits. He let us off easy for now. We've got to find a way out of here, it will be worse when he returns. He's already started drinking and he gets more irate and out of control the more alcohol he consumes. And you, my sweet girl, I can't have him hurting you. He won't be gentle and I can't even imagine what awful things he'll try to do to you."

"I'm going to see if I can get to the shelves. I think I saw some broken glass over there when he was moving the flash light around." I stated as I tried to form a plan.

~*Dylan*~

Corey, Quinn, and I sat on the bar stools around the kitchen island when Officers Tracy and Jones entered, their faces expressionless.

"Anything new?" I asked.

"Not really. We have roadblocks set up. If he tries to get off the mountain we'll find him. The reality is though he might have already left the mountain. We don't know how long they were gone before you got here. The storm isn't helping either" Officer Jones replied.

"Are you getting a search team out there?"

"Dylan, it's getting dark. The storm is making visibility difficult. We'll have to wait before we start a ground search."

Standing up abruptly, fury radiated through me. "Are you kidding me? You guys have been here for over an hour and haven't even thought of doing a search tonight?"

"Please calm down. We know you're upset and worried. We've got patrols increased, and we'll be starting a door-to-door search. That's all we can do right now."

"Based on what you've told us about your father, it's very likely he'll reach out to you. When he does, we'll have something more solid to go off of." Officer Tracy added.

"Yeah, and what if he doesn't? Then what?"

"We'll continue our search."

"This is ridiculous. I can't just sit around here all night. They could be out there in the snow right now freezing to death. Forget it, I'll do it myself." I reined in my anger and focused it on the tasks at hand. "Corey, call Sara. Have her meet us here with Jake, and have her bring you your gear. I'll run to my house and get mine."

"Jake? Who's Jake?" Quinn asked.

"Jake is Sara's search and rescue dog," Corey replied as he pulled his phone out.

"Wait, what? What are you doing?" Quinn asked.

"We're going to find my mom and Mia and bring them home." I replied calmly.

"Dylan, you're in no frame of mind to go out and do a search. We don't need to be looking for you too. Leave it to the professionals." Officer Tracy calmly placed his hand on my shoulder.

"I am a professional. Corey and I are part of the local search-and-rescue team. This is what we do." I shrugged Officer Tracy's hand off as I marched out of the kitchen.

CHAPTER
TWENTY-SEVEN

~*Mia*~

Pushing myself up against the cold concrete wall; my head pounded. I sat next to the empty shelves, my legs cramped and numb from being restrained. Dylan's mom moved slowly toward me, her breathing was labored.

"How are you doing, Jolene?"

"My side hurts pretty bad. I think Randy might have cracked a rib."

"Okay, just rest for a minute. Let me see if I can find that piece of glass. Or at least I hope it was glass or something sharp."

Scooting along the face of the shelf my hands felt across the floor. The effort to move to the perimeter of the room had warmed me slightly and my teeth had finally stopped chattering. My fingers searched along the cold, dirty floor. They touched something that was hairy and squishy. Holding back a scream I thought to myself maybe it was better it was dark so I didn't have to see what I'd just stumbled on. Thoughts of spiders and bugs would just creep me out further.

"Any luck?" Jolene asked.

"Not yet."

I continued to move down the shelf. Finally, near the last vertical post my finger caught something sharp.

"Wait, I found it. I think this will work."

Carefully my fingers searched around the edge as I gently picked it up. It appeared to be a piece of a mason jar. One side was smooth but the other had a sharp point to it. I breathed a sigh of relief. We weren't out of the woods yet, but I now had at least a glimmer of hope that maybe we might have a chance.

~*Dylan*~

Returning from my cabin, I had my backpack full of supplies in tow. I'd changed my clothes and now sported warmer layers and my hiking boots that were more suited for the harsh weather we were about to venture into. I had shoved aside my emotions and was focused on finding the two most important people in my life. I'd deal with my father after my mom and Mia were safe.

Corey and Sara sat at the kitchen table as they sorted through their supplies. Jake, a five-year-old yellow lab that was trained for search and rescues lay at their feet. Quinn looked up from across the table as I entered the kitchen.

"Mia's parents and Zach are in the living room. The officers are giving them an update. They arrived a few minutes ago." Quinn stated.

"Okay. Sara, thank you for helping and bringing Jake right over."

"We'll find them Dylan." Sara's voice was calm and determined.

"We're about ready Dylan. Jake is going to need something of Mia's and your mom's for a scent." Corey stated as he finished zipping his pack and set it on the floor next to Sara's.

"Let me see if Mia had a jacket or something in her car."

Turning I briskly left the table; I grabbed Mia's keys off the counter and left through the kitchen side door. I unlocked Mia's car and opened the passenger door. I picked up the jacket and scarf that was tossed on the seat and sat down. I shut the door and allowed myself a minute to regroup. Her car smelled of her perfume, I closed my eyes, and breathed in the scent.

Memories of our short time together flooded my thoughts. Her warm brown eyes as they twinkled when she teased me. The cute dimples in her cheeks when she smiled. She was always so happy and carefree.

No matter how bad a situation was—she'd find the good in it. I admired her strength and the love she so freely gave. I knew we needed to hurry, every minute counted. I had to find her—there was no other option. I carefully folded her scarf and exited the car, locking it behind me as I re-entered the kitchen.

Next to the kitchen door was a hook that held one of my mom's sweatshirts that she wore a lot around the house. I pulled it off the hook and smelled it to make sure it hadn't been just washed. I saw Mia's mom out of the corner of my eye and looked up as she stood at the edge of the kitchen. Her eyes glistened with tears. I didn't know what to say to her. She made the first move as she closed the distance and stopped right in front of me. She opened her arms and pulled me tight against her. Shocked, that she wasn't angry or yelling at me. I tentatively wrapped my arms around her and returned her embrace.

"Find my baby, please. Your friends told me you're going out there to look for her. Please, bring her back safely." Her tears slid unchecked down her face.

"I will, I promise. We'll find her," I whispered.

Mia's mom pulled back and wiped the tears from her face. "I know you will. You've made her really happy, Dylan. Happier than I've ever seen her."

I broke eye contact as I looked past her to the flurry of activity in the living room. "It's my fault she's missing."

"No, Dylan, look at me. This is not your fault. You can't blame yourself."

"We need to go. It's getting darker, and the storm is getting worse. Please help yourself to whatever my mom has in the fridge and pantry. I'll send you updates. Here, take Mia's phone. I'll text her number."

Brushing past Mia's mom I reached the kitchen table. I handed the scarf and sweatshirt to Sara. I was focused on our next steps. I knew attempting to search for Mia and my mom in the storm that was brewing outside was not the most ideal situation and was possibly dangerous. Corey, Sara, and I had been on searches in worse conditions before. This wasn't new to us. It was what we trained for.

"Let's go. We'll start in the master bedroom. That's the door that was unlocked. We'll see if Jake can pick up a scent from there."

"I'm coming with you." Quinn stood up with Sara and Corey.

"Quinn, you're not trained, we are. Stay here with Mia's parents, they need support."

"Dylan, you can't stop me. I'm coming too. An extra person can't hurt. Who knows what we're going to find out there."

"This isn't a game, Quinn. The weather is lousy and getting worse. We don't need to be held up."

"I'm not going to hold you up. Just tell me what you need me to do."

Sighing, I gave in. I looked over Quinn's clothing, he was wearing boots, and was dressed warm. He'd come in with a heavy jacket. It wasn't the best clothing, but it would do. I didn't need Quinn trying to follow us, and I was pretty sure that's exactly what he'd do if I held my ground. It was better to just bring him along. "Fine. But if I tell you to do something, don't question me, okay? Every decision, every move out there, can be life or death."

"I understand."

Sara led with Jake into the master bedroom. She held the items of clothing for Jake to smell. Corey, Quinn and I stood in the doorway and watched as Jake moved around the room, into the bathroom, and then to the sliding door. After a few minutes Jake sat at the sliding door and waited for Sara to open it.

Jake moved across the back deck and down the stairs, out into the snow covered forest. I handed my extra flashlight to Quinn as we descended the stairs. We followed behind Sara and Corey. The temperature outside had already dropped several degrees since I had returned from my cabin. The snow was still light, and if we were lucky it would stop. And I hoped beyond all hope that Mia and my mom weren't out in this weather exposed to the elements.

A HEALING SPIRIT

I continued to saw through the rope that was wrapped around Jolene's wrists. The last piece of twine snapped apart, and relief flooded me. Specs of blood had dripped to the floor where the rope had cut into Jolene's wrist, but her wrists were free.

"Can you reach the knots around your ankles?" I asked.

Jolene gasped as she leaned forward. "Yes, I can reach them." She whispered.

I was worn out. I laid my head back on the ground and rested for a minute. It had taken a lot longer to cut through the rope than I had thought it would.

After Jolene freed her legs she reached over to my wrists and untied the knots. Relieved, I released my ankles and was finally able to stretch. Sharp needle-like pain shot through my legs as I moved my limbs. Exhausted, we both lay there side by side.

"This was not the relaxing evening I had planned with Dylan." I stated trying to find some humor in the whole situation.

Dylan's mom sighed. "Pretty far to the opposite I'd say."

"Do you think Randy will come back right away?" I asked.

"I think we have some time. I could tell he'd had a lot to drink. If he drinks more he'll probably pass out."

"Let's see if we can budge the door. Any chance we'll get lucky and it will be unlocked?"

"Doubtful. But let's find out."

I stood first, my legs were shaky. The movement caused my blood to flow quicker and my head throbbed harder with the excursion. I closed my eyes to stop the nausea that overwhelmed me. I hadn't eaten anything since breakfast, and I had no idea how late it was. After a minute I felt more stable, and I reached my hand out to help Jolene up. Wrapping my arm around Jolene's waist to help hold her up I was careful to not push on her ribs. We moved slowly to the wooden stairs in the corner of the room.

Jolene leaned against the wall for support as I climbed the stairs. The large wooden doors above were slanted, and reminded me of a barn door. I pushed on them and they only budged slightly. A sliver of a gap appeared between where the doors joined in the middle. Cold air trickled through the slit.

"There's some sort of lock from outside. I don't think we're in a basement though. I can feel cold air, and when he came in I remember a burst of freezing air that followed."

"What if we both try to push the doors open together?"

"It can't hurt. We don't have much choice. Our only other option would be to wait."

"I don't want to be here when he returns. We're better off trying to get out of here." Jolene sighed. "We might not get another chance."

I shifted to the side, as Jolene climbed the stairs and stood next to me. Together we shoved and pushed. The crack widened slightly, but the doors wouldn't budge.

"What if we push with our backs? Do you think we might get more strength that way?" I asked.

"Let's try it."

"Careful when you turn … these stairs are steep." I anchored myself by grabbing the rough wood handrail on the side. "On the count of three, ready?"

"Yes." Jolene braced herself against the cold concrete wall.

"Okay, one, two…three."

We pushed against the doors, with all our strength, and we were rewarded by the sound of wood as it cracked.

"One more time, Jolene."

The pressure on the hinged lock broke loose from the weathered wood slats. The doors flung open slightly and then slammed shut. We turned and shoved the doors and sighed with relief as they burst open. The doors crashed against the sides of the concrete opening.

The icy wind blasted our face as we peeked out of the opening to survey the surroundings. It was pitch black outside. Light snow flurries drifted in the wind. Looking around I saw nothing but forest, with the exception of a small cabin not far away. It looked abandoned, but yellow light lit up one of the grimy windows. There was a truck parked in front, but no road was visible.

"I bet he's in that cabin." I whispered. "Do you have any idea where we are? Does any of this look familiar to you?"

"No, there's so many small dirt roads and tiny cabins in the area. We could be anywhere on the mountain."

"Do you think there's any way we might be able to try to get the keys for the truck?"

"I think that's risky. We can see if he happened to have left the keys inside the truck. Sometimes people up here will do that. They'll leave the keys up in the visor."

"Okay, let's go."

We crept quietly through the snow, the wind bit through my sweatshirt and sent shivers through me. We used the large tree trunks as shelter as we circled around to the front of the cabin. No light was visible from the front. We hunched over and made a quick dash across the open drive to the truck.

I grabbed the handle of the driver's side and the door opened. My heart pounded as I climbed in, thankfully the interior cabin light didn't come on. I checked the visor, the glove box, the console, nothing. A jacket lay on the floorboard of the passenger side and I grabbed it. I slid from the driver's side and quietly shut the door.

I shook my head at Jolene. "No keys." I whispered.

A door slammed shut on the cabin, followed by several loud curses. We peeked over the hood of the truck and watched Dylan's dad stumble through the snow to the dark cellar that we had just escaped from.

"Mia, we've got to go. Now."

"Here take this jacket, it was on the floor."

"No, you take it. I've got warmer clothes on than you do. Come on, we don't have much time. He's going to realize we're gone any minute now."

"Run Mia!"

"Come on Jolene, I'm not leaving you behind. Let's go!"

We stumbled in the darkness. Our hands were interlocked as we ran into the shelter of the trees that lined the gravel road.

A HEALING SPIRIT

Randy was tormented by Mia's insolence. Even several hours after he had left them in that root cellar, he was still riled up. Another twelve-pack sat empty on the kitchen counter, and Randy's temper had reached a full-blown rage.

How dare that girl talk to him like he was nothing? Who did she think she was? He charged through the back door. The snow had iced over a portion of the porch, which caused him to trip down the remaining steps, falling face first into the snow. He cursed into the wind as he stood up and continued to stumble toward the underground cellar with his flashlight in hand.

He pulled his keychain out of his pocket and leaned over to unlock the latch on the doors. But found the lock skewed and detached from the wood.

"What the bloody hell?"

Randy tossed the doors open and entered the cellar. His flashlight stopped in the center of the room where rope lay, but the rest of the room was empty. "NO!" he yelled.

Realization that they were missing sobered him almost immediately. He stumbled on the last step as he ran toward the cabin.

"I know you dirty whores are out there somewhere. You can't hide from me!" Randy screamed into the dark night.

The kitchen door slammed shut behind him as he grabbed his handgun from the table and returned outside to hunt down his prey.

CHAPTER TWENTY-EIGHT

~Dylan~

Jake continued to lead our group through the trees. Sara would stop him occasionally and let him smell the clothing to refresh the scent. We had been walking in almost complete silence for close to four hours. Corey was the first to break the silence.

"Dylan, I think we need to stop for a few minutes. Let Jake rest and give us a chance to eat a snack and get some water."

"Okay, we'll take a quick break."

"Do you guys even know where we're at?" Quinn asked.

"Yes, we have our GPS." I replied as I lifted the pack off my back and unzipped it. Pulling out a bottle of water and a protein bar I handed them both to Quinn. I then extracted a small tarp and laid it on the ground for the four of us to sit on.

"How do you think he moved both of them this far? I thought for sure we'd end up on the road by now." Quinn asked.

"It looks like he had a snowmobile at the back of the cabin." I answered as I chewed on my protein bar.

"How do you figure that?" Quinn asked baffled.

Corey chuckled. "We've been following the tracks."

"Oh. I hadn't noticed," Quinn replied, looking a bit embarrassed.

"They are subtle. With the wind and the new snow, they are almost completely covered. Some areas they have been more visible than others," Sara replied.

"Corey, remember last year when we were on that rescue with the missing teenagers on the lower trail. One of them had fallen and broken their arm. They had stumbled on a small abandoned cabin. Aren't we near there?" I asked.

"Yeah, I think we are."

"It would make sense that he'd move them somewhere close."

"Either that or he stashed a vehicle and used the snow mobile to get to it and then left the mountain." Corey stated.

"I don't think he's left the area yet. I can't tell you why, it's just a feeling I have." I felt like we were getting closer. Even though there weren't any additional signs I just knew we were close.

"Your gut feeling is rarely off. Let's keep moving I think that cabin is only a bit further." Corey stated.

"Ready Sara? Quinn?" I asked as I stood up, anxious to keep moving.

"Yes." They both replied together.

Picking up the tarp, I folded it and repacked it in my backpack. I lifted it and we continued to move through the winter night in silence.

Twenty minutes later a clearing appeared in front of us. A small cabin sat along the edge, light streamed out the rear, and a truck was parked in the front. A gunshot stopped us in our tracks as the sound echoed through the forest. Panic sliced through me. *"No!"* I whispered to myself.

~*Mia*~

Jolene and I ran into the forest, blinded by the snow and freezing wind. Jolene started to fall behind. I was worried about her ribs–if she had fractured one–running like this could easily puncture a lung. Wrapping my arm around her waist I continued to pull her along.

"Come on Jolene, we've got to keep moving. He's gaining on us."

"I'm the one he really wants. Just go … you'll be able to move faster without me." Jolene gasped; her breaths were short, more labored the further we traveled.

"I'm not leaving you," I stated firmly.

The beam of light from Dylan's dad's flashlight searched the darkness in a sweeping pattern. Risking a glance behind us I realized the flashlight had found me, leaving me completely exposed and vulnerable.

"I can see you. You can't get away from me!" Randy yelled into the wind. He stumbled as he moved forward.

I saw the gun as he pointed it in our direction, adrenaline pumped through my body, my heart hammered in my chest. Our chance of escape was slipping away quickly.

The gunshot echoed through the snow-laden trees before I had a chance to turn away. My arm burned as I pulled Jolene around another tree and searched for protection.

~Dylan~

"Sara, you stay here with Jake. Call 911 and give them our location. Corey, Quinn, let's go." I barked the orders, my voice sounding calm and in control when inside I felt like the world was shattering around me and there was nothing I could do to stop it. A piece of me felt like I was a young child again–helpless–as I watched my dad hurt my mom. Pushing aside those memories I wouldn't let my dad win this time. I was no longer defenseless.

The three of us ran toward the sound of the gunshot. We reached the side of the cabin and stopped at the corner to survey the area. A truck sat in front, the faint signs of a gravel or dirt road cut a path through the dense trees. I noticed a shadow of a man as he staggered up the hill. The beam of his flashlight bounced in front of him. Several curses were audible as the figure stumbled over broken tree limbs and snowdrifts.

"Is that him?" Corey asked.

"I think it is. I can't be positive, it's too dark and he's too far away."

"I don't see anyone else." Quinn stated. "Now what do we do?"

"We're going to follow him. We have to be quiet, move to the back of the truck first. We'll use that for cover, then we'll bolt to the trees across the road." I replied.

"Let's do this. Ready, Quinn?" Corey asked.

"Yes."

"Okay, follow me." I instructed as I crouched down and ran to the back of the truck bed first. Corey and Quinn directly behind me. I watched as the shadow fell to the ground. The beam of light bobbed in the sky, before it disappeared. A curse ripped through the air as another gunshot went off.

"Is he moving?" Corey asked.

"I don't think so. Something is wrong, come on."

I approached cautiously. My boots crunched in the snow, my focus straight ahead as I maneuvered through the trees. Corey and Quinn were on my heels. As I reached the area where the man had fallen, my flashlight swept the area. I focused the light on the large man that lay face down in the snow. A dark reddish pool stained the snow where he had fallen. The light washed over the man's head and the side of his face was visible. I gazed down at the unmoving body of the nightmare that had plagued me for years.

"It's him." I whispered as I slowly moved closer. I used my foot to roll my dad over, every instinct on alert. Blood saturated my dad's chest. The butt end of the gun was pressed into the snow. My dad's hazel eyes were open and fixed.

Corey stepped closer and kicked the gun out of reach. "Does he have a pulse?"

I stared at my dad, as he lay unmoving in the snow. My heart pounded as I stood there face to face with my past. I felt like I was on an emotional rollercoaster. My dad wasn't as dangerous looking as I had remembered. I realized that the fear I had lived with for so long was gone. There was nothing left inside me now but fury and resentment.

The past few years in prison had not been kind to him. He looked older, and worn out. I knelt, pulled off my glove, touched my dad's wrist and felt no pulse. The contact of his skin started to send me in a panic and I focused on shutting it down. I wouldn't let myself feel anything for this man. He was nothing to me.

"No, he's gone."

"Any sign of Mia, or your mom?" Quinn asked.

I noticed Quinn kept his distance, as he stood a few feet away. He was holding himself together pretty good. People had different reactions when seeing a dead person for the first time. I was almost positive this was the first time Quinn had ever been in this type of situation before.

Standing up, I pulled my glove back on and walked away. I buried my emotions, unwilling to waste anymore of my energy on him. My flashlight searched the ground ahead of us. Small dark spots further ahead caught my attention. I marched through the snow toward the spots. When I reached them I crouched down to get a closer look. My blood ran ice cold. Someone else was injured and the likelihood was it was either Mia or my mom.

"It's blood." I stated as I stood up. My eyes scanned the trees around us. I listened for any movement in the area, but nothing stood out.

"MIA! MOM! ARE YOU OUT HERE?" I yelled and waited for a response. Nothing. My dad had to have a reason for traipsing through the snow at night without even a jacket on. They had to be out here somewhere.

"Corey, go back and get Sara and Jake and meet up with us. Quinn and I will continue to follow the blood trail."

~*Mia*~

We climbed the hill, with no direction in mind but to get as far away as possible before we were found. I slipped on a sheet of ice that brought us both to our knees. As we sank into the cold snow, the wetness soaked our jeans. Our hands were exposed and mine tingled. I knew hyperthermia was a very likely possibility for us, but I'd rather suffer that than being in the grasp of a madman. Exhausted, we hauled ourselves up and continued to push forward when the sound of a second gunshot pierced the area.

"He's still behind us, but that sounded a bit further away."

"I'm not sure how much further I can go, Mia."

"Just a little further, I think I see an overturned tree ahead. Maybe we can hide under there."

"Okay."

We continued to trudge through the wet snow. The drifts were deeper the further we moved up the mountain. A tree trunk sprawled ahead of us as it spanned what appeared to be two small mounds on the ground. We circled to the backside and found a small crevice under the tree. I kneeled and dug more snow out to give us additional space and planned to use the excess snow to help conceal us. My fingers were numb with cold. Jolene sat with her back against the log for support, her hand rested on her side.

"Oh Mia, you're bleeding."

"I'm fine. It's just my shoulder. It's nothing." I looked up at Dylan's mom. I didn't even feel the burning in my shoulder any more. My mouth twitched in a slight smile. "I've been in worse pain."

"Such a positive attitude. Most people would be crying by now, but not you. You just shrug it off and keep moving. You are just what Dylan needed. I can't tell you how thankful I am that you came into his life."

"I'm the lucky one. Here, I think we can make this work. Come, see if you fit under here or if I need to dig further." A voice drifted on the wind, causing my heart to race. "Jolene, did you hear that?"

"Hear what? Is he getting closer?"

"I don't think so, that sounded almost like Dylan."

"How would Dylan be out here?"

"I don't know. Wait, there it is again."

"I heard it to, I think you're right."

Standing up I looked over the tree trunk, and saw two flashlight beams as they flickered through the snow. Two different voices shouted my name.

"DYLAN?" I yelled back.

"MIA!"

I heard his voice, but couldn't see him. I started running toward the flashlight beams and his comforting voice. Finally, I could see his strong frame as he ran towards me. I met him halfway as I flung myself into his arms.

"You're here, you're really here." Tears rolled down my face as I sobbed into his chest. All my previous composure slipped as I felt his warm embrace hold me securely.

"Oh baby, are you okay? Let me look at you." Dylan carefully pulled me back so that he could examine me. His hands ran down the side of my face and continued to trace down my arms, when he touched my shoulder I flinched.

"Careful. My arm's bleeding."

"We need to get you out of here. Where's my mom?"

"I'm right here Dylan." Jolene staggered around the tree and walked the few steps to reach us. "Where's your dad? He was right behind us."

"He's dead."

"What? How'd that happened?"Jolene asked as she visibly slumped to the ground.

Dylan released me as he pulled his mom up from the wet snow. Supporting her weight against him.

"He fell, it looks like the gun went off and hit him in the chest. Come on, we need to get you both warmed up." Dylan stated.

I searched Dylan's eyes as he looked back over at me. His voice was emotionless as he talked about his dad. My heart broke for him. I knew no matter what he said it had to be traumatic for him to find his dad dead.

~Quinn~

Standing just behind Dylan I watched Mia, as she wrapped herself in Dylan's arms. I knew at that moment, that Mia had found her true love. Dylan wasn't such a bad guy. I knew now that he would take care of her and treat her right. In the end when I really thought about it, that's what mattered the most to me was Mia's happiness.

Mia looked over Dylan's shoulder and her eyes caught mine. She slid out of Dylan's arms, and stepped to the side as Jolene hugged her son. Mia walked directly to me. She stopped a few steps in front of me, her eyes never leaving mine.

"Quinn?" Her voice was soft and still shaky.

"Hey, Mia. You okay?"

"Yeah, I'm alive, that's a good thing, right?" She smiled slightly.

"Yeah, you sure have been a magnet for excitement lately." I grinned.

"Well, I think I've had enough to be honest. What are you doing up here?"

"Dylan called me. I came as soon as I heard you were missing."

Mia glanced over her shoulder. I looked up and caught Dylan watching us. He stayed a few feet away, giving us some space. I respected and appreciated it. Mia turned back to me.

"I've missed you. Missed our friendship. Are you okay? I never meant to hurt you."

"We're good, Mia. I'm sorry that I was so angry before. Dylan's a really good guy. I'm happy for you, really I am. He's the one that found you. You'd probably still be out here if it wasn't for him."

Mia leaned up and hugged me. My eyes closed as I wrapped my arms around her. I released her, knowing that her heart belonged to another. I would support her in whatever her decision was. That's what friends were supposed to do. The ache I felt in my heart would go away eventually. At least I sure hoped it would.

"Thank you." She whispered as she stepped back breaking the contact.

Dylan walked over to us, his mom at his side. "Let's get out of here," he said as he wrapped his arm around Mia.

I couldn't agree more. I was cold and tired. But relieved that we'd found them and they seemed to be relatively okay.

⁓

~Dylan~

On our way back to the cabin I had skirted the location where my dad had fallen. I didn't care to see him and I didn't want to put that image in my mom's or Mia's head. They'd been through enough.

The ambulance had taken my dad's body away. The police were collecting evidence as they moved in and out of the small cabin and the underground cellar that Mia and my mom had been kept captive in. They had already transported my mom to the hospital for evaluation and X-ray's. Elliot had cried on the phone when I'd called him to let him know we'd found them. He was on his way to meet my mom at the hospital.

Mia's mom had sobbed on the phone when I called her. I couldn't even understand what she'd been trying to say. She had handed the phone off to Mia's dad who thankfully was easier to talk to. They were waiting for us to return to my mom's cabin.

Corey and Sara sat at the kitchen table, while Jake was sprawled out at Sara's feet, snoring quietly. Quinn paced the room. He hadn't been able to stay in one spot for long. I was actually surprised at how well Quinn had done as we had hiked through the forest, especially since he'd never been trained before.

I sat on the couch in the living room of the tiny cabin while we waited for the cops to let us go home. Mia was nestled on my lap. Her head rested on my chest. I couldn't let her go. I'd almost lost her tonight and the thought alone sent chills down my spine. She was a rare jewel and I knew I'd treasure her and always try to keep her safe.

The paramedics had cleaned and bandaged Mia's shoulder. She had been lucky that the bullet had only grazed her. My hand traced over her hair as I held her, I felt her relax as she drifted to sleep. She'd been through a lot today. I knew she must be exhausted, both physically and mentally.

I leaned down and kissed her forehead. Anger radiated through me as I noticed the bruising on her cheek. She'd been in harms way because of me. But she was alive, and she was here in my arms where she belonged. I knew I needed to let my past go, to move forward.

My nightmare couldn't hurt me anymore. My dad would never be able to reach out and harm anyone else that I loved. That by itself gave me a sense of peace that I'd never truly known before. My past would no longer threaten my future or my happiness.

Mia had been a soothing presence for me. She had given me her unwavering support and love. She was full of life, hope, and laughter. Her spirit had been infectious, as it weaved itself into my heart. I knew I'd be forever changed because of her. Mia stirred in my lap, she turned her head upward, her deep brown eyes searched my green ones.

"Dylan?"

"Yes, Baby."

"Thank you, for rescuing me. Not once, but twice."

"I'll always be there to rescue you."

"I love you; words can't even begin to express how you make me feel." Mia lifted her fingers to trace the stubble that lined my cheeks.

"I thought I'd lost you. I couldn't breathe, or focus. You've wrapped yourself so tightly around my heart, the thought of you not being a part of my life nearly shattered me. But I hope these rescuing adventures are good and done with. I think you've shaved several years off my life." My fingers traced along her body as I held her.

"I guess we'll have to wait and see. I've been told that I seem to be a magnet for adventure."

"Yes, you certainly have been." I chuckled.

I caught her lips against my own, my hand supported the back of her head. The kiss was full of emotion, and a promise of more. She affected every inch of my body. I knew I'd never be able to get enough of her. I blocked out the world and commotion around us, at that moment it was just the two of us, secure in our embrace and love.

CHAPTER TWENTY-NINE

~Mia~

Several weeks after Dylan's mom and I had been kidnapped my nightmares were finally starting to disappear. Discussing them with Dylan was difficult because he still blamed himself. Bailey had been a huge help after I had opened up to her. I knew she could relate to my night terrors since she had lived with them for so long after her family was killed.

Bailey had been the one to encourage me to see a professional therapist. I had decided to visit the same one that Bailey had seen. After a few visits I'd finally been able to convince Dylan to come with me. He'd been hesitant at first, but had finally agreed.

Sitting in Dylan's jeep I watched him while he slowly walked across the green grass of the cemetery where his dad had been buried. The therapist had suggested that Dylan write a letter and say everything he wanted to say to his dad that he never got a chance to say in person. Then to read it out loud at his dad's grave.

For Dylan, there was so much left open and raw that he needed to find some sort of closure. The therapist had explained that although his dad was gone, if Dylan could express his anger and emotions verbally it would help him begin to let go and start the healing process.

I really hoped it worked and that maybe Dylan would finally be able to let go of his anger and grief over the loss of his dad. Dylan asked me to give him a few minutes alone. I knew he was struggling. Though Dylan didn't have very good memories of his dad as he grew up–he was still his dad–and he was dead.

In one of my counseling sessions we had discussed how most victims in similar situations still desired a relationship with their parents. No matter how badly they'd been treated. There were usually always some good memories there. Things often weren't horrible every day. That's what makes those types of situations worse is that the victim focuses on the good times. Eventually though, the bad begins to outweigh the good. The victim still hopes that maybe things will get better and change for the good. As long as the parent or significant other is alive there's still a chance to repair a relationship. Once they are dead that hope dies with them.

I had learned so many things from the therapist as I tried to deal with my own nightmares. But I wanted to try and help support Dylan through his nightmares as well.

I now knew that blame is a big issue where there is domestic violence. I'd seen that first hand with Dylan. The victim often shoulders the blame or feels like if they had just done something more or been a better person then things would have gotten better. That somehow they were the ones that caused the violent behavior. Letting that blame go and realizing that none of it was their fault or in their control is a big step forward. I knew Dylan dealt with that most of all.

Especially the whole kidnapping situation. He felt responsible and that guilt was eating him up.

Dylan stopped midway across the lawn and his shoulders slumped as he looked down. I watched as he held his paper in front of him. Then he was ripping it up and throwing it on the ground as he crushed it with his foot. He sunk to his knees, his hands in the grass and his head hung down.

I couldn't take it anymore, my heart was breaking into a million pieces. I opened the door and quickly walked to Dylan. I could smell the recently cut grass and the slight smell of orange blossoms from a nearby orange grove. The smell of spring and new beginnings floated around me as I walked through an area full of endings. It was an odd sensation.

As I got closer I could hear him sobbing, not just crying but sobs racked his body. I walked up quietly behind him and placed my hand on his shoulder. He grabbed it and held tightly. I stood there silent, giving him my support and my love. Tears formed in my eyes, not because I was necessarily sad that the crazy man who'd kidnapped me was dead. But for all the loss and heartbreak that I knew Dylan was going through.

After a few minutes he finally stood and I stepped into his warm embrace. I wrapped my arms around his waist, my head against his heart as it beat strong under my ear. His head rested on the top of my head.

"I don't know why I'm crying. He was never a good dad."

"It doesn't have to make sense Dylan. No matter what, he was your dad. It's okay to be angry or sad. He doesn't control you or rule your life."

"I feel better, at least a little bit. I feel exhausted though."

"That's okay."

"I don't ever want to turn out like him." He whispered quietly in my ear.

I leaned back slightly and searched his clear green eyes, full of pain and anguish. I knew that was Dylan's worst fear was to someday become like his father.

"Dylan, you are nothing like your dad. You never will be like him."

"I try so hard to keep calm. But sometimes I'll feel this deep rage from somewhere dark. I can't explain it. It's like a caged monster and it's trying to find it's way out. What if one day it breaks through? What if it's just a matter of time Mia?" His voice breaking in anguish.

Reaching my hand from where it rested at his waist I wiped away a lingering tear on his handsome face. My fingers traced down his cheek that was clean shaven today. I lingered on his scar at the side of his chin and ended with my index finger on his lip.

"It's never going to happen Dylan. Your heart is too big. You're too caring. We all get angry sometimes. We're human. You don't think I never lose it? It's not something that rubs off on you. It's not a flu virus. Just because your dad was like that doesn't mean you are destined to become the same way. You make your own destiny. Don't give him that control over you. He's not worth it."

We stood there, silent for a minute as he studied me. His hands shifted to my lower back as he pulled me closer and his warm lips sealed over mine. The kiss was raw. I melted into his strong frame. When he finally broke the kiss I was out of breath.

"How'd you get so smart?" he questioned.

"I've been around you long enough to know you. All of you. To some people it might seem like a short span of time. But I think when you're in the middle of a life and death situation a bond develops that is unbreakable. And we haven't been through one, but two of them."

"I love you Mia, more than I thought I was capable of. You broke down–no actually–you ripped apart every wall I constructed around my heart."

"Well, you know if you're going to do something might as well do it with full gusto right?" I smiled.

Dylan finally chuckled and I knew he was going to be alright.

"I love you too Dylan. And not just because you seem to continue to sweep me off my feet with your repeated heroics." I grinned as I leaned up on my toes to brush my lips against his.

<u>EPILOGUE</u>

~Dylan~

$\mathcal{T}wo$ months had passed since that fateful January night. I had finally relaxed. My nightmares at night had stopped, and I felt peace like I'd never felt before in my life. My mom had recovered quickly. Although she had a fractured rib, she had been lucky.

Elliot had been inconsolable the first days after the abduction. He had blamed himself for not being at the house. A few days after my mom was released from the hospital Elliot had proposed. I had never seen my mom so happy. I was glad that she had someone beside me who loved her. I knew Elliot would take care of her, it was obvious to anyone that watched them together that they were both crazy for each other. I had felt a huge burden lift from my shoulders.

A few weeks previous Mia told me she wanted to get back on the chairlift before the season was over. I was actually a little shocked that she was ready to try it, but then again I wasn't totally surprised. That was Mia, facing her fears head on. I never questioned her, just asked her if there was anything that I could do to help. I knew that first trip up on the chairlift was going to be the hardest for her. I told her when she was ready I'd be there right with her each step of the way.

~*Mia*~

The days flew by in a blur, and spring was in the air. The day was bright, and warm, the snow was starting to melt. I stood next to Dylan at the bottom of the ski slope as I observed people load the chairlift. My heart pounded, but I figured we had been standing there long enough. I held my poles in a death grip as I slowly snapped, first one boot into my ski, and then the other boot.

Before the ski resort closed for the season I had been determined to face my fear head on and ride the chairlift once again. Dylan stood next to me, his strength and support radiated from him as he smiled down at me. He'd seen me at my worst and was still here by my side. I never knew that I could love someone so deeply as I loved him.

"Are you ready, Baby?" he asked me in his soothing southern drawl.

"I hope so. My heart is racing a mile a minute."

"You can do this. I'll be right here with you."

I smiled as I tilted my head to look up into his sparkling green eyes. My hair swirled around my shoulders in the wind as I pushed it out of the way. I reached my gloved hand over to Dylan's face as I leaned up to kiss him.

"Thank you," I whispered.

"For what?"

"For everything. I think I would have probably chickened out by now if you weren't here with me."

"Mia, you can do this. I've never met anyone so fearless and positive as you."

"My brain tells me one thing, but my body isn't listening. My legs are wanting to turn around and bolt from here." I chuckled.

"I'll be right with you the whole time."

"Okay, let's do this." I pulled my goggles over my eyes and then pushed forward on my skis to the line that waited for the chairlift.

The line moved quickly, and it was our turn to load. I pushed my rising panic down, and moved into position with Dylan at my side. I turned my head to watch the chair swing around the corner. Seconds later it was directly behind us, as I sat down on the seat my arm grabbed the armrest to her right. My skis dangled in the air as they no longer touched the snow. I looped my left arm behind the back of the chair as Dylan had suggested. This gave me better anchorage onto the lift and kept me sitting back as much as possible. I took a deep breath, sucking in the cool air as I tried to calm the rapid beating of my heart. I looked over at Dylan who sat on my left.

"You did great. Are you okay?" Dylan asked.

"Yes. That wasn't as bad as I thought."

I looked forward, and kept my line of sight straight ahead. I refused to look down. I knew I wasn't ready for that yet. The wind whipped around me, the cold chapped my cheeks and I felt alive. I had always loved skiing, the freedom, the thrill of racing down the hill. I refused to let one small accident take that away from me.

At the top of the mountain, I braced myself, and let go of the chair only at the last minute. All my instincts took over and I skied down the small slope to an area where I would be out of the way of skiers and snowboarders that were exiting from the lift. I glanced up and grinned at Dylan as he slid to a stop next to me.

"I did it! I feel like my heart is about ready to jump out of my chest. But I did it Dylan!"

"I knew you would. You don't ever let anything stop you from what you want. You tackled your fears head on. It took me a lot of years before I was able to do that."

"It's because I have you by my side. It's a lot easier to be strong when you know there's someone there to support you."

"I'll always be here for you Mia, no matter what."

"And I'm here for you as well, Dylan, always. But right now, I think I'll race you to the bottom." I laughed and without giving Dylan any other notice I turned and pushed off down the hill.

I felt the burn in my legs with each turn, but the freedom I felt was like no other. This was what I loved, what I'd grown up doing since I was little. I crisscrossed the white, snow covered slope. My eyes watered from the frosty wind as it whipped against my face. I felt alive as I breathed in the crisp air. Nothing was going to stop me.

The further down the mountain I went the more in tune my body became to the rhythm. With each turn I was braver and more daring. I reached the bottom in record time; snow flew away from me as I skidded to a stop. I turned as Dylan came to a halt next to me.

"I won." I beamed at him.

"I might have let you win." Dylan grinned back.

"Oh yeah, well I guess we'll have to go again." I teased.

"In a bit. First, I have a surprise for you."

"A surprise? Ohh, I like surprises."

"Come on, this way. Then after we'll get back on the slopes. Let you try something a little more challenging."

"I can't wait."

I followed Dylan through the main building near the resort lodge as he stopped at a conference room.

"Are you ready?" Dylan asked.

"Yes, I'm totally baffled though. Why are we at a conference room?"

"You'll see."

Dylan opened one of the double doors and ushered me in. The large conference room table was full. There were two seats open in the middle of the oval table. I looked at the group of people that stared at Dylan and me. I didn't recognize any of them. Confused I turned back to look up at Dylan.

"What is this?" I whispered.

"Mia, this is a group of ski association representatives. They are responsible for research and development for ski safety."

"Okay, and how does this apply to me?"

"Remember when you said you wanted to do something about chairlift safety?"

"Yeah."

"I did some research and found this group. I told them your story and they wanted to meet you. In fact, they want you to work with them. They'd like you to help them with ski safety education, as a type of spokesperson."

"What? Me? Why me?"

"Why not you? Here, sit down I know it's a lot to take in. I'll let them explain."

Dylan led me to the two empty chairs. He pulled one out for me as I sat down in complete shock. Dylan sat down next to me. He grabbed my hand under the table and squeezed it. I listened in awe to the group. I had never realized how much time and attention was spent on safety and all the different factors, pros and cons for each safety device.

An hour later, I had agreed to work with the group. I was honored to help in any way I could. The group left and Dylan and I were the only ones left in the room. I sat in silence as I stared out the full height glass windows that were located at the end of the large room. The chairlift that I had fallen from was visible in the distance. The snow-covered slopes were speckled with moving color.

Dylan touched the side of my face, pulling my attention away from the view.

"Hey, are you okay? You look like you've seen a ghost. This was supposed to be a happy surprise."

My eyes misted as I turned to look into Dylan's deep emerald gaze.

"Yes, I'm okay. It is a happy surprise. I knew I had to do something, be a part of something after my accident. You made that happen."

"I only put the pieces together Mia. You are the perfect person to help them. You're full of life and energy, and you have an amazing story that people will listen to."

"I never even thought about all the little things they were saying. There really isn't any one solution is there?"

"No, each area, each lift, has it's own challenges. But they are listening and they are trying new things to improve safety. And that's what's most important. It's working together with the resorts, the owners, the skiers and snowboarders to make progress and move forward."

"You are amazing. I love you Dylan. I don't even have the words to express how much you mean to me."

"I'm not sure I can say I'm glad you fell nearly on top of my ski patrol hut. But I guess if you hadn't, I'd never have had the chance to find the love of my life. For that, I'll always be grateful. Your laughter and love brighten each day and when we're apart I can't wait until we're together again."

Dylan pulled me up from my chair. His left hand traced the loose tendrils of my hair that drifted along my shoulder. His right hand tightened at my waist as his lips captured mine. My arms slipped around Dylan's neck as I returned the kiss. Electricity raced through my body down to my toes. I fit perfectly within his embrace and I knew I never wanted to be anywhere else.

We had found each other on a dark day, but together we would turn that day into something bright and good.

A HEALING SPIRIT

Author's Note:

This story, while fictional, is inspired by true events. On Saturday, April 3, 2010, Keely Proctor, eight years old, and a black diamond skier, fell thirty-two feet from a chairlift in the local Southern California mountains. Numerous miracles would play a role in her recovery.

Keely fell right near a ski patroller's hut, which allowed immediate care. She was riding the lift with a friend, and her friend's father who happened to be a pediatric doctor. Who, after getting off the lift, was able to assist the ski patroller's in her care. She was transported down the mountain in an ambulance and prepared for airlift to the local children's hospital.

The shortest road down the mountain was closed due construction. On that closed road the helicopter would meet the ambulance. The weather that day was windy and electric lines were nearby. In most cases, it would have been a civilian medic flight that would have arrived. Had they been the ones to answer the call they would very likely not been able to land that particular day. Instead, it was the sheriff's volunteer squad that arrived, which was much more experienced in unfavorable conditions.

Keely was transported to the local hospital on a seven-minute flight, while her parents and siblings drove an hour and a half down the mountain. Later they would find out that the helicopter pilot knew Keely; he had a child who went to school with her.

After arriving at the hospital Keely was still awake and conscious. Enough so that her spirit flared when the nurses continued to call her by the wrong name as she yelled back to them "It's KEELY!" And spelled each letter for them.

When Keely's parents finally arrived they were in full denial of how serious her injuries were. Keely was prepped and underwent an unsuccessful surgery. The following hours were full of bad news and being told their daughter was bleeding out. She bled through thirty units of blood. Two different trauma teams attended her.

Finally, after several discussions the second team came up with the idea of using the Factor VIIa clotting agent in an effort to save her. This clotting agent helped the surgery team to go back in and stop arterial bleeds in her liver.

Easter Sunday, Keely, on life support rested. The community came together that day in prayer groups and blood drives.

Monday, Keely was back in surgery to remove her damaged kidney. She spent a total of ten days on life-support and twenty-one days in the hospital.

While Keely recovered in the hospital, the family learned that one of the first ER nurses who cared for her was a family friend. A student doctor that had been part of the team to care for her also visited to make sure she had survived. The doctor informed them that Keely had been within a couple of minutes of losing her life.

The local blood bank would later inform the family that they'd never had such an outpouring of support with the number of people donating blood in Keely's honor.

Today, Keely is an active teenager and enjoys playing soccer, dance, and continues to ski with her family. She has given speeches on her accident, and is a spokesperson for the local blood bank.

Skiing is a dangerous sport. No matter what safety precautions are taken accidents will still happen. While restraint bars are an option, there are other issues that should be considered. In order for restraint bars to be the most efficient they require a vertical bar that's located between a person's legs, otherwise a person or specifically a child could still slip under the bar. Additional weight added by the bars also impacts the structural integrity of a lift and must be considered. There's also the concern that with a restraint bar that those using the lift might feel more secure and not be as careful as they might be without the bar.

Signage and education on proper loading and how to sit on a lift can also be increased. Terrain and configuration of a lift also has to be considered, as well as there are some lifts that bars will never work on.

Life in general is full of risks, and accidents happen. But it's how we move forward and what we do with our lives when we're tested to our limit that is the most important.

For more information check out:

www. skipeace.com
www.nsaa.org/safety-programs/
www.kidsonlifts.org/

www.nsp.org/slopesafety/skiandsnowtips.aspx
www.nsp.org/slopesafety/chairliftpsa.aspx
www.fs.usda.gov/Internet/FSE_DOCUMENTS/
stelprdb5172694.pdf

Acknowledgements:

A Very Special Thank You to **Terri Proctor,** for sharing their family's story. From the initial interview to the reviews during the writing process, her help and support was crucial for this story.

Donna Newlin, for her input and review of the processes and procedures for ski patrol. Donna was a member of the ski patrol for twenty years and retired after serving as patrol manager for eight years. She has been an active member of the local sheriff's search-and-rescue team since 1999 and has participated in hundreds of missions.

Jennifer Blackey, RN, BSN, OCN® for her input and review of the basic medical terminology and processes. As well as catching typos and inconsistencies.

Jennifer Glenn, LCSW, CCFC, who's a trauma specialist and works with kids and teens post–domestic violence, for her input on the real impacts of domestic violence and after effects of trauma to kids and teens specifically.

Teighlor Polendo, Jenny Cunvong, Breanna Blackey, and **Kathryn Cooper** who went the extra mile spending hours reading, marking up drafts, and being blunt when dialogue or sequencing was off.

My editor **Erica Orloff,** for her ideas and support, when after the first edit I reworked the entire format.

And to the rest of my beta readers, Thank you! You helped strengthened Mia's story.

About the Author:

MELISSA A HANSON lives in Southern California with her husband and two sons. Growing up in Southern California, inspiration for the city of "Riverview" is based on her hometown, Redlands.

Melissa's journey to writing began with a passion in reading that started in sixth grade. In high school she started writing, but writing took a back seat when she decided to pursue a career in architecture. Almost twenty years later, her first novel was written.

A Healing Heart was her first completed novel, and is book 1 of the Riverview Series. It is Bailey and Collin's story.

A Healing Spirit, is book 2 of the Riverview Series. It is Mia and Dylan's story.

A Healing Touch book 3 of the Riverview Series. It is Natasha and Troy's story.

Each book is a stand-alone novel.

While Melissa spends most days designing buildings, she still loves reading and creating stories.

Facebook: www.facebook.com/mahwriting
Instagram: www.instagram/melissa_a_hanson
Web: www.mahwriting.com

Book 1—Bailey & Collin's Story

a healing
heart

Riverview Series Book 1

Book 2—Mia & Dylan's Story

a healing
spirit

Riverview Series Book 2

Book 3—Natasha & Troy's Story

a healing
touch

Riverview Series Book 3

MELISSA A. HANSON
MAH
WWW.MAHWRITING.COM

www.ingramcontent.com/pod-product-compliance
Lightning Source LLC
Chambersburg PA
CBHW061021120726
47910CB00006B/2050